# SET YOUR BOOK FREE!

## Hello Stranger!

You've caught a travelling book. I'm a very special book. You see, I'm travelling around the world making new friends. I hope I've made another friend in you.

Please go to: www.bookcrossing.com and enter my BCID number. You will discover where I've been and who has read me, and can let them know I'm safe here in your hands. Then...

### READ and RELEASE me!

**BCID:** _____

Registered by: _____

Where: _____

When: _____

**BLOOD OF NYX**
Druscilla Morgan & Roy C. Booth

Indie Authors Press

London | Chile | USA

BLOOD OF NYX

A catalogue record for this book is available from the British Library.

**ISBN: 978-1-910910-06-1**

1st Edition

Indie Authors Press policy is to use paper that are natural, renewable, and recyclable products and made from wood grown in sustainable forests. The logging and manufacturing processes are expected to conform to the environmental regulations of the country of origin.

London | Chile | USA

# ACKNOWLEDGMENT

THIS book has been a deeply personal journey, from its inception through to the prose printed before you now. There are many who have traveled the winding path with me—family and friends who have shared my dreams and frustrations, encouraged and supported, critiqued and commented. Each has contributed to the story of the House of Nyx. Each and every contribution has been invaluable. With deep and heartfelt gratitude, I'd like to thank them all. I couldn't have done it without them.

AND I'd like to thank you, the reader, for embarking on this journey. Welcome to the world of Nyx.

**- Druscilla Morgan**

FOR Cynthia, who has been incredibly supportive of this project from the start.

AND a tip of the hat to Axel Kohagen, John F. Mollard, David E. Beard, Rabecca Wilcowski, and Howard Preston.

**+- Roy C. Booth**

# PROLOGUE

## ODI ET AMO, EXCRUCIOR

SHE lay beside him, watching the shallow rise and fall of his chest. His cheeks, flushed with youth and lust only an hour before, were pale alabaster. On his neck, blood flowed in rivulets trickling from two small, puncture wounds. Slowly, he turned his eyes towards her.

"You said you wouldn't."

"You believed me?" Her eyes were sad. She reached out a hand and stroked his cold brow. His breathing now slowed, small, slight movements, like a dying bird.

"Foolish boy! Did I not warn you? When we take your heart, we take your soul."

He looked at her, his fading eyes flickering with shadows of confusion, the loss of blood dimming his thinking. She could see the fear, the incomprehension in his eyes.

"I told you, when you first offered yourself, that it is you who lays upon my altar. Did you suppose I would sacrifice myself?"

"I had hoped..." His voice faded, rustling like autumn leaves upon the ground. She knew his time grew near and could not help the smile crossing her blood stained lips. The foolishness of mortals never ceased to amaze her. She stopped stroking his brow and leaned close, her breath cold in his ear.

"And how shall that which is immortal sacrifice itself? On whose altar shall I lay?"

He turned his head away, but not before she caught the glimmer of tears. Pulling her hand away, she thought for a moment. When she leaned forward again, her voice held a ferocious intensity.

"I give you a choice I have given no other."

His eyes turned to her once again. This time, they flashed with anger.

"Go to hell, vampire," he said with a hiss.

She laughed. "That would be a homecoming, foolish man. I, the daughter of Nyx, am born of Hell."

He stared at her with empty eyes. She wondered if he actually understood the decision he faced. Of course, it was only his decision because she wished it to be so. She leaned closer, her lips brushing his ear.

"I have infected you," she whispered. "I can return you to life, but you will belong to me. You will be destined to wander through your days seeking the taste of me, my touch. Or you can go now to your grave without love, without comfort. Without me."

His breathing shallowed, barely discernible. She knew the end drew nigh.

She raised her voice, ever so slightly. "Edmund, you can become one of us. You will still hunger insatiably, your soul will know no rest, but you will be with me for eternity, or I can simply let you die, alone."

Again his voice rustled from his throat, underpinned by the distinctive wheeze of impending death.

"Want. To. Be. With. You."

She smiled a small smile of victory, even as she sadly shook her head. She had given him the chance of death, of escape. Foolish mortal, consumed by passion even unto his dying breath. With a heavy sigh, she turned up her wrist and in one swift movement, pierced the flesh with a sharp fang. Blood sprayed from her vein, spurting through her skin in a volcanic eruption of life. Laying her head upon his chest, she counted, "Four. Three. Two. One."

As the last beat of his heart struggled to keep him, she pressed her wrist firmly against his open mouth. Her blood flowed into him, an internal baptism. It took a moment, and she thought she had lost him, but in a sudden convulsing movement he began to take in the sweet plasma, with difficulty at first, but swallowing thirstily, the warm liquid strengthening him. It dribbled from the sides of his mouth, trickling down his throat and neck where his own blood lay. The two mingled upon his skin, completing her task.

His eyes opened, aglow with a new luminosity. He gazed up at her and a small wry smile crossed his blood-soaked lips.

She smiled back, and as she leaned down to kiss him, whispered, "Welcome to eternity."

***

# CHAPTER ONE

LUCIUS watched the girl bend to pick the largest pink rose. Her movements were fluid and graceful, but her gentleness was betrayed by a decisive snap of the rose's stem. She was a beguiling contrast of dark eyes and golden blonde hair, living poetry of flesh and blood. Her scent wafted to his nostrils, exciting his senses. He breathed her in deeply, holding her in his being for a moment before releasing her back to the summer breeze. *Let her enjoy her last moments of freedom.*

"Margrethe! Come inside! A well-bred young lady does not expose her skin to the rigors of the midday sun!"

The girl straightened, turning in the direction of the voice. He followed her gaze to the older woman who had broken the spell. The mother, mistress of the house and a creature of immense ego and minute intelligence, stood hands on hips, her middle aged curves framed indignantly in the doorway. Her fading beauty was not enhanced by the harsh light of day, nor favored by the constant scowl she wore.

"You will be the death of me yet, young lady! Not even a thought for the wearing of a proper hat!"

"Oh, Mother, stop fussing! I've not been out here long." The girl sounded bored, immune to her mother's dramatic posturing.

"I insist you come in *now*, I will take no argument!" The shrill voice rose an octave with impatience, accompanied by a practiced foot stomp for added emphasis.

Reluctantly the girl turned towards the house, crushing the innocent bloom in her hand. Petals fell to the ground in a shower of soft pink. He longed to gather them up and give them to her, and then beg her to put them back together again. Was it no less cruel to crush the beauty of a flower than to crush the soul? Soon she would know she belonged to him. She was the only satisfaction for his hunger. His justification. His need.

He watched the girl's retreating figure even as his mind drew her to him. Suddenly, she hesitated and turned in his direction. The sight of her slender body, lit by the sun beneath the gossamer fabric of her dress, made him catch his breath. She seemed to hear him, cocking her head towards the copse of trees where he concealed himself. Their eyes met though he remained hidden from her sight. The primal hunger rose in him, and he knew he could wait no longer. The girl hesitated again, her dark eyes hovering over his hiding spot, then, slowly, she turned and followed her demanding mother into the house.

A murky gloom engulfed her as the door closed behind them, the cavernous hallway swallowing her blonde hair and gossamer dress in its shadows. She left a fragrant trail behind her, a scent of lavender and skin, of warm blood coursing through delicate blue veins. Again, it inflamed his senses. Reeling from his unexpected need for her, he turned back toward the coach, crunching the lush undergrowth heedlessly beneath his boots. His eyes did not linger to feast upon the beauty of nature. In his mind's eye, he saw only her face, her eyes, her neck. His steps became more urgent. Ancient Silas waited, knowing his master's impatience at being thwarted. Already he had trouble keeping the horses steady as

7

they shifted restlessly, sensing their master's mounting turmoil and tossing their heads every so often in defiance of the reins.

"The time is now, Silas!"

He strode up to the coach, a terrifying figure in his haste. His cloak wrapped itself in the breeze, a threatening cloud around his powerful form.

"Damn you to the depths, man! What in Hades are you waiting for?"

Silas hastened under his master's dark gaze, leaping quickly to the driver's seat. The Master's temper was legendary, even in the darkest corners of the underworld and Silas had no wish to further fan the fires of hell. In a sweep of black, Lucius climbed into the coach. Silas gathered up the reins and with a sharp command, urged the horses on. Eager to be gone, the impatient steeds lunged forward, and the darkness headed towards its prey.

Those who know not the bounds of time are able to move seamlessly through space. The coach reached the faded grandeur of the house within a few short minutes, its occupant oblivious to the manicured gardens with their exotic flowers and marble statues lining the gravel drive. His eyes remained fixed ahead, envisioning the feast before him. He would tread carefully, raising no suspicion or fear. This was a scene well-rehearsed, the new neighbor calling to pay his respects as expected of a gentleman of superb standing and impressive breeding. It would all be too easy. He had chosen the human family name of Ruthven, unwilling to expose his true identity. The Ruthven line was sufficiently tainted by blood and scandal to suit him well, yet, he hoped, would arouse no suspicion by its familiarity. They of flesh and blood were ignorant of the darkest devices of the undead, supposing that which they could see before them to be the sum of existence. The fools! That which they thought to be theirs had been his from the beginning of time. He merely returned to claim his own.

At first he had sought only the estate itself as befitted the only son and true heir. The girl, a mere obstacle to be removed, the unfortunate result of his father's human marriage, an institution that had no consequence or power in his dark world. Yet that had all changed from the moment he first laid eyes on her. Within a short time, he had found himself uncharacteristically entranced by her beauty. She held a magnetism for him that transcended any familial bonds. After only a few days of watching her, she had ceased to be his half-sister and had become the object of his desire. He knew the danger, he knew it would incur his mother's legendary wrath, but he simply did not care. He wanted her. And, as always, Lucius of the House of Nyx would have what he wanted.

The coach stopped in front of the mansion's grand entrance. There was a crunch of gravel when Silas jumped down from his driver's perch and opened the coach door. Barely able to contain his hunger and excitement, Lucius, Lord of Nyx, stepped from the coach. His dark gaze traveled up the stone steps to the marble portico and massive oak door. The place had a sense of grandeur undiminished over the years. There was a timeless ambiance, a feel of permanence, and, more importantly, indestructibility. Lucius breathed it in deeply. It felt right. It felt good.

It felt like home.


MARGRETHE watched the black coach sweep down the driveway. There was a sense of urgency in the gait of the horses, their manes streaming behind them like dark flames. Apprehension gripped her, as though destiny itself was approaching her door. She turned quickly from the window, seeking the familiarity of the cozy drawing-room.

"Mother, we have visitors!" There was an edge to her voice that quickly drew her mother from the bowels of the kitchen.

"Visitors? Who is it, Margrethe? We are hardly ready to receive visitors! Oh, my goodness!"

"Well, Mother, we will have to be ready." A crunch of gravel announced the arrival of the coach at the main entrance. Margrethe turned back to the window, leaning forward on tiptoe to catch a glimpse of the occupants. Her mother pressed herself against the window beside her, both women peering through the glass expectantly.

"It is a well-appointed carriage, Margrethe. Clearly, our visitor is of some prominence and good social standing. I will gather the servants. Ready yourself to receive guests! Quickly, girl!"

Margrethe did not reply. Her gaze fell upon the coachman as he jumped from his seat and opened the coach door with a respectful flourish. She held her breath as the occupant emerged. A dark boot, well-polished, came into view, followed by a black imposing figure in understated finery. His face was obscured by an outrageously fashionable hat. Margrethe twisted and strained but, in spite of her contortions, his face remained hidden from view. Again, she felt the strange wave of apprehension. Her mother's voice barked through her thoughts, jarring her back to the warmth of the drawing-room.

"Margrethe! Go and change now, lest our guests mistake you for the gardener!"

"*Guest*, Mother. There is only one visitor. A gentleman."

Lady Elizabeth Winchester fixed her daughter with a disdainful look. "A gentleman caller is even more reason for you to make yourself presentable!"

Margrethe sighed. Her mother's tone brooked no argument. Dutifully, she headed upstairs to choose a dress suitable for receiving a gentleman visitor.

LUCIUS tried to fix an interested expression on his face as his hostess generously brought him up to date with the local gossip and matchmaking news. The woman was an interminable bore, and Lucius couldn't stop his gaze wandering towards the ornate staircase. There was no sign of the girl, his prey.

"My son Beaufort is due to return this week. You must meet

10

him, Lord Ruthven! He's been at Cambridge, completing his studies."

Lucius's attention suddenly snapped back to the annoying woman. *What son?* He knew of no son! Part of the beauty of his plan was that there were no men to protect his prey, no interfering would-be hero. *Well, not until now.*

"Ah, you have a son, Lady Winchester." Lucius said, forcing a smile. "My, an academic, too. You must be very proud of him."

"Oh, I am." said Lady Elizabeth Winchester, beaming widely. "He will be following his father into politics."

"His father?" *By the gods, it is getting worse! A father now!* Silas had assured him there were no men to be seen. He knew where the girl's true father was, the sad, pathetic creature his mother had turned. The one through whom he and the enchanting Margrethe shared familial blood, the reason he, Lord of the ancient Clan of Nyx, had suffered ridicule at the hands of those who should be beneath him.

"Yes." Lady Elizabeth Winchester drew a quick breath; the first Lucius could actually remember her taking. Her ample bosom heaved dramatically. "I remarried three years after Margrethe's father mysteriously vanished."

Lucius feigned surprise. "Vanished?"

Lady Elizabeth Winchester cast her eyes downward for a moment. When she raised them, they were limpid pools of sorrow. It was a brilliant performance.

"Margrethe's father vanished soon after our marriage. Margrethe was conceived on our wedding night." Her voice choked a little. "Poor Margrethe never even knew her father. There was no warning, no explanation."

*How fortunate for Margrethe!* Lucius thought bitterly. It was he who had to suffer her father's weak, mortal nature! She at least had been spared the misery of the creature's company for all those years, while Edmund had become the bane of Lucius's dark

11

existence. Edmund Charlesworth was a worthless shadow of a creature, no longer human, yet not wholly vampire. He clung to his weak human morals like a timid child clings to its blanket, refusing to feed with the rest of the clan. Claudia had finally resorted to bringing him goblets of goat's blood, reasoning that he had consumed such fare each time he'd eaten meat in his human existence. Edmund had reluctantly drunk the blood, his face contorted with horror and distaste. Lucius remembered his disappointment when the man had accepted the goblet. He would much rather that his mother had let the useless creature waste away.

He'd once dared to ask his mother why she had turned her human lover. He remembered clearly the coldness of the gaze she fixed upon him before replying that such things were beyond his understanding and that if he ever asked again, she would assign him to the darkest depths of Hades. He wondered fleetingly if his mother *would* send him to the Underworld when he returned with his half-sister by his side. He suspected she might but, for the first time he could remember, he was willing to take his chances. In any case, Hades would have more warmth than his mother and as such held little fear for him.

"And I had Margrethe to think of. It was a good match, and my Beaufort is a good husband." Lady Elizabeth Winchester wiped an imaginary tear from her eye.

Lucius was a little confused. He had lost the conversation while deep within his bitter thoughts.

"I am sorry, Lady Winchester, I thought Beaufort was your son."

Lady Elizabeth Winchester stared at him, wide-eyed for a moment, then burst into laughter!

"Why yes, he is! Beaufort is named after his father, Lord Beaufort Winchester the First."

*Winchester!* Of course, the woman had remarried! Silas had told him it was her maiden name. Damn the idiot to hell, he'd deal with him later!

Lucius recomposed himself.

"Ah, I see. How fortunate that you found happiness after such an unexpected and mysterious loss."

"Yes, mysterious, indeed." Lady Elizabeth Winchester's voice trailed off. Lucius followed her glance through the open doors to the hallway. Margrethe stood at the base of the staircase, her golden hair a halo of light beneath the glass skylight above her. Lucius drew a sharp breath. His cold blood raged within him, beating against his ears. His senses reeled.

"Ah, Margrethe, come and meet our guest. Lord Lucius Ruthven, let me introduce my daughter, Lady Margrethe Charlesworth-Winchester."

Even the mention of his father's name did nothing to spoil the vision before him. Lucius knew beyond any shadow of a doubt that he must have her. Possess her. She was no longer his prey, she was his desire, his destiny. As she turned her gaze towards him, he evidently saw the flames of his passion reflected in her dark brown eyes.

"I'm honored to make your acquaintance, Lord Ruthven." She dipped her slender body in a well-practiced curtsy as he bent to kiss her hand. His lips brushed her skin like ghost's breath. Her hand felt warm in his grasp, the fine veins forming a delicate pattern across alabaster skin. Soft hands, delicate hands that could snap a rose and crush its beauty to dust.

His breath stopped.

At that moment, Lucius knew that he loved her.

***

13

# CHAPTER TWO

MARGRETHE watched their guest through lowered eyelashes while carefully maintaining the demure demeanor becoming to a young lady. He was handsome, no doubt about that! Finely chiseled cheekbones, a straight and noble nose, and shoulders that looked like they could carry the world. The outline of his body, robust and muscular, revealed itself now that he'd divested himself of his cloak. His clothes were finely cut of the best cloth. He was fashionable, with a slightly rakish air, as were many of her brother's friends. But any similarity to any other man she'd met ended there.

Something about Lord Lucius Ruthven made Margrethe strangely uneasy, yet at the same time, drew herself irresistibly to him. Perhaps it was his eyes, dark, fathomless caverns aligned perfectly on his handsome face. Every time he looked at her she found herself wanting to sink into them and explore their depths. Occasionally he gazed at her with an intensity that brought a blush to her delicate cheek, and tightness of her breath. Her usual coldness to any man's attentions melted away, and she found herself hoping to catch his eye. She listened with fascination to the tales of his travels and adventures in faraway places that she only imagined. He was well educated, entertaining, charming, intriguing, and terrifying.

Yes, terrifying.

He seemed to see through her, to know her very inner being. It felt as though every one of her thoughts lay naked before him, open and vulnerable, totally at his will and mercy. And stranger still, Margrethe found herself willing to be so.

No, Margrethe had never met a man quite like Lord Lucius Ruthven.

Her mother's voice broke through her thoughts. "Margrethe, perhaps his lordship would like to hear you play? Margrethe is quite a talented pianist, Lord Ruthven."

Margrethe found herself blushing yet again. Their guest's attention landed entirely upon her now, and an amused smile played at the corners of his mouth. Margrethe's blush deepened.

"I would like nothing more than to hear the Lady Margrethe play," he replied warmly. His eyes burned into her, and suddenly Margrethe welcomed the distraction of performing. She went over to the piano near the window and sat down, arranging her dress around her. Even when nervous, Margrethe's movements were fluid and graceful. The light from the window cast its diffused glow on her seated form, giving her an ethereal air. Slowly, she laid her fingers on the keys and began to play. The soothing strains of *Green Sleeves* drifted into the still air of the drawing-room. It was the first tune Margrethe had learned and still her favorite. Gradually, as she lost herself in the familiar melody, Margrethe forgot the dark eyes feasting upon her. It was only when she had finished and turned to her mother and their guest that Margrethe caught the look upon his face. It was hunger, raw and primal, frightening, yet exciting. It was there and gone in a moment, quickly stifled by polite applause from her small audience.

"Beautifully played, Miss Winchester!" Margrethe watched as Lord Lucius Ruthven rose from his chair, deftly gathering his cloak and hat. His powerful form seemed to take up the entire room.

"My apologies, dear ladies, but I must make haste. The pleasure of your company and hospitality has kept me longer than I expected." He bowed deeply to her mother before again taking Margrethe's hand. His touch felt cool, yet she burned. Not just her skin and her veins, but every part of her being seemed to come alive and dance like a flame.

"You will attend the ball in honor of my son's homecoming, will you not, Lord Ruthven? It would be our great honor to have you as our guest." Lady Elizabeth Winchester's voice held a slightly pleading note. The opportunity for large social events proved rare, and the chance to have foreign aristocracy attend them even rarer.

"Of course, Lady Winchester, I look forward to it." Behind his sociable smile, Lucius bored into the woman's thoughts, compelling her to allow him a moment alone with her daughter. He must have Margrethe alone to seal her connection with him, to draw her so deeply within him that she could never leave.

It took not even a minute.

"Margrethe will see you to the door, Lord Ruthven. I am afraid I find myself tiring so easily these days."

After accepting her apologies and farewells, Lucius followed Margrethe's slender form down the dark hallway and out into the glaring sunlight. Silas patiently waited with the horses. Lucius spared him barely a glance. His attention remained on his prey.

"Thank you for a most entertaining and enjoyable afternoon, Miss Winchester." He watched as a warm blush stained her delicate cheeks as it had so many times during his visit. She teetered but a step away from being his.

"It has truly been our pleasure, Lord Ruthven. We rarely receive visitors of your, standing." She shifted uneasily. Lucius sought to reassure her.

"And I have rarely enjoyed such warmth and hospitality." It was true. Vampires were not known for their warmth or hospitality.

Most of his friends, family, and associates would be happier to fight him for a feed than share their goblet.

"And," he continued, "I am looking forward to attending your brother's homecoming." He gave her his warmest smile, and she smiled back.

"You will indeed come?" She appeared childish, expectant, hopeful.

"Of course, I would be delighted! But only on one condition."

Her eyes narrowed slightly. "And what would that condition be, Lord Ruthven?"

He gave a slight bow. "That you will dance with me."

He saw relief flood over her. The smile returned, brighter than before.

"Why, of course, Lord Ruthven. That would not be a condition at all, but a pleasure."

*The first of many pleasures,* thought Lucius. Her proximity made it difficult to contain his desire. He fought to maintain composure.

"And, of course, you will meet my brother."

*Oh yes, the brother.* This time, when Lucius smiled, it contained slightly less warmth.

"Are you close to your brother? I mean, your half-brother." The distinction seemed important for some reason.

Margrethe seemed to hesitate. When she answered, however, her tone became measured and careful.

"Yes, I am. Even though he is my half-brother, I am but three years older, and we have a close relationship. He is very protective of me. Perhaps too protective sometimes." Her voice trailed off, as though she'd said too much.

"Then he is much to be admired as one who guards the most precious of jewels."

Lucius smiled softly at her, resisting the urge to cup her chin in his hand and crush her ruby lips to his. The thought of the brother held him back, and he couldn't help but wonder at the nature of their relationship. Brother or lover? Could there be more than familial affection between them?

Such things were common in vampire society, for hunger had to be satisfied by whatever means necessary. The Elders were disapproving, but the younger fledglings had no such misgivings, indulging themselves in carnality and bloodlust where ever possible. Of course, in the human realm, such things were forbidden, but the half-blood between Margrethe and her brother made it a possibility.

"I look forward to meeting your brother, Miss Winchester." Again, Lucius flashed his best reassuring smile.

He most definitely wanted to make Beaufort Winchester II's acquaintance.

Oh, yes, indeed.

THE coach made its way through the picture-perfect countryside. Beaufort Winchester II's attention would certainly have been captured by the lush, green perfection of the Cambridgeshire scenery passing before him had it not been for a formidable hangover and the disturbing letter in his hand. Instead, he shut his eyes tightly against the incessant sunlight, grimacing at each thundering beat of the horses' hooves. His stomach swayed with the coach, each lurch producing a rising nausea that threatened to overtake him. He opened his eyes only to glance at his traveling companion, who seemed to be faring a little better. Fredrick "Freddie?" Hannington's dark head was thrown back in a deep sleep. A droning snore emanated annoyingly from his throat. Beau envied Freddie his momentary respite from self-induced misery. He would like nothing more than to sleep like his friend, but every time he shut his eyes, the letter in his hand came to life in his mind. Images of his dear Margrethe swam before him. Margrethe in the arms of a handsome, dark stranger. Margrethe gazing lovingly into

18

mysterious, unknown eyes. Margrethe drifting away.

Beau forced bleary eyes once more on the contents of his mother's letter. There was the usual excited babble about his return home and the forthcoming holiday festivities, followed by even more excited babble about a ball thrown in his honor. Then came the part where Beau's heart had traveled to his stomach.

*The ball will be the perfect opportunity for you to meet our handsome new neighbor, Lord Lucius Ruthven. He is of aristocratic birth and his family owns estates the world over. I do believe he is quite enamored of our Margrethe and she of him.*

Beau felt his stomach tighten again. Sweet, innocent Margrethe, untouched by the corruption of the world, pursued by a complete stranger who, for all his mother knew, could be after the family estate. Aristocratic indeed! Beau would certainly be looking into this man's pedigree, whoever he claimed to be! He would enlist Freddie's help once he'd sobered up. Freddie had a knack for uncovering the dark secrets of others and an even greater knack for using those secrets to his own best advantage. Freddie would smell an aristocratic rat in no time. Beau sighed. Damn his mother's impulsive, romantic nature. If only his father spent more time at home! Lord Beaufort Winchester the First cited his parliamentary duties as the reason for his frequent, long absences. However, Beau suspected his father spent much of that time in the company of certain "professional" ladies while enjoying all the benefits that his social stature afforded. All extremely discreet, of course. Sins behind the polished oak doors of exclusive men's clubs. Sins quietly accepted and never spoken about in genteel circles. Fashionably ignored sins. A life he never wanted for his sister! A loud, guttural snore suddenly broke the silence as Freddie jolted himself out of his slumber, cutting into Beau's disjointed thoughts. With a startled look, Freddie shook his head and peered out the carriage window.

"Where are we? Are we nearly there?"

"We have about another hour's travel, Freddie. You may as

well sleep." Beau wasn't sure that his pounding head could tolerate his friend's annoying chatter.

"Sleep! Oh no, old boy, I am quite awake now!" He beamed at Beau, who could not help but wonder at his friend's amazing recovery. Oh, the wonders of sleep! Freddie's sharp eyes caught Beau's pale, sickly complexion.

"I say, old boy, you do not look at all well! Tch! Should have caught some sleep yourself!"

"Yes, I should have," Beau muttered darkly. It was going to be a long hour.

"It is not like you to overindulge, Beau," Freddie continued, "but you certainly excelled yourself last night! Oho!" His observation accompanied a raucous guffaw of laughter that hurt Beau's head. The resulting wince didn't go unnoticed. Unfortunately, it only drew louder derisive laughter.

"So what sorrows were you drowning, Beau, old man? What frivolsome evil wench has broken your heart?"

"Let it go, Freddie, there is no wench, 'frivolsome,' evil, or otherwise." Beau gripped the letter tightly in his hand, scrunching it in his fist as though to hide it from prying eyes. Freddie saw the movement immediately and swooped.

"Ah, there's the answer to your misery! That confounded mysterious letter!" Freddie made a grab for the letter, but Beau's wits were still sharp enough to snatch it away in time.

"Come on, old boy, I know it's that letter that has upset you! You changed as soon as you took delivery of the wretched thing. All your good humor left you, you were quite difficult and churlish all evening. Not even drinking eased your misery or ours in tolerating it." Freddie eyed him balefully, and Beau hung his head. He knew his friend was right. He had been a miserable drunk, morosely sitting in the corner with occasional angry outbursts at the capricious nature of fate. He couldn't even remember stumbling to his bed and availing himself of its downy comfort, boots and all.

"You fell asleep on the floor next to your bed. We just picked you up and threw you on there, you were too drunk to know or care."

*Well!* thought Beau, *that answered that!* He raised a hand.

"Please, Freddie, spare me the details!"

"Then tell me what's in the letter that's upset you so!"

Beau sighed. Clearly Freddie wasn't going to let the subject rest.

"It is a letter from my mother. Apparently my sister has a suitor." Beaufort tried to keep his tone neutral.

"Why, that is wonderful news, old boy! Smashing! A good match I hope, though I must say, I had an eye for your sister myself." Beau stopped him with a sharp look.

"I have no idea whom this suitor is, or if he is indeed suitable!" This time, Beau could not disguise the irritation in his voice. "And sorry, *old boy,* but I do not regard you as a suitable match for my sister!"

"No need to be offensive, old chum!" Freddie retreated to the corner of his seat, and for a short, blessed time silence reigned, punctuated only by the occasional dark look in Beau's direction from the offended party.

Beau had no wish to explain his chagrin at his mother's "good news" to his friend. To be truthful, he admitted difficulty understanding it himself. He and Margrethe had always been close. She was the elder, yet her vulnerability and the loss of her father brought out a certain protectiveness in Beau that bordered on obsession. Her beauty fascinated him, causing him to wonder at their shared blood. Beau was by no means displeasing to the eye, with his sandy blonde hair and blue eyes, but his features lacked the luminosity and perfection of his half-sister's. Her gold hair contrasted with his sandy locks, her eyes velvet brown pools to his pale blue sky. An aura of sadness clung to her, a fragility that covered mysterious depths. Margrethe never spoke of her father, nor of his strange disappearance, yet he knew it haunted her. He saw it in her eyes, in the shadowy half smile she gave when he told her a joke or pointed out a funny hat. Always something missing.

So he protected her in the best and only ways he could. He shielded her from the lads who gazed at her with eyes full of ill intention. Beau followed her through the rolling fields of their estate to ensure she didn't fall and injure herself. He explored the neighboring woodlands with her lest she be waylaid by ruffians or lose her way home. He accompanied her to town to protect her from pickpockets and charlatans, shielded her ears from harsh words, tried to shield her mind from harsh thoughts. She had pain enough.

And should this stranger show any disrespect or duplicity towards Margrethe, should he prove to be false in honor, word, or deed, then he, Beaufort Winchester II, would protect his beloved sister from Lord Lucius Ruthven and his ill intent!

\*\*\*

# CHAPTER THREE

"YOU forbid me?" Margrethe stared at her brother in disbelief. "You cannot be serious, Beau!"

"I have never been more serious in my life, dear sister!" Beaufort's jaw tightened with determination, his blue eyes clouding dark with anger. Margrethe realized his seriousness.

She had been nervous about telling her brother about Lucius. Her new neighbor had been a daily visitor, and she had awaited each visit with increasing delight. His attentions were respectful, but his eyes, oh, his eyes lit a fire inside her that wouldn't be quenched. Margrethe found herself seeking quiet moments in his company, so enchanted by his knowledge and experience. His symphonic voice carried her away to exotic places, filling her mind with new visions. Cambridgeshire suddenly seemed so small, so stifling. She found herself longing for new horizons. She found herself longing for Lord Lucius Ruthven.

Her mother, of course, had given her beaming approval. Margrethe sometimes wondered if her mother's eagerness to see her wed was born of a desire to be rid of her daughter and the memories of her unfortunate conception. She was, therefore, not entirely surprised when her mother declared Lucius to be utterly charming and clearly of quality stock. He was, in her opinion, an entirely suitable match for Margrethe. In fact, it would be sheer folly not to accept his proposal, or indeed to fail to work towards such an end. Her mother's motives mattered little to Margrethe. She had fallen in love with the dark, mysterious aristocrat. He stirred her blood in a way no other had or ever would.

But how to explain this to her brother? Beau had always been fiercely protective of her. Margrethe had humored him at first, amused by his youthful loyalty and adoration. As she grew older, however, his attentions became less amusing. In fact, they became annoying at first, then strangely discomfiting. When he'd finally gone away to study, Margrethe had breathed a silent sigh of relief. Her sense of freedom only curtailed during Beau's infrequent visits when, as now, he would often be accompanied by a fellow student. Most of Beau's friends were immediately attracted to Margrethe, who might have returned the attentions of one or two had Beaufort not held them off like an angry guard dog.

"Beau, you cannot *forbid* me." Margrethe's voice became quiet but firm. She had resolved to stand her ground. "Mother has already given her approval."

Beau stood up and propped himself next to the fireplace, gazing at his sister with cold fury. Margrethe couldn't remember ever seeing him look at her that way before.

"I gave you more credit for intelligence, Margrethe." His voice became low and dangerous. "I may not be able to forbid you, but I will most certainly stop you from making such a terrible, foolish mistake."

"You will stop me?" Margrethe's eyes narrowed. "And how on Earth will you stop me, Beau?"

He said nothing. Margrethe stood up, too, facing him squarely, looking him in the eye.

"I will marry whomever I wish, and I wish to marry Lord

Lucius Ruthven. It is that simple, Beau, really. And so it shall be, with or without your approval."

"You do not know this man! You know *nothing* about him! Have you lost your mind?" Beaufort took a step toward his sister. Margrethe backed away, for the first time uncertain. She'd never seen this side of Beau. He'd always been gentle with her, always seeking her happiness. Why did her happiness mean nothing to him now? She'd expected some resistance, but not this.

"He is from a reputable family, Beau. They own property the world over. He has just bought Grantham Hall. Clearly, he is a man of substantial means and he has done nothing but treat me with the utmost respect." Margrethe stopped for a breath. She felt as though she were pleading, justifying.

"And I love him!"

Silence fell as Beau continued to stare at her, then a strange madness seemed to overcome him. His eyes suddenly darkened with a wild, crazed look. The blood drained from his face, leaving him pale and ghastly. Her brother, her champion, no longer existed. Instead, a frightening stranger stood before her, filling the room with barely contained rage.

Margrethe took another step backward.

"You *love* him?" Beaufort took a step after her, then stopped abruptly, his entire body shaking.

"Had I known you were so generous with your favors; I would have encouraged Freddie in his pursuit of you! Better to throw you to him than to a total stranger who, for all you know, could be a trickster after your inheritance!"

"He is no trickster, Beau!" Margrethe managed to protest. "Why, you have not even met him, yet already you judge him and cruelly at that!" Tears of anger and frustration welled up in her eyes.

"I do *not* need to meet him, Margrethe! I already know of his kind. This has happened all too fast. He is a wolf, a predator. But do not worry, I will most certainly meet him!"

25

"And I will most certainly marry him!" she spat back, anger finding her voice for her. "Mother has already written to Father seeking his approval, which I'm sure will be forthcoming, so there's nothing you can do to stop me!" She sounded churlish, even to her own ears.

"Then have him, Margrethe! Have your dark stranger!" Beau's voice rose in anger. "But remember this: You have made a choice. You may have a suitor, but you no longer have a brother!" With that, he turned and stormed from the room, slamming the oak door behind him. The heavy boom resonated in her head along with his words, *you no longer have a brother.*

Margrethe succumbed to her shock and sorrow, to the tears that, for the entire confrontation, had threatened to fall. She sank back into the plush chaise, burying her head in her hands, allowing the wracking sobs to overtake her until she spent all her energy.

The next two days were spent in a flurry of preparation for Beau's homecoming ball. Margrethe busied herself with decorations and the all-important task of choosing a gown. To all around her, she seemed happy enough, but inside she grew more and more hollow. Her mother, of course, noticed nothing amiss, attributing Margrethe's occasional lapses of attention to the flush of youthful love.

*Just because your heart's aflutter, Margrethe, there is no need to daydream at such a busy time.*

Margrethe sighed. If only it were daydreams pulling her away from the hustle and bustle around her. She longed for distraction, but nothing could tear her mind away from the terrible scene with her brother. They hadn't spoken since Beau had stormed from the drawing-room. In fact, he had been conspicuously absent, preferring Freddie's company to that of his family. The two men had ventured out early in the day, pursuing such manly interests as hunting and fishing. They would return late in the evening, eating a quick supper in their rooms before spending hours in conversation

26

behind closed doors. The women's preparations held little interest for them, but Margrethe suspected that Beau's frequent absence was in no small part due to their argument.

Occasionally they would cross paths, a mumbled greeting, eyes turned away. The estrangement became more than Margrethe could bear. Her heart, never before challenged, tore in two. She longed to be with Lucius, but could she bear the loss of her brother? Her only hope depended upon their meeting. Perhaps they would find each other's company more acceptable than expected. Perhaps they would even find the beginnings of friendship. Margrethe hoped so with all her breaking heart.

BEAU stared at his friend in consternation.

"Truly, Freddie, now is not the time for your amateur sleuthing!"

Freddie leaned back in his chair, inhaling the aromatic smoke from his pipe, breathing it in deeply and holding it before exhaling in a practiced stream. With a dismissive wave of his hand, he hushed his critic.

"On the contrary, Beau, now is precisely the right time for my sleuthing. Do you know anything of the Ruthvens?"

Beau had to admit he didn't. "And I suppose you do?"

"Well, as a matter of fact, I do know something of the Ruthvens. Quite a notorious bunch, really. Traitors, true rotters from the earliest days and not known for their stability. Or even wealth."

Beau raised a quizzical eyebrow. It sounded both ominous and outlandish at the same time. Of course, everyone knew of the Ruthvens from their dusty old history books. But the family had lost its power many years ago, and much of their fortune with it.

He said as much to Freddie if only to show he was not completely uninformed.

Freddie nodded. "That's quite right, old boy. They did lose

everything, including the family estates. One confiscated, one burnt to the ground. The Ruthvens carry a curse upon their backs. But just recently, one branch of the family has been accepted back into political and social favor."

"And is this *Lord* Lucius Ruthven born of that same branch?" Beau asked.

"Aha! *That* is why you need my sleuthing skills, my dear man!" Freddie claimed triumphantly.

"Hrm."

"Now don't roll your eyes! This is of vital importance. It's Margrethe's happiness, perhaps even her safety, which is at stake!"

"Margrethe has made her choice!" Beau snapped.

"You know you don't mean that, Beau."

No, he didn't mean it. Even in the heat of his anger, the thought of any terrible fate befalling Margrethe filled him with dread. He wouldn't let anyone harm her, even if it meant he had to depend on Freddie's dubious sleuthing skills. Annoyed at his own transparent emotions, Beau glared at his friend.

"Very well then, Freddie, play detective if you must! I need to know more about this stranger who has captured my sister's heart so easily. But I warn you, this is a serious matter! I need facts, not conjecture and rumor!"

Freddie looked offended. "But, of course, old boy! I've given this matter serious consideration. Much indeed! I have a vague social connection to the Ruthvens. My uncle's wife has known them for years, grew up with one of the Freeland Ruthvens."

Beau stared at his friend blankly and then raised an eyebrow. "Freeland Ruthvens?"

"Well, some say the line died out years ago, but there was a sister. Oh, never mind! My point is I can use that family connection, tenuous though it may be, to question this man directly and to the point. I'll soon know if he's genuine or not."

Beau remained unconvinced. "And you will do this when?"

Freddie smiled smugly. "I think the ball will provide the ideal opportunity."

"It would provide an excellent opportunity to warn this man to stay away from my sister," Beau muttered darkly.

Freddie gave a snort of laughter. "I hardly think so! Causing a scene at your homecoming ball is *not* a good idea, Beau! Oh, no! It might be prudent to wait until we have more information before you go on the attack!"

"I suppose you're right, Freddie, but it's difficult to stand by and watch my sister seduced by an opportunistic stranger."

"Of course it is, which is why we still stand idle no longer!" Freddie ashed his pipe decisively. "Tomorrow night we shall meet this Lord Ruthven and see what he's made of. I can assure you, Beau, if this man has any skeletons in his closet, I'm the man to rattle them!"

Beau didn't answer at first. Instead, he turned his gaze to the window. A full moon lit the familiar landscape, casting its eerie glow into the room. A cold shiver passed through him. Whatever this stranger hid in his closet, Beau ascertained it was much more dangerous than skeletons. No logical reason allowed for him to come to this conclusion, just a nagging feeling something very, very wrong and improper shrouded Lord Lucius Ruthven.

"I'm not so sure that I can wait until tomorrow night, Freddie. I need to know more before I meet this man."

Freddie looked at his friend cautiously. "What do you have in mind, Beau?"

"I thought we might do a spot of hunting near Grantham Manor tomorrow morning." Beau returned his friend's doubtful gaze with a boldness he didn't quite feel. The idea had just occurred to him and he'd given the wisdom of it scant thought.

Fortunately, his idea appealed immediately to Freddie's sleuthing instincts.

"Wonderful, old chap! There can be no harm in checking the

place out."

Beau rose heavily from his chair. "Then we had best get some sleep, Freddie. We should start out early, say, at the first light of day. After all, my friend, it is by the last shadows of the night that darkness settles its debts."

Even as he said them, Beau's words seemed to carry a warning as ominous as the dark shadows that flickered in the candle lit room. He couldn't repress an involuntary shiver, an imminent feeling of danger. It nagged relentlessly at his already tormented thoughts. His words seemed to unsettle Freddie too. He mumbled a somewhat subdued good night, leaving Beau to snuff out the waning candle. As darkness fell over the room, he thought he sensed another presence beside him, oppressive and stifling.

*It is by the last shadows of the night that darkness settles its debts.*

Pursued by a childish feeling of terror, Beau reached hastily for the door handle and escaped into the comforting half-light of the hallway. As the door closed behind him, he could have sworn he heard a dark, guttural voice call his name.

***

# CHAPTER FOUR

LUCIUS gazed out of the window with an expression of distaste. The dying days of autumn were unusually warm and sunny, assaulting his eyes each morning with an unaccustomed brilliance. How he longed for the cold, gray chill of winter with its pale, misty nights! These interminable days of sunshine were torture for his dark soul. Like all vampires, he avoided the sun whenever possible. However, due to his partial human heritage, he was not as vulnerable to the accursed rays as a Full Blood, being able to withstand the unmerciful glare without fatal results.

Irritated, he turned away from the offensive sun, redirecting his dark, brooding thoughts to his pursuit of the delectable Margrethe. The arrival of the meddling headstrong brother had concerned him momentarily, but his frequent out of body visits assured him that the relationship between Margrethe and her brother had chilled significantly. Lucius also knew it had chilled because of him. This gave him some small satisfaction. It meant that her heart, if not wholly his, was at least torn in two.

It sufficed.

Easier now to divide and conquer.

Tonight he would attend the ball in honor of the invasive brother. He would be charming, witty, and attentive, a perfect gentleman, the perfect suitor for Beaufort Winchester II's sister, the exquisite Lady Margrethe. If there remained any resistance, Lucius did not doubt for a moment he would break it down, either by persuasion or by force. He'd never met a human yet immune to his telepathic power and Beaufort Winchester II would be no different! At least only one Winchester male stood in his way. The father, the lord of the manor, was conspicuously absent, immersed, no doubt, in affairs of either a political or sensual nature. The brother's friend, an egotistical imbecile by all accounts, posed no challenge. Again, there appeared to be little threat to Lucius's conquest of the fair Margrethe. The friend proved foolish and prone to excess, the brother hot-headed and willful.

Lucius allowed himself a small smile. Yes, all in all, he enjoyed this satisfying progress of events.

He stretched luxuriously, basking in his imminent success.

"Master!" The urgency in the usually tired, ancient voice broke through Lucius's pleasant reverie.

He sighed. "Yes, Silas?"

His servant's agitation did not go unnoticed. "The Watchers have returned from the perimeters, Master. It seems we have some uninvited guests."

"What?" Lucius jumped to his feet, his attention now fully upon his manservant. The ravens were never wrong! They faithfully watched his dark sanctuary, alerting him to any danger or disturbance long before even his own finely tuned senses picked up any threat. They were especially effective against vampire hunters and had saved Lucius from danger many times. If a warning came from the Watchers, it must be heeded immediately!

"Saddle the horses, Silas! The ravens will lead us to the intruders!" The manservant hesitated, but not for long as his master's fury quickly fell upon him!

"Move it man, before I beat you more senseless than you already are!"

There was no mistaking the dangerous look in his master's eyes. They burned with the fire of Hell, a seething mass of darkness that Silas knew could explode upon him in an instant.

As quickly as his old bones would allow him, Silas moved!

FREDDIE shouldered his gun and pushed through the thick undergrowth, swearing intermittently as the bramble hedges ripped at his arms and legs. Beau watched him thrashing around and couldn't help wondering if he could make himself more conspicuous. It would be bad enough if their prey were only pheasants or hares, but today their prey proved far more dangerous. And elusive.

They had started out in the early hours, under the cover of the gray morning light. Just under a half hour walk from home lay the Ruthven estate, but Freddie had insisted on saddling the horses anyway. They'd ridden until the forest had become too dense. Tethering the horses, they continued to trek through the forest wilderness on foot. Clearly unused to such rigor, Freddie regularly tripped on tree roots and uneven rises of ground. Amusing at first, it soon became tiresome, slowing them down and announcing their presence to any living creature within a mile.

"For God's sake, Freddie, do you think you could muster up a modicum of stealth? I'm surprised they haven't sent out a welcoming party!"

Freddie stopped and turned abruptly, glaring at his friend.

"You might be used to traipsing around in the God forsaken wilds of the forest, Beau, but I most certainly am not!"

A retort froze on Beau's lips as the sharp snap of twigs cracked through the stillness. Freddie heard it too and raised a finger to his lips. Both men sank to their knees, keenly scanning the surrounding forest. Not even a bird stirred. All remained quiet. Too quiet!

He motioned Freddie to stay, then, still crouching, scrambled towards the dense copse of trees in front of him, trying to hold the shotgun close. It snagged on branches, hampering his progress as he paused to carefully free it. Finally, he made it to the thick wall of trees. With a last glance at Freddie, he pushed through the twisted branches and emerged into a clearing. The stillness persisted, heavy and ominous. Again, he scanned his surroundings. At any other time, it would have been a peaceful, secluded spot. Now, with his senses electrified and his heart pounding, he found no peace. The small clearing contained only unseen danger. A rustle of leaves caught his attention. Turning in the direction of the sound, his heart pounded even harder. Nervous sweat smeared his hands. He swore under his breath and gripped the gun more tightly. What had he heard? An animal? Or something else?

Breathing.

He was sure he could hear breathing. He strained his ears, head to one side. There it came again, behind him! Beau's heart leaped to his mouth, and he spun in fear, mindless of the jagged branches behind him. The gun slipped from his grasp and disappeared into a confusion of bramble bushes. Panicked, Beau grabbed for the barrel. Vicious thorns tore at his hand, and he swore in pain and fright. Suddenly, one side of his head exploded. The blow lifted him off his feet, throwing him helplessly into the vicious tangle of bramble beneath. Waves of pain and darkness engulfed him. He struggled to stand, only to be felled by a blow even more violent than the first. The brambles ripped through his wool jacket, piercing his arms and body. He screamed in agony as they tore at his skin, leaving rivers and streams of blood in their wake. Through his pain, he dimly caught sight of a dark figure kneeling over him, his last memory before the dark bliss of unconsciousness claimed him.

FREDDIE watched as his friend disappeared into the thick

undergrowth. He wanted to follow but wasn't keen to endure any more sarcastic comments, so he stayed in one spot, eying the surrounding forest nervously. It grew deadly quiet. Not even a breath of wind, only a cold stillness that clung to his skin, as if wet silk. Freddie shivered. He gripped the gun tightly, relishing the security of the cold metal against his skin. Not that he was a good shot, but at least it would be enough to scare off any predatory creature. At least, he hoped it would be. He checked his pocket watch. He'd give Beau ten minutes, no more.

A sudden cry rent the silence. A cry of pain and fear.

Freddie spun on his heel. A cold sweat broke out on his brow. His heart pounded in his ears, drowning out all other sounds.

"Beau?" He tried to call out, but only managed a miserable croak.

A crunch of leaves startled him. He spun on his heel, his heart leaping from his chest into his mouth, stifling his scream. Cold, black eyes met his, red-rimmed and fathomless, framed by deathly pale skin. The skin stretched over a grotesque deformity that perhaps once could have been called human. Freddie's eyes widened in terror. He pressed the trigger instinctively. The shot blasted his eardrums, shattering the early morning with its violence. It should have destroyed the creature's chest, yet the thing remained horrifically intact and alive. It reached a taloned hand towards the now cowering man. Dropping the useless gun, Freddie tried to scramble backward. His crab-like attempt at escape proved hopeless. With the guttural cry of a thousand demons, the creature flung itself upon its hapless victim. Freddie's stifled scream became a bubbling gurgle of blood and air as his throat ripped open. Blood sprayed in wide, graceful arcs, spattering the yellowing leaves nearby with delicate crimson patterns. The creature buried its fangs deep within the bloodied mass, feeding hungrily. Sharp talons ripped into the body, tearing through chest muscles and intestines. Finally, with both anger and thirst satisfied, the creature raised its head. Blood smeared the handsome cheekbones. The dark eyes, so cold and ravenous only moments ago, were glazed with contentment.

Lucius stood and wiped his mouth with the back of his hand. A useless gesture really, given that his hands were drenched in blood. The red plasma and bits of gore soaked his skin, his coat, his hair. One could say he was literally bathed in blood. The thought made him chuckle to himself. Rich, dark clots dotted the bloody mess on the back of his hand. Lucius licked at a particularly delicious looking morsel. He'd get Silas to move what remained of the body. Of course, it would be impossible to link the man's unfortunate disappearance to himself. And he would show the same shock and horror as everyone else when no sign nor hair ever appeared of the hapless Freddie. Hunting parties would be sent out, and he would join them, determined to find the missing man. He smiled at the irony. Of course, the most delightful touch to the whole scenario lay in his returning Margrethe's injured brother to the safety of his home and family. Margrethe would be eternally grateful, and Beau would be none the wiser that his rescuer was, in fact, also his attacker. It was a beautiful plan and even if the meddlesome brother harbored any suspicions, they were unlikely to be believed. In fact, suspicion over Freddie's strange disappearance may well fall upon Beau himself! In any case, Lucius was sure that the disappearance of his best friend served sufficient warning to Beaufort Winchester II not to cause any further disturbance in Lord Lucius Ruthven's dark world.

"Silas! Dispose of the remains somewhere on my property! Be sure to place them where they will be undisturbed and undiscovered. Feed them to the dogs if you must." Impatiently, he shrugged off his blood-stained coat, handing it to his manservant. "Take this, too! Get rid of it!" Silas took the coat and turned to gaze dully at Freddie's remains. A man's throat was now a blood-soaked, gaping hole surrounded by jagged flesh. The ripped apart chest, exposed glistening muscle, sinew, and bone. Not much remained recognizable as human.

Without comment, Silas leaned down and placed the coat over the bloodied mess before lifting what remained of the man in his arms and melting into the morning mist. Lucius stayed in the clearing, breathing in the cold morning air as it closed behind his departing servant. With breakfast now completed, he would return Beaufort Winchester II to his family. Within moments, he knelt beside the prone figure of Margrethe's brother. Beau's jacket, ripped by the bramble thorns, exposed slithers of pale skin caked in dried blood. His face exhibited a maze of scratches. One had narrowly missed his right eye. With a sigh, Lucius bent and picked up the young man. Balancing him easily in his arms, he closed his eyes and let the ether draw them through the thickets and trees to the Winchester driveway.

Margrethe saw them first.

"Mother! Come quickly! It's Beau! Something has happened!" She flung the oak door open with a strength that defied her slender build. Lifting the annoyingly voluminous nightdress, she flew down the stone steps, tears springing into her eyes.

"Lucius! What happened! Oh, my! Is he all right?"

A dark frown creased Lucius's brow. "I don't think he's severely injured, dearest. It looks as if he's sustained a nasty blow to the head, though. He's scratched to pieces, too."

Margrethe stopped in front of him, her eyes pooled with tears. She reached out and gently touched her brother's scratched cheek.

"Oh, poor Beau! What could have happened?"

"I would guess, dear Margrethe that your brother fell and injured himself. He has a concussion so we'd best get him to bed and call the doctor."

"Of course!" Margrethe turned and hurried towards the house. Shifting the weight of his burden, Lucius followed her. The morning sunlight filtered through her embroidered nightgown, revealing delicious hints of well-formed legs and a lithe, supple body. Lucius felt an ill-timed flush of desire and tried to focus on his deceitful role as rescuer and hero.

Elizabeth Winchester met them at the door. The sight of the prone body of her son sent her into immediate hysterics. With a calm air, Lucius suggested that she find a servant and dispatch them to fetch the doctor without delay. With the flustered woman temporarily distracted, Lucius and Margrethe hastened Beau through the dark hallway and up the winding staircase. Even in the panic of the moment, Margrethe couldn't help but marvel at the ease with which Lucius carried his burden. He seemed to take the flight of stairs in no time. Margrethe caught up to him to open the bedroom door, but he was already inside, laying her brother on his unmade bed. As Lucius began to tug off Beau's muddied boots, Margrethe reached out and gently touched his shoulder. It sent shock waves of electricity through him. Lucius gave an involuntary shudder of longing.

"Lucius, thank you."

He kept his back to her. For some reason, he could not bear to look at her right now.

"It was nothing, Margrethe. It is merely good fortune that I found him."

"Where was he?"

Lucius hesitated before turning to look at her.

"He was a little way inside my property. It looks like he was hunting. His shotgun was caught up in a bramble bush."

"Hunting?" Margrethe looked puzzled. "Then where is Freddie? Beau would not go hunting alone, I am sure of it."

Lucius shook his head.

"I saw no sign of Freddie, or anyone else, Margrethe. Only your brother."

Without a word, Margrethe turned and ran from the room. Throwing Beau's boots into a corner, Lucius followed her out of the room and into the bedroom next door. Margrethe stood in the middle of the empty room, hands on hips, a frown creasing her lovely brow.

"Freddie's not here!"

"No, it would appear not." Lucius kept his voice even. "Perhaps he is at breakfast or has gone for a morning stroll on the grounds?"

Margrethe turned to face him. Her dark brown eyes were wild, frightened. Her fear engulfed him like an aphrodisiac, he breathed in its fragrance and swirled it round in his veins.

"Or maybe he went hunting with Beau! Lucius, we must find him! Something's happened to poor Freddie, I know it has!"

She trembled now. Lucius stepped towards her, drawing her in close. He could smell roses in her hair. He buried his face in the fragrant softness and kissed the top of her head gently.

"Do not worry, sweet Margrethe, we'll find him. I will arrange a search party immediately." He stepped back and gazed deeply into her eyes. "My darling, your brother needs you now. I am sure the doctor has been summoned. Stay at Beau's side and nurse him back to health. You are the best medicine he could have at present, my love."

Margrethe looked up at him with an expression of pure trust. He leaned and kissed her lightly on the lips. Her debt was his now, as was her love. With a final embrace, Lucius turned once more from his desire and left to form a search party.

# CHAPTER FIVE

BEAU became aware of two overwhelming sensations as he slowly resurfaced to consciousness. The first, a headache that throbbed and pounded relentlessly throughout his entire aching skull. The second, the gentle touch of a soft, delicate hand on his forehead. He knew Margrethe's touch immediately. Many times throughout his childhood, Beau had felt the same soothing gesture of healing, and it never failed to bring relief, no matter how great his suffering. Until now! The headache grew merciless, and even the weight of Margrethe's delicate hand on his forehead became nearly too much to bear.

He stirred restlessly, groaned and opened encrusted, bloodshot eyes. Margrethe stared at him, worry clearly etched upon her face. She jumped at his groan.

"Beau! You are awake! Thank God!" Mindless of his pain, she threw herself upon him, smothering him with a hug that normally would have warmed his heart and soul. Now, however, it felt somewhat claustrophobic, restricting his breath and his ability to think.

"Margrethe, please!" He pushed her away none too gently, then doubled over, wincing. His headache threatened to split his skull in two! He wanted so desperately to have a moment to think, to work through what had happened. And that was the question, what had happened? Lost in his confused thoughts, Beau missed the flicker of hurt in his half-sister's eyes. He gazed around the familiar bedroom, trying to orientate his fragmented thoughts. Strange scenes flashed in his mind. A confusion of brambles, a gunshot, a dark, mysterious figure kneeling beside him.

"What happened to me? Why does my head hurt so?" Margrethe hesitated only a moment before reaching for his hand.

"Dearest Beau, I wish I knew! Lucius found you a little way inside his property, unconscious!" We've no idea what you were doing there or what happened. You had your gun with you, so it seems you were hunting when perhaps you fell?"

*Lucius!* The mention of the hated name jolted his mind sharply out of his befuddlement. *Of course!* He and Freddie had gone to the Ruthven mansion to find out more about Margrethe's mysterious suitor.

Again, a flash of memory. Pain, falling, someone kneeling beside him.

"Or perhaps I *was* felled!" muttered Beau, darkly. At last his gaze settled on his sister and he saw the tears pooled in the corners of her beautiful eyes. A horrific thought jolted him upright.

"Freddie! Margrethe, where is Freddie?"

Margrethe tried to hush him with a restraining hand.

"Beau, do not upset yourself!"

"But I was with Freddie." Beau persisted, "Is...is he all right?"

Margrethe lowered her eyes. Their answer proved enough. He pushed himself upright, grabbing her delicate wrist in a deathly grip.

"Margrethe, where is Freddie? Tell me!"

Margrethe slowly raised her eyes to his. She looked genuinely distraught.

"We don't know where Freddie is, Beau. Lucius is out searching for him now."

"Lucius!" Beau's temples throbbed even harder. "By the gods, that man need search no further than his own memory!"

Margrethe's eyes widened. "Beau, whatever do you mean? It

was Lucius who found you. I can assure you he is as concerned as I am. As we all are!"

The pain in his head reached volcanic proportions. With a withering look, Beau pushed his sister's hand aside! "Damn it, Margrethe, why do you place your blind trust in that man? I was on his property when this happened!"

"Indeed, you were and fortunately so, or who knows when you would have been found!"

"Oh, yes! How opportune that his lordship, Lucius Ruthven, found me after my mysterious fall!" Beau's voice dripped with sarcasm. "Which again begs the question, where is Freddie? Why did he not find him also?"

Margrethe's voice choked with tears. "Beau, I honestly do not know! Lucius said he saw no sign of Freddie when he found you. If it were not for Lucius, you might have lain there for ages! Besides, it was you who was trespassing on his property, Beau! Lucius has done no wrong!"

"Oh, I seriously doubt that." Beau fixed his sister with another withering look. "I'm going to search for Freddie myself. I do not need Lord Lucius Ruthven's help! None at all!"

"Beau, do not be ridiculous! You are in no condition to go anywhere!" In spite of her tears, Margrethe's voice held firm resolve. "Lucius will find him. He's organized a search party, and they are scouring the woods now."

"Feh! Oh, I'm sure he will find him, Margrethe. In fact, I am sure he will lead them right to him!" Beau swung his legs over the side of the bed, wincing as the movement sent sharp blasts of pain through his temple yet again. Margrethe did not miss his grimace.

"For God's sake, Beau, please lie down! And if not for God's sake, then for mine!" Her concern skyrocketed. Surely the blow to Beau's head had made him irrational. The thought that Lucius would harm either her brother or Freddie—utterly ridiculous!

Suddenly, Beau noticed a bright red smear on his sister's

42

nightgown. He peered at it bleary-eyed.

*Blood!*

His eyes weren't so bleary anymore.

"Margrethe, what's that on your night dress?"

Margrethe stared at him blankly for a moment before turning her gaze downwards to the sheer white material that covered her. A small frown creased her brow. Beau answered for her.

"It is blood, Margrethe! Blood! Where did the blood come from?"

She looked puzzled for a moment. Reaching down, she scrubbed at the stain like a demented Lady Macbeth. For a moment she seemed to struggle for an answer, then a light dawned in her eyes. She pointed at her brother's arms, now swathed in bandages.

"You, Beau! The blood stains must have come from you!"

"And your dear Lord Lucius Ruthven? Did he have blood on him, too?"

Again her brow furrowed as she tried to recollect the moment she'd first seen Lucius with Beau in his arms. Her memory turned hazy, given the panic of the moment, but she did remember seeing blood on Lucius's shirt and hands.

"Well, of course, he did, Beau! He carried you here, you were bleeding!"

"How much blood was there, Margrethe?"

She strained her thoughts. There had been a fair amount of blood on Lucius's shirt, but no more than would be expected from Beau's wounds. She said as much to Beau. He regarded her stonily.

"Are you sure, Margrethe? Perhaps it was not my blood on his shirt."

Exasperation overtook Margrethe. "Of course, it was, Beau! How could it not be?"

"Maybe it was *Freddie's* blood!" Beau's eyes were hardened steel. Margrethe felt a wave of despair wash over her. Even after his rescue, Beau still regarded Lucius Ruthven with suspicion and hatred. She put it down to childish jealousy and the blow to Beau's head.

"It wasn't Freddie's blood Beau, it was yours! And perhaps you should show some gratitude to Lucius for saving you instead of condemning him!" Frustrated now, she rose from the chair she'd pulled up to the side of his bed. Her tears had dried, replaced by a steely look equaling her brother's angry gaze. "I have heard enough of your ridiculous talk! Mother wishes to see you. I will call her and leave you alone for now. Perhaps we can talk when you are more rational."

"It is not I who is irrational, Margrethe. Your blind faith in this man is irrational!"

"Oh, that is enough! Stop it, Beau, stop it now!" With one last fiery glance, she turned on her heel. Beau heard her say something about fetching their mother before she strode from the room. *Damn! Why could she not see it?* And now he would have to endure his mother's histrionics. Beau seethed inwardly. All he wanted to do was find Freddie. He had no time for arguments or for the emotional outbursts of women. But it was too late, his mother's ample form already filled the doorway of his room.

"Beaufort, my dearest boy! Oh, thank God you are alive!"

Defeated, Beau slumped back onto the sheets, all thoughts of escape quashed by his mother's appearance. She began fussing around him, plumping pillows and admonishing him for putting himself and his friend in such danger. And the ball, what of the ball? She couldn't possibly cancel everything now! Beau closed his eyes and succumbed to the pounding in his head and ears. There would be no reasoning with Lady Elizabeth Winchester, nor with Margrethe. He would just have to deal with Lord Lucius Ruthven later, knowing full well his preening mother wouldn't let him join the search. Any further argument only served to increase his pain and boiling anger. Wearily he waved a hand at Elizabeth.

"It is fine, Mother, do what you must."

44

"Well, Beaufort, everything is arranged! And it will provide a welcome distraction from all this drama. I am sure Lord Ruthven will find Freddie and all will be fine. You need not attend, of course, people will understand."

"Yes, yes, of course, Mother, of course," Beau replied with a calm that belied the seething frustration and anger within him. "I am sure it will all be fine in good time."

But he knew it wouldn't.

LUCIUS returned to his mansion to clean up and organize the horses. Silas had readied the two most reliable steeds and now waited in the courtyard with reins in hand, anticipatory as always of his master's wishes. With a curt greeting, Lucius bid him to wait while he divested himself of his bloodied clothes. He quickly splashed his face with the water in his toiletry basin, scrubbing at a couple of stubborn clots that still clung to his skin. The clear water turned pink, a testament to deeds ill done and hidden. He wondered momentarily if Margrethe had noticed the amount of blood on his face and hands, but he quickly dismissed the thought. Entranced Margrethe would see only what he wanted her to see. He tipped the contents of the basin out the window. They splashed onto the courtyard below, startling the ebony horses and Silas, who struggled to bring them back under control. Freshened and changed into clean attire, Lucius joined his manservant in the courtyard. Together they mounted the horses and rode out to the neighboring estates, gathering willing helpers as they went. It took just nigh on two hours, but finally a small band of men thrashed their way through the rich forest undergrowth, some on foot, others mounted. They spread out, covering the outskirts of Lucius's property first before spilling into the vast breadth of the Winchester estate.

As they parted bramble bushes and called out Freddie's name, Lucius turned to Silas and whispered, "I hope you hid him well! I have no desire for him to be found."

45

Silas gave his master a small, sly smile. He knew too well the workings of Lucius's mind and had acted accordingly. The hounds had eaten their fill.

"No trace of him shall be found, Master."

Satisfied, Lucius asked no further questions. He wanted the ball to go ahead tonight, and the discovery of Freddie's bloodied and ravaged remains would most certainly put that and the rest of his plans in jeopardy. It suited his purposes far better if Freddie's fate remained unknown, open to theory and gossip.

With a loud shout, he urged the searchers on, drawing them away from the perimeters of his land and moving them gradually closer to the Winchester mansion. By lunch time, they were exhausted and discouraged. Lady Elizabeth Winchester's cook had prepared a feast of ham and baked bread, with onions and condiments to assuage their hunger. They ate wordlessly, each man intent on his own thoughts and fears. The search then resumed, spreading back once more to the Ruthven estate. Lucius wanted to be sure that no trace of the missing man ever became found on his property. After a few more fruitless hours of searching, it ended, called off due to impending darkness. Lucius smiled as he watched his neighbors return to their own homes to ready themselves for the Winchester ball. Lady Elizabeth Winchester had been most insistent at lunch that the event should continue, assuring them that it was the only way she could show her gratitude and provide some relief from the grave situation. Lucius had barely been able to maintain his solemn expression at her words, grave situation indeed! A shallow grave, perhaps, covering the barely recognizable remains of the annoying and invasive Freddie. Away from prying eyes, he now allowed a burst of laughter to break forth. Silas glanced at his master. He didn't need to inquire as to the reason for his mirth, knowing well his master's black humor. Together the two men returned to the dark, cool halls of the Ruthven mansion and began to make their preparations for the ball.

MARGRETHE stared at her reflection in the mirror. A wan, pale ghost stared back, black eyes pooled in alabaster skin. She twisted a curl listlessly, wondering for the umpteenth time at the possible inappropriateness of the ball. Her mother remained undeterred, of course, and Beau had insisted on attending, in spite of his fragile condition. A tear rolled silently from her eye, trailing down her powdered cheek, splashing onto the polished oak surface of the dresser. It was supposed to be such a happy occasion, a time of merriment and dancing. Instead, her dear brother came home injured, his erstwhile friend went missing, and her beloved fell under suspicion. Margrethe sighed heavily. There seemed to be no solution, the two most important men in her life were bound to enmity. Lucius could not be at fault! Beau's reactions were extreme and unfounded. Jealousy lay at the core, she felt. Beau had always been her protector, unfailing in his love and support. She had always been able to count on him, no matter what the situation. Now, he seemed like a stranger, an angry and irrational stranger who had no care for her feelings at all! His loyalty to her no longer existed. He seemed angered by her love for another man when she had thought he would be happy for her. And now, his accusations against Lucius were driving a deeper wedge between them, forcing her to choose sides. It was beyond her how she could do so—her heart torn, her mind confused. Lucius was attentive, loving and kind towards her and her family. She'd been given no reason to doubt his sincerity or his love for her. Beau, on the other hand, had pushed her away, even frightening her at times with the violence of his anger. This Beau she did not know and unsure she ever wanted to know.

Part of her hoped that Beau would remain in his room. Only then would Margrethe truly enjoy the ball and the company of Lucius. She feared a direct confrontation between the two. The thought of either being hurt, be it emotionally or physically, greatly tested her! She could not throw off this overriding feeling of fear, no matter how she tried to reassure herself. She couldn't bear it. An ominous presence hung over the Winchester household. Its cold fingers gripped her heart, filling her with growing dread.

Margrethe shivered and reached for her new gown, a beautifully sewn creation of silken embroidery and pearls. She held it up against her tired body, trying to distract herself from her dark thoughts. The pale blue of the gown complimented her porcelain skin. Her blonde hair fell in a cascade of curls over her delicate shoulders. Margrethe sighed again and stepped carefully into the dress, pulling it over her slender hips and full breasts. She reached behind, closing the clasps at the back with experienced fingers. Stepping back, she examined her reflection. The image of beauty that stared back at her belied the dark turmoil within. Satisfied with her well-disguised despair, Margrethe turned to the door and opened it. She could hear the last minute preparations and even as she began to descend the winding staircase, the first carriages were announcing the arrival of the first guests with a crunch of gravel. Taking a deep breath, Margrethe steadied herself and plastered her prettiest smile on her face. Thus armed with the required social grace, she made her way to the ballroom to greet their guests.

# CHAPTER SIX

LUCIUS gazed around the room, taking in women in their ornate gowns and the men, stiff as penguins in their finery. He cut quite the figure, immaculately attired in the latest London style, his coat elegant and finely cut, complimented by an embroidered waistcoat and stiff-collared shirt. A stylish cravat and well-tailored trousers completed the man about town effect. He immediately became aware of quite a few coy glances from the female guests, radiating heated interest from beneath their lowered lashes. Their desires were of no concern to him, for his eyes were fixed intently on his prize as she entered the room. Margrethe, a vision of breathtaking beauty, dulled all other attempts at femininity. Her dark eyes scanned the room, searching out her lover, experiencing a wave of relief when she finally saw him. They moved towards each other, oblivious to the stares and whispers around them. She moved with effortless grace. Her pale skin glowed against the fine blue silk of her gown, her hair swept up into a fashionable pile of plaits and curls. She appeared a little wan, no doubt from the stress of the day, but it did nothing to diminish her appeal. If anything, it just increased her allure, lending her a becoming fragility. Lucius felt an unaccustomed wave of protectiveness wash over him as he took her hand and pressed it to his lips.

"Margrethe, you leave me breathless with your beauty!" He did not lie, having felt the fire of lust many times in his life, always disguised as desire until the object of his attention succumbed to his advances. Such fever quickly faded when his appetite became sated, enabling Lucius to move onto fresher prey without so much as a backward glance. Margrethe, however, was different. Somehow she had crept into his dark soul and warmed his icy heart, sending flames of desire through his senses with a simple look or a touch.

She had become so much more than prey, and he couldn't imagine this hunger being satisfied by any other.

Margrethe smiled at his words, but her eyes seemed sad and somewhat distant.

"Beau has decided to join the festivities," she said simply.

*Ah, so that was the source of her concern.* Lucius fixed what he hoped to be a caring expression on his face.

"So your brother is well enough to attend the ball? Should he not be resting?"

"Yes, he should." Margrethe nodded at a peacock of a woman and her portly husband as they passed by, their inquisitive stares unmistakable. Lucius's presence normally would be of great interest in itself, being a stranger to the area, but his association with Margrethe made him more of a curiosity to Margrethe's friends and neighbors. Even if he had not planned to make his intentions clear before now, Lucius could see that the pressure most certainly would be upon him to do so.

"I would feel much happier if Beau would rest, but he insists on being present," she continued. "Of course, Mother encouraged his attendance. She has hopes that he may find some of the young ladies attractive. There are several good matches here tonight."

"None as perfect as you, Margrethe." The compliment slipped smoothly from his tongue. She smiled at him again, and this time it reached her eyes.

"You are so good to me, Lucius, I don't know what I would have done lately if you had not been here for me."

"I will always be here for you, my beloved."

"Will you indeed?" a voice interrupted sharply. The smile died on Margrethe's lips. Lucius turned to come face to face with Beau. The two men stood and stared at each other for a moment, each frozen in silent contemplation of his rival. Beau's wounds had been tended to, but they still looked angry and raw. Even his expensive coat couldn't disguise the bandage on his arm and nothing could disguise the look of hatred in his eyes. Lucius quickly covered his own distaste.

"Beau! What a relief to see you up and about." Lucius held out his hand. Beau ignored the gesture and Lucius let his hand fall back to his side. Margrethe shifted uncomfortably.

"Really, Beau, you could at least be civil." She whispered the entreaty, but her voice held a certain steeliness that Lucius hadn't heard before.

"Civility would indicate respect, Margrethe, and I have none whatsoever where this man is concerned." Beau made no effort to lower his voice and several guests standing nearby glanced in their direction. Margrethe's face reddened perceptibly, but Lucius retained a calm composure, seeing clearly where this situation could be turned to his advantage. If Beau chose to alienate himself further from his sister, it would only drive her more quickly and deeply into his arms.

"Beau, that is enough!" Now her tone turned icy. "Come, Lucius, I'll introduce you to some more savory company. I imagine that will not be difficult to find!" With a dismissive toss of her carefully coiffed head, Margrethe slipped her hand onto Lucius's arm, steering him gently but firmly away from her brother. Beau stared balefully after them as they merged into the gaiety of the social whirl. A drinks waiter passed by. Beau reached out for a sweet wine, sweeping the glass off the tray and into his mouth in one swift movement. Before the waiter could escape, Beau quickly grabbed another drink and made his way through the crowd of revelers A few of them cast him strange looks as he pushed past. The rumors had already started. Freddie's strange disappearance caught on like wildfire as the current topic *de jour* at dining tables throughout the countryside, whispers of an accidental shooting and a hasty burial. He had even heard a vile reference to a lovers' tiff, no doubt accountable for the amount of time spent with his dear friend behind doors. Little did people know that the arrival of his loathed rival had driven him to retreat to his chamber with Freddie. Their plot to uncover the truth about Lucius, hatched in those late night sessions of drinking and debate, had been foiled before it began.

For a moment, Beau wondered what they would've found it they hadn't been set upon. Freddie's disappearance may have been a mystery to some, but for Beau there was no mystery. Lord Lucius Ruthven had somehow discovered their plan and murdered Freddie. The only question in Beau's mind concerned why he had been spared. He still had no memory of events beyond a sharp pain to the back of his head. People questioned him about it relentlessly, of course, including the local constabulary. Beau loathed to reveal too much, lest people think him mad for his suspicions. He stuck to his cover story of a hunting trip gone wrong and an unfortunate fall that had completely wiped his memory. The explanation still left him open to suspicion and innuendo, but, for now, it remained the safest course of action. His rival had already ingratiated himself with the locals. Lucius was charming, wealthy, and handsome. People seemed to need no further assurance of Lord Ruthven's good character, as though mesmerized by his presence. Even his own mother and sister held the wretched cad on a pedestal while looking at their own relation with doubt and disgust in their eyes.

A sudden burst of raucous laughter broke through his thoughts. Yes, it was his mother, indulging in too much sweet wine. To think the woman dared lecture him on his own drinking. Beau slipped through the crowd, cutting across the dance floor, disrupting a polka waltz. He tapped his mother on the shoulder. She turned a flushed face towards him. Her laughter died in her throat when she saw him. She regarded him with narrowed eyes.

"Why Beau, you are not circulating." Her tone dripped disapproval. She took in his disheveled hair and wild eyes and stared at the half-empty glass in his hand. "You *are* drinking, though, I see."

"But, of course, Mother. As are you." He stared at her own near empty glass of wine pointedly. Her eyes narrowed more.

"Then perhaps you should lift your spirits a bit, my dear son. This is, after all, *your* homecoming celebration."

"Ah, yes, Mother. My homecoming. And what a homecoming it has been." Beau's voice rose an octave.

"Clearly, it has been too much for you, Beau. Perhaps Lord Turley could escort you to your room. I fear you are overwhelmed and need rest."

A stout, gray-haired man stepped forward to do her bidding. Beau waved him away.

"No need to trouble yourself, Lord Turley, I am well able to find my way to my own chambers." He turned to his mother and bowed theatrically. "I shall bid you good night, then, Mother. You are quite right. I am, as you put it, overwhelmed." *Yes, overwhelmed with frustration, pain, and anger,* he thought.

Gathering his last threads of sobriety, Beau turned and waved his hand at the room. "Good night, my dear friends, enjoy the revelries on my behalf."

Drowned out by the strains of the chamber orchestra and ceaseless idle chatter and laughter of the guests, his voice barely resonated with anyone. A few people nearby heard his farewell, nodding at him uncomfortably. Shakily, Beau made his way to the nearest door and wove across the hallway. He stopped at the stairs for a moment, glancing back. Through the door, he caught a final glimpse of Margrethe in Ruthven's arms. She looked deliriously happy.

With a final gulp of his drink, Beau threw the glass on the floor. The crystal shattered, the pieces scattering across the mosaic tiles. He regarded the glittering remains, a strange feeling of satisfaction gripping him. One day, he would destroy Lord Lucius Ruthven. He would dash him to pieces like the fine crystal glass. With that comforting thought, Beau turned and made his way slowly and painfully up the stairs.

Blissfully unaware of her brother's departure, Margrethe

whirled around the dance floor in a dream. Lucius pressed his hand firmly against the small of her back, drawing her body close to his in a cushion of warmth and unspoken longing. They moved in unison, their steps flying effortlessly together with poetic grace. So immersed was she in her dream that the admiring stares of the other guests went unnoticed. Lucius, however, *did* notice and reveled in the admiration. They were a beautiful couple, the raven-haired lord with his finely chiseled features and his delicate blonde partner. This was his homecoming, not Beau's. Lucius smiled. The guest of honor was barely missed. Instead, all eyes were on his sister and her mysterious suitor. Men looked on with admiration tempered with envy, women with jealousy, tinged with reluctant admiration for the fortunate Margrethe Winchester. Lucius smiled again, a beaming smile, and swung Margrethe around in a graceful arc. The waltz ended in a melodic swirl of violins, and the couples parted. Margrethe drew reluctantly away from Lucius, the warmth of his body still imprinted on hers. As he led her to the edge of the dance floor, the tinkle of a bell drew everyone's attention.

"A moment if you please, my dear friends!" Lady Elizabeth Winchester's voice rose shrilly above the murmur of guests and clinking of glasses. She waited for a moment for the noise to die down before continuing.

"I would like to thank you all for coming here tonight to celebrate Beaufort's homecoming. Regrettably, as most of you know, Beau has been through an unfortunate experience recently and is feeling unwell. He has retired to his room to rest but insists that you all enjoy the ball in his absence."

A sympathetic murmur erupted to the first part of her statement and a patter of applause to the last, which Lucius found mildly amusing. Their dear friends seemed happy enough to continue the festivities without their drunken, surly guest of honor. It seemed Beaufort Winchester II had fallen out of favor while he, Lucius, reigned as the man of the moment. It was a most satisfying state of affairs and, strangely enough, achieved largely through the efforts of Beau himself, the irony of which was not lost on Lucius. Once again, he was grateful for Beau's incredible stupidity.

The orchestra started to play again. Lucius turned questioningly to Margrethe, but she shook her head. Her face, slightly flushed, complemented her unsteadiness.

"Do you need fresh air, my love?" Lucius asked, his brow furrowed with concern.

Margrethe nodded, following him like a child as he led her through the double glass-paned doors to the balcony. After the oppressive heat of the dance floor, the fresh air hit them like a blast of Antarctic air. Margrethe caught her breath sharply and Lucius gathered her close to him, wrapping her in his arms. She clung to him wordlessly, burying her face in his chest. Gently he stroked her hair. His gaze fell not upon her, however, but upon the magnificent grounds of Winchester Hall. Soon it would be all his, along with the delicate flower wrapped in his arms. It had been too easy, really. He'd expected a challenge of sorts, a fight of some kind. Instead, he faced a strong but naive young beauty, her empty-headed, vain mother, and her churlish, moronic brother. Their father so often absent as to be non-existent. Yes, all too easy. He felt Margrethe move in his arms and broke away from his thoughts, looking down at her with a gentle, caring expression. It was not all an act, for he did indeed care. Too much, perhaps, but it was of little consequence, for all he sought he conquered and more.

Margrethe returned his gaze adoringly. Her next words shocked him back from his reverie.

"Take me with you, Lucius."

He stared at her, uncomprehending.

"Take you? Take you where, Margrethe?"

"To your real home, Lucius. To your family home. I want to be with you. I want to be a part of everything you are."

He hesitated for a moment before lifting her chin gently and looking deeply into her eyes. She was more than a little affected by the wine, but the adoration he found there resounded pure and strong.

"Are you certain, my flower? You truly know not what you ask."

"I am certain. I care not about obstacles. Take me away from here, from my mother, from Beau."

Her eyes were pleading now, almost desperate. It wasn't what he had planned, but…

"If it is what you wish my adored one. You know I will do anything for you."

He leaned down and kissed her lips. She returned his kiss with a passion that belied her experience, the heated searching of his tongue parting her lips easily. A fire engulfed them both, inflaming the deepest parts of their beings. Lucius pulled himself away. When he managed to speak, his voice was ragged with desire.

"Then we will go now, my love. Come with me, take my hand. Silas has the horses."

Still burning, Margrethe grabbed his hand, oblivious to the cold night air. Together they ran down the worn marble stairs into the darkness, the sounds of laughter and music fading behind them.

***

# CHAPTER SEVEN

THE early morning sun filtered through a crack in the brocade drapes, slashing Beau's face with a shard of blinding light. He opened his eyes reluctantly against its bright assault, squinting and turning his head away towards the blessed darkness of his room. The house was silent, a stark contrast to the festivities of the night before. He took a moment to orientate himself. He had slept deeply, yet a strange lethargy enveloped him. He struggled against it, willing himself to sit up and swing his legs over the side of the four-poster bed. His feet hit the floor with a dull thud. Beau sat very still, listening for any sign of the usual morning activity.

There was none.

Perhaps everyone else felt poorly after the ball. The champagne had flowed freely, even before he'd retired to his room. No doubt, the resulting sore heads wouldn't provide any incentive to rise and greet the day. Beau felt little enthusiasm to do so himself. His thoughts wandered to the events of the previous night and he scowled at the memory of Lord Lucius Ruthven and his sister. Clearly, Margrethe had been overwhelmed by champagne and infatuation. To choose a manipulative stranger over her family was completely out of character, and her rejection had stung Beau badly. He hoped she would see things differently in the light of day. He would talk to her later and try to appeal to her common sense, if indeed she had any left. With a sigh, he rose heavily to his feet, shrugging on the silk dressing gown draped on the chair beside him. He felt like death warmed up, but through the fog of his thoughts he became aware of a vague hunger. Perhaps a pot of tea and some breakfast would bring him back to the land of the living. He padded over to the door and opened it quietly, peering out into the hallway. Again, he listened for any sound of activity, but only silence greeted him. It seemed he would have to wake the servants before he could even have the pleasure of a hot cup of tea.

Disgruntled, Beau made his way to the staircase, pausing for a moment at Margrethe's door. No sound or movement there, either, so he continued down to the kitchen. He decided against rousing the servants, preferring to have the time to himself to gather his thoughts. He lit the stove and waited for the water to boil. As the water splashed into the kettle, the rich scent of the aromatic leaves revived his senses. The simple task proved strangely comforting, unfamiliar though it was, and he wondered momentarily if perhaps a servant's life was worth more in its simplicity than one of landed nobility and wealth. With another sigh, Beau decided to take his tea on the terrace. He would resolve things with Margrethe when she awoke and hopefully appeal to whatever good sense remained.

***

# CHAPTER EIGHT

"FOOLISHNESS!"

His mother's voice snapped at him like a whip. Ice cold chastisement, that one word dripping with fury. Reluctantly he lifted his eyes, for he knew to not do so would only incur more wrath. His mother's eyes bore into him, dark cauldrons of fire and ice. It took all his courage to meet her gaze.

"I'm sorry, Mother."

"Sorry!" Claudia spat the word at him in disgust. "You haven't even begun to understand the meaning of sorry! Have you *any* idea what you have done?"

Lucius nodded. "Yes, I understand."

"You understand nothing! How could I have bred such ill witted progeny? It cannot be from my womb you were spewed! Oh, by the dark gods, no!"

Spewed from the bitter womb, weaned on despair. Ah, yes, sadly, he knew too well he'd sprung from his mother's womb!

"Take her back!" Again, the words were spat at him, burning like acid.

Lucius steeled himself. "I will not take her back, Mother!"

Deadly silence settled in. Her cold gaze bore into him. He forced himself to hold his ground though his own eyes longed to lower themselves. When he spoke, he could feel the weakness in his words. His last defense

"I cannot take her back, Mother. We are betrothed."

Claudia let out an unearthly scream. It pierced the stone walls, shredding the dark silence in a cyclone of rage.

"*Betrothed?* You pathetic ingrate! How dare you take a human to be your wife, let alone your own half-sister!"

Lucius gazed at his mother in horror. He'd never seen her this angry. Her fury paralyzed him. He tried to speak, but even his vocal chords were frozen in terror as his mother's face contorted into a mask of demonic fury.

"I should throw you both into the depths of Hell!" She drew closer. "You know I can do that, do you not, Lucius?" Her tone demanded an answer. Lucius only managed a monosyllable.

"Yes."

"Tell me you have not had her yet!"

Lucius's silence substantiated answer enough. He hung his head, waiting for the furious assault. He didn't have to wait long.

"So it is not enough for you to fuck your human half-sister, you then have to go and pledge yourself to her! You could have at least finished the creature off! Lust is one thing, but this?"

"I love her," Lucius said quietly.

"Love?" Claudia stared at her son incredulously. "What do you know about love?" she hissed, her words full of venom and disgust.

Lucius swallowed. This fared well not at all.

"We began to share our passion, but I was inflamed beyond my control. The bloodlust, the desire—they all became one, and I tasted her..." His voice trailed off.

Claudia's eyes narrowed. "Then why is she not dead?"

"Because I turned her."

Again, a silence, more deadly than before.

When Claudia spoke, her voice dropped low, dangerously low.

"You *turned* her? You mean she is one of *us* now?"

Lucius nodded miserably, trying to muster a hasty defense.

"It is no different than you turning my father." He regretted the words as soon as they were out.

He did not see the blow that struck him. He grabbed helplessly at thin air as the momentum lifted him off the floor and flung him backward. A sharp crack resonated as his skull hit the hard stone wall on the other side of the room. It sounded like Chinese fireworks going off in his head. He felt the stickiness of blood trickle down the back of his neck. It seeped into his crisp, white collar, staining it a beautiful crimson. There was no pain, just numbness and stickiness. He remained slumped against the wall, struggling to regain his senses.

"Where is she? WHERE IS SHE?" His mother's voice rose in a demonic wail. "If you don't bring her to me, I will find her and fix this myself! You idiot! You ungrateful, moronic...you...you...!"

Lucius waited for another blow, but it never came. Somewhere through the fog that used to be his thinking, he heard a door close. As his strength returned, he realized he was alone in the room. That frightened him more than anything. He had no idea where his mother had gone or what she would do. Vaguely, he knew he had to reach Margrethe before Claudia did. He tried to stand, but the room spun around him, pulling him onto the floor. He tried to crawl towards the door, but his strength vanished. Darkness closed around him, beckoning him to oblivion. He reached for the brass door handle and just managed to feel the cold metal brush his fingertips before he lost consciousness.

MARGRETHE lay listening to her own breath in the silence. In, out, in, out. Yes, she drew breath, just as she always had since her first gulp of air as a newborn babe, yet she felt different. There but not there. Alive but dead.

She shifted uncomfortably. A sharp pain drew her hand to the side of her neck. As her fingers found and probed the two small scabs marring her perfect skin, the pain stabbed her again. She withdrew her hand hastily. What had happened last night? Foggily, she searched her memory. She could remember the ball, the argument with Beau. She remembered stepping outside with Lucius, she remembered his warm, soothing embrace, the scent of him, his whispered words of reassurance—then nothing! Frowning, Margrethe raised herself on her elbow and surveyed her dim, unfamiliar surroundings.

Richly embroidered brocade draped the windows, blocking all but a small sliver of light that cut through the dark red silk sheets on which she lay. Beyond the oak four-poster bed, the room sparsely, but tastefully furnished. A heavy dark dresser of considerable age dominated the room. A simply carved writing desk and what looked like to be a genuine Persian rug were the only other furnishings she could make out in the gloom. Expensive, yet functional. Whoever had decorated it had good taste and sparse needs.

Each turn of her head brought the stabbing pain her neck. Again, Margrethe's hand strayed to the two strange scabs. As her fingers gently brushed over them, a flash of memory erupted. Lucius upon her, waves of passion washing over her as he exposed her neck, grazing the exposed flesh with his lips, his teeth.

*His teeth! Lucius! Did Lucius leave the marks? It was the only explanation.*

Once unleashed, the passion between them had been overwhelming. Margrethe had held back her desire for so long that the mere touch of his lips on her neck had caused her entire body to shudder with unforeseen delight. His hands had explored the most secret parts of her, and she had opened herself willingly to his touch.

Brazen desire had washed over her, drowning her in an ocean of sensuous delight. Lucius had been gentle, hesitant even at first, but the taste of her skin had seemed to light an unquenchable fire in him. His touch had become more urgent, his kisses more brutal. She had given herself up to him and let him devour her. Their bodies had come together, crashing like waves upon a wild shore. She remembered her nails tearing at his flesh as he entered her. Her sharp cries of pain and pleasure had pushed him further to the edge. Her small, delicate body, crushed against his powerful torso, had shuddered with him as he reached his climax. There was a moment she was certain she had fainted, so intense her pleasure. She had lost herself in lightheaded abandon as her lover's seed coursed through her. She remembered his head buried in the soft fall of her hair, the pain between her legs, the warmth of her soul and the blood. Blood on the sheets. On the pillow. In her hair. It had been warm, sticky, sensual.

Horrified, Margrethe threw back the bedclothes and stared down at the bloody mess between her legs. The blood smeared along her inner thighs and up around her stomach. Her breasts too had crimson streaks across them. So much blood. Margrethe stifled a scream. Climbing carefully out of the crimson soaked sheets, she made her way to the only mirror in the room and reluctantly raised her eyes to her reflection. The face that stared back at her belonged to a stranger. Her eyes had darkened to the deepest black. Black circles framed the lower lashes. Her porcelain skin was even paler than usual. A delicate flush no longer accented her cheeks, and her lips now possessed a strange, bluish tinge.

Numbly, Margrethe turned away from the mirror and surveyed the room more closely. She recognized Lucius's clothes strewn across an ornate velvet chair. His boots were tossed carelessly nearby. There was, however, no sign of Lucius. An embroidered velvet lounging robe lay at the foot of the bed. Margrethe reached over and pulled it towards her, hugging it to her strangely cool body.

Crushed against her cold skin, it seemed to afford no warmth, so she hastily shrugged it on, wrapping the cord around her waist. Tying the robe securely, she turned her attention to the door. The handle proved as cool as the touch of her hand. She'd somehow expected it to be locked, but it turned easily. The heavy oak door swung slowly open, revealing a gloomy stone corridor. There were no windows. Candelabras attached to the walls lit up the entire hallway. The flickering light threw darting shadows across what looked like alcoves or doorways. These shadowy recesses lined the corridor as far as she could see.

Margrethe drew a breath and listened. All was as silent as the grave. Not even the early morning bird songs penetrated the thick, dark walls. Reassuring herself that there appeared to be no other living creature around, Margrethe drew another, sharper breath and stepped out into the hallway. The coldness enveloped her immediately. She expected her flesh to raise in goose pimples, but suddenly, inexplicably, the coldness seemed to melt away. Her skin remained smooth, unmarred by bodily reactions to temperature. Margrethe marveled for a moment at her unfamiliar adaptability to her cold environment until the nearest alcove caught her eye.

Framed by a simple, double carved arch, the alcove contained a life-size statue of a woman. Crafted in fine marble, she stood stiff and straight, staring blindly ahead with her desperate, empty eyes. Her hands were folded in front of her, as though folded in death. Her mouth gaped slightly open, forming a small, surprised "o." She stood carved in magnificent detail, so well, in fact, that when the light caught the marble features they seemed to come briefly to life. The lifelike flicker in the eyes would have produced a shiver if Margrethe were physically able to do so. When one's entire being is immersed in coldness, shivering becomes a memory of physical discomfort.

Margrethe reached out a hand and touched the marble cheek. The empty marble eyes stared straight into hers. Their white depths seemed to hold a silent cry. Was it loss? Despair? The statue made Margrethe uneasy. She snatched back her hand and stepped away, turning her attention to the rest of the corridor. A little further along, she noticed a larger carved door frame. She crept towards the heavy oak door, her bare feet whispering along the stone surface. She paused and strained her ears for any sound or sign of life. None could be hard. Hesitating for only a moment, Margrethe turned the iron latch. As the door swung open, a blast of warm air hit her, like a furnace against her cold skin. A roaring fire illuminated the room. Before the fire stood a man, his back turned towards her. He stood motionless, bathed in the fiery glow. She hesitated, uncertain as to whether he sensed her or not. She prepared to turn and quietly slip away when his voice drew her to a halt.

"You never get warm. No matter how close you stand to the fire, you never get warm."

Margrethe wasn't sure if he addressed her or someone else. A quick glance around the room told her he must indeed be speaking to her as there was no one else present.

"I'm sorry?" It came out as both an apology and a question. She felt like an intruder, a disturber of the peace.

He turned towards her slowly, his voice measured and deliberate.

"The coldness. It never goes away. Ever. No matter what you do." His eyes met hers. Dark, eyes, so like her own. Empty, dark, lifeless eyes.

Margrethe took an involuntary step backward. The eyes that mirrored her own narrowed slightly, as though in puzzled recognition.

"I do not believe I have made your acquaintance, young lady."

"No, sir, you have not. My name is Margrethe Winchester. My mother is Lady Elizabeth Winchester, formerly Elizabeth Charlesworth."

Even in the orange glow of the fire, the man's face visibly paled. The empty black eyes widened, becoming instantly more unnerving. Margrethe had the strange feeling she'd said something horribly wrong. She stood silently, unsure of what to say or do.

He stared at her for a moment or two. Then he finally spoke, his voice low, barely above a whisper.

"Did you say Charlesworth?"

Margrethe nodded. "Yes, my mother remarried after I was born."

The man staggered backward, holding his head between his hands as though trying to block out her words.

"Dear God, no, surely not!" His retreating back found a wall, and he leaned against it, head still cradled in now trembling hands.

In spite of her fear, Margrethe felt a surge of concern. He looked terribly unwell, perhaps even on the verge of collapse. She stepped forward, reaching out a hand in support. He pushed her away and stared at her wildly.

"I am Edmund Charlesworth."

Margrethe stared at the stranger. In the light of the room, she could see, even more clearly, the resemblance between them.

"Charlesworth?" she dumbly repeated. The enormity of his words crashed over her, sending sickening waves of realization through her stomach.

"You are my father." It was a statement, not a question. It was unmistakable.

The empty eyes raised to meet hers.

"Yes, Margrethe, I am your father."

Margrethe found herself suddenly overwhelmed by a cascade of emotions. Joy, fear, elation, horror. They all danced and played within her, each taking turns at reeling her mind around a chaotic dance floor. Elation won, and she ran towards the slumped man, a little girl longing for the embrace of her long-lost father.

He didn't stop her. Edmund allowed himself a moment to

remember the warmth of human emotion, the embrace of a loved one, a moment he knew must be all too brief. Finally, reluctantly, Edmund pushed his daughter away, holding her at arm's length.

"What are you doing here, Margrethe? How in God's name did you get here?"

"To answer your first question, Lucius brought me here. I cannot answer your second question, for I have no memory of getting here."

"Lucius?" Edmund frowned. "Why on Earth would Lucius bring you here?"

Margrethe blushed and lowered her eyes as her lover's name brought back flashes of dark, unbridled passion. Her flustered reaction did not go unnoticed.

This time, Edmund did push her away, his face contorted, etched with horror.

"You and Lucius? You are…?"

"Yes, we are betrothed."

"No, surely not! It can't be true!" Edmund Charlesworth slid further down the wall and curled into a crouching position, rocking back and forth. "No, no, no."

Margrethe stood helplessly, at a loss of what to do or think. Silently, she waited for the rocking and moaning to stop.

When it did, Edmund Charlesworth looked up at his daughter with the saddest eyes she'd ever seen. When he spoke, his voice carried the burden of knowledge best left unknown.

"Lucius is my son, Margrethe."

She stared at him blankly for a moment as the truth dawned on her.

His eyes.

So like hers.

So like Lucius.

Lucius was this man's son. And she was his daughter.

Suddenly, she understood all too well the despair of the man before her. She had found her father. And she had given herself to the man she loved—her half-brother!

***

# CHAPTER NINE

CLAUDIA paused for a moment and caught her breath. Her instincts had drawn her to her son's room in the west wing of the castle, where she now stood before the ornate oak doors to his chamber. Her finely tuned ears picked up no sound or sign of movement beyond them. She sniffed the air. The distinct scent of lavender and human odor assailed her nostrils. Her burning anger rose up again like bile, and she flung the doors open, prepared to unleash her rage against the unwanted mortal bitch. An empty room greeted her, denying Claudia the chance to attack her prey. Had the human whore sensed danger? She was one of them now and even in the earliest stages of vampiric evolution, she may well be able to use her enhanced senses to advantage.

Claudia's took in the contents of the room with a single, penetrating glance. The bed, with its tousled silk sheets and haphazard pillows, bore the marks and smell of copulation. There were blood sprays on the sheets. Invisible on the deep red silk, the metallic scent of their crimson stain gave away their presence. The idiot! He'd indeed fucked and turned her! There were clothes strewn across the floor and furniture. They all belonged to Lucius. Not a female garment was visible. Claudia strode across the room, kicking an abandoned shirt out of her way. She stopped and listened again for the sound of breathing. Nothing. Clearly the creature had made her escape.

Infuriated, Claudia turned all her senses to her prey. Intuitively, she sensed movement across the grounds, somewhere near the high stone wall that surrounded the castle. The vampire focused on the psychic sensation. A delicate figure manifested. Her face was hidden, and her movements hurried. Claudia allowed the visualization to clarify itself. The girl climbed feverishly. She still bore the awkwardness of a human, but she had the speed of a vampire. Claudia watched with unworldly eyes as the girl dropped down over the wall and into the thick cover of the surrounding forest.

For a moment, Claudia thought to follow her, but unlike Lucius, who suffered only small discomfort in daylight due to his human genes, Claudia dared not venture out during the advent of the sun. She of Hades, the daughter of darkness, could bear no daylight. It tore at her eyes, her skin, her breath. It savaged and devoured her, and she had learned quickly to avoid its intensity, knowing that the light, and only the light, could lead to her ultimate destruction. It was her one and only weakness. The darkness of the forest would protect her to a point, but it proved a risk that she wasn't prepared to take. Temporarily thwarted by her prey's escape, Claudia turned back towards the hallway, intending to unleash her frustration on her moronic son.

It wasn't Lucius, however, who crossed her path, but her equally moronic husband. Claudia wondered at the chances of human genes and stupidity triumphing over the genetic line of Hades, but it seemed that human stupidity was a powerful thing.

She prepared to push past Edmund with her usual lack of regard, but something in his eyes stopped her. Her husband stared at her with a strange mixture of grief and fury. The grief was not so unusual. It had flickered in his eyes for a while after his turning until the light went out, leaving only dark surrender and emptiness. Fury, on the other hand, she'd not seen or sensed in Edmund until now. Her husband had never dared show any such signs of displeasure towards his wife, for he knew all too well from whence she came and the destruction she bore in the dark, empty place that would be her soul, should she have one. Thus cowed by fear and resignation, he usually stayed compliant and easily managed.

However, Edmund showed no such fear now as he stared at Claudia. She allowed an icy smile to cross her face, more of a warning than a welcome.

"Edmund? Is something wrong?"

He seemed unable to answer. His ragged breath came hard and shallow, hissing through his lips like an angry serpent. Claudia drew closer, inclining her head at a mockingly ridiculous angle.

"I am sorry, dearest, I cannot quite hear you."

"How...dare...you..." The words were barely formed through his thinned lips, but the intensity behind them made them clear and strong.

"How dare I? What, pray tell?" She phrased it more of a challenge than a question.

"Was it not enough to draw me into this lifeless existence? Must you take my only daughter as well?"

His words took Claudia by surprise, quelling her urge to swipe him aside.

"Your daughter? What of *your* daughter, Edmund?"

"She is here. You brought her here!"

Claudia fixed her husband with a dark stare.

"I did not bring her here Edmund," she replied calmly. "Lucius brought her here in a moment of pure idiocy that can only have come from his human side."

Her slight seemed to go unnoticed by Edmund, who continued to stare at her with trembling anger.

71

"Lucius? Yes, of course, he would bring her here at your behest!"

The urge to hit him intensified. Somehow, Claudia resisted, retaining her calm exterior. Instead, she attacked him with her words.

"Not at my behest, dear Edmund. I had no part in this. It was Lucius who chose to bring your daughter here and bed her!" Even as the words spilled out into the vast hallway, she saw the pain in Edmund's eyes. Humans were made so vulnerable by their emotions. It was their greatest downfall, along with their inherent stupidity.

"And how *do* you know your daughter is here, Edmund?" Her question shot out at him, catching him in his vulnerable, emotional state.

"She came to my chambers." The words fell out as though compelled. Already, he knew he'd said far too much.

"Ah, so you spoke with her, Edmund? Does she know who you are?"

Edmund tried to clamp his lips shut yet, somehow, the word still escaped, like a traitor through the gates.

"Yes."

He didn't expect the roar of laughter that suddenly erupted from his dark spouse. His eyes widened in surprise when the sound pealed through the darkened hall.

She couldn't help her outburst. *Dear Edmund*, she thought gleefully, *you have done my work for me and banished her by her own hand.* The sheer beauty of it amused and pleased her. Still laughing quietly, she leaned forward and took Edmund's face between her hands. Her cold touch felt dead on his skin. That touch had once stirred such passion in him. Now, it stirred only deep revulsion.

He tried to back out of her grasp, but he remained caught. Unable to turn his eyes right nor left, he met her dark gaze head on. Her eyes, as always, gave away nothing with their emptiness. *The eyes are the window to the soul or lack thereof,* thought Edmund.

"Edmund, you have done well. Your daughter has fled from her shameful coupling with her half-brother. You shouldn't trouble yourself, she will no doubt flee to her mother and bother us no more."

*Unless she is with child.*

The thought rose, unbidden, and refused to retreat. Even as she thought it, she knew it to be so. It shook her and poached her next words. Suddenly preoccupied with the thought of unwanted spawn, Claudia released Edmund from her grasp but not her gaze.

"Edmund, you should go and rest." Her voice dropped to a monotone. She stared at him, unblinking. Edmund stared back, nodding dumbly in response. All his words and fight appeared spent. He had become, once again, the lifeless shell that covered the darkness where his soul once lived. Wordlessly, he turned and walked slowly back to his chambers.

Claudia stood for a moment, deep in thought as she watched his retreat.

Why had she not thought of the possibility of a child? If it were so and her intuition told her it to be so, Lucius would pursue his lover and child to the ends of the Earth. Even worse, the creature's child would have a claim to both the human inheritance of land and wealth and the vampiric inheritance of eternal solitude and living death, with all the power that allowed one to exist in such a state.

Claudia's thoughts tumbled over each other. Lucius could not know of this turn of events. Not yet. If he knew his lover had fled, he might try to bring her back. The human wench could not return. Not her and not the abomination that even now grew in her womb. Claudia tried to gather her troubled thoughts. She would somehow keep Lucius and Edmund apart. It wouldn't be too difficult as the two avoided each other wherever and whenever possible. When their paths did collide, their words were either heated or few. If they were to collide now, the result could be explosive. Claudia wasn't prepared to take any chances. Stealthily, she glided along the hallway to Edmund's chambers. The heavy oak door remained shut. Claudia placed her ear against the worn wood. Beyond the grain, the sound of rhythmic breathing reached her finely tuned ears. Without taking her ear from the door, Claudia carefully reached inside her bodice, extracting an iron key, worn with age as the door. It slid into the keyhole easily and silently. A slight click sounded as the lock turned. Claudia listened for a moment more. The breathing continued its steady rhythm. Satisfied that the matter was safely contained for now, Claudia tucked the key back in its hiding place and turned back down the hall, walking resolutely towards the sitting room where she had left her son lying semi-conscious.

MARGRETHE stopped under a huge oak and leaned against it. Her ragged breathing tore at her ribs. Her legs were numb, but her stockinged feet felt bruised and sore. She vaguely registered the strange absence of a heartbeat where her heart should have pounded with exertion, in all a fleeting distraction from the effort of regaining her breath. Finally, after what seemed like an eternity, her lungs were able to fill with air and her chest rose and fell normally.

Somewhat relieved, Margrethe raised her head and surveyed her surroundings. She had run blindly, thrashing through the thick undergrowth with little thought to direction or destination. Shock and survival had driven her through the dawn, into the arms of the wilderness which now damply embraced her.

The first rays of the sun had no warmth in them. They filtered reluctantly through the trees, cold, pale fingers of light that didn't even begin to reach the dark depths of the forest. Margrethe shivered. She had fled in her dress, hurriedly shrugged on, and a light wrap hastily snatched from a chair. The wrap was long gone, caught haplessly on the same thorny branches that had torn at her feet. She looked down, expecting to see bleeding cuts and scratches, but aside from her torn stockings, barely a mark appeared on either foot. Only a couple of slightly red marks betrayed any sign of her battle with the undergrowth.

Absently, Margrethe rubbed the marks, almost expecting to wipe them away. They remained beneath her fingers, but as she cast her mind back to the events of the night before, they gradually faded and disappeared. This miraculous healing passed unobserved as she remembered, with sadness, the verbal altercation with Beau. She had drunk too much wine. She'd smiled, danced and pretended that all remained well. In truth, the only enjoyable part of the ball was the loving attention of her dear Lucius. She remembered feeling a little faint. Lucius had taken her out to the balcony. She remembered the sting of cool air on her face as he tilted her head gently and brought his lips down to hers. She flushed at the memory of the delicious kiss that wound its way through her entire body, lighting a fire within her that she'd never experienced. She had fallen willingly into the depths of his passion, returning his kisses with a hunger she never knew existed. She remembered the touch of his body as she pressed against him like a wanton tavern hussy. The fires had roared through her body, igniting her like a falling star. And so she fell, into his embrace, into the depths, into his power.

Margrethe suddenly noticed her feet. A small, puzzled frown creased her brow. The marks had completely vanished. She rubbed at her feet again as if to make the marks reappear. They didn't. Neither did her memory of that fateful journey to Lucius's mansion. Well, that had been her assumption at the time as to their destination. However, this place, this foreign landscape, was far from home. She could remember the thunder of horses' hooves, the sway of the carriage—it seemed like a lifetime away. Then she arrived in his bedchamber, drowning in his feverish kisses as they divested their clothes on any available surface. He had murmured words of love in her ear as they edged toward the silk covered bed.

She had returned them, along with desperate kisses. She agreed to be his wife as he entered her, the question spilling from his lips as he plunged deep within her, drawing a small gasp of surprised pain, soon quelled by tidal waves of passion rolling across her senses. He had tried to hold back, she had sensed it, but the vortex took them both. He had bent his head as his seed spilled into her and she remembered the sharp, sweet sting of his teeth as she exploded like a star. They had fallen asleep in each other's arms, spent and sensuously satisfied.

The memory of his bite drew her hand to her neck. The marks had subsided. Again, like her feet, the results of some kind of miraculous healing. These things, along with the seeming lack of heartbeat, drew her mind towards questions she feared to ask. And now, to find her father under such circumstances and then find out that her lover was, in fact, her half-brother. Margrethe buried her head in her hands. The memories, deliciously sweet a moment ago, were suddenly stained with shame. She vowed inwardly never to think of that night again but, even as she did so, she knew it would haunt her to the end of her days.

*The end of her days.*

The words drew her back to her curious body changes. And her fiancé's bite. Her brother's bite, she remembered, cringing. *Dear God, forgive me for my foolishness!* She'd heard vampire tales. Even as a child, she and her brother had frightened each other with tales of ghosts and dark, undead creatures. Margrethe strained to remember those stories, but the damp morning air chilled her to the bone. At least with her feet healed and her breath returned, she could continue to find her way out of the forest and keep warm. The chill seemed to have less hold on her while moving.

The gloom had lifted a little, but the trees still hid among the shadows. She was tempted to go back and find her lost wrap, but the thought of who or what may be pursuing her stopped her. Would Lucius come after her when he discovered her gone? Would he find out she knew about their true relationship? Did he even know of it? Perhaps he'd never been told.

So many thoughts whirled through her head. She pushed them away, trying to focus on some sort of plan or even sense of direction. A dull, thudding sound reached her ears. She strained a little more. It seemed to come from quite near, just to her right. She followed the rhythmic sound, *thud, thud, thud,* until it suddenly stopped. Margrethe stopped, too, listening intently and praying it had not stopped entirely. Nothing. Just the sound of the awakening forest. The call of birds. The rustle of leaves. But no *thud*.

Suddenly, a man's voice broke through her rising despair. She scrabbled through a thicket of bushes and emerged seeing a most welcomed sight. There, before her tired, hurting eyes, was a small clearing. In the middle of said clearing a small daub house. The voice belonged to a short, stocky man standing next to an old cart laden with wood. The four horses pulling it looked tired and old, even a little malnourished. Margrethe suspected the man's harsh voice belied an equally harsh manner. A small, plump woman emerged from the cottage with something wrapped in a checked cloth. She handed it to the man, who placed it on the seat of the cart. With a wave and a gruff farewell, he climbed up into the cart. With a crack of the whip, the laden cart and its angry driver wound their way out of the clearing and into the forest.

Something had held Margrethe back from making her presence known. She hadn't felt comfortable about the man. In her current, delicate state of mind, harsh words were not what she needed right now, while a motherly, womanly touch fulfilled her needs. Waiting long enough to be sure the man had truly gone, Margrethe emerged from the undergrowth and made her way across the open clearing to the cottage.

The woman didn't hide her surprise as she opened the door to the ravaged girl. She quickly recovered, clucking with sympathy and cutting off any words of greeting Margrethe may have offered.

"Oh my, you poor lamb! Look at you! Where did you come from? No, no, don't try to talk, there's time enough later for that. Come, come and sit by the fire and get warm!" With that, she kindly bustled Margrethe inside and deposited her on a small wooden stool in front of the fire. The woman placed a patchwork blanket around her shoulders, and Margrethe drew it close around her, allowing the warmth to wash over her. The light of the fire played upon her pale skin, but the warmth didn't seem to reach her chilled bones. Nonetheless, these ministrations brought her comfort, and she welcomed the sweet ale placed before her, drinking thirstily from the roughly hammered tankard. The sticky liquid seemed to wash away the dull ache behind her eyes. Thankfully, she drew a breath and exhaled. For now, she was safe. From here, she would find her way home.

***

# CHAPTER TEN

LORD Beaufort Winchester the First gazed at his wife in utter disbelief.

"What do you mean you did all you could? By the gods, woman, you did all you could to encourage this folly!" The roar of her husband's voice echoed painfully in Elizabeth's head.

"Please, dear, my headache."

"No headache could be as great as the one you've caused me!" thundered Lord Winchester. "Have you any idea what this has cost me? Hm, do you? And at such a time too, with the Labor Party breathing down our necks!"

Lady Elizabeth Winchester felt tears spring to her eyes. Her husband had sometimes been impatient with her but never before had she seen him in such a fury. After such a long time apart, this was hardly the reunion she would have desired. Her husband saw her tears, but they inspired no sympathy in him whatsoever. Instead, they goaded him on to even greater anger.

"Don't you dare suppose tears will save you, Elizabeth. Don't you dare!" He waved a finger at her. "This is the final straw! Not only do I return to a scandal involving my son and his missing friend, but

I am also greeted with the news that my stepdaughter has eloped with a stranger to God knows where! So yes, my lady, spare me your tears and give me an explanation!"

"T-they were to be betrothed, Beaufort."

"Marriage? Oh, wonderful!" Her husband threw his hands in the air. "And I suppose you gave their pledge your blessing!"

Elizabeth avoided his gaze.

"Well, yes. They are so in love."

"Enough! This is no explanation!" Lord Winchester bent over, leaning his arms on either side of her chair. His eyes bore into her, compelling her to lift her gaze to his.

"Elizabeth, I want to know what happened to that missing boy. I want my son's name cleared of all suspicion so that this family's reputation can be restored *and* I want to know where my stepdaughter is. Furthermore, I expect your full co-operation in all these matters."

"But, of course, Beaufort. I am your wife."

"Yes, you are, such is my fortune." Lord Winchester straightened up, not taking his eyes off Elizabeth for a moment.

He sighed. "Where is Beau?"

Wretchedly, Elizabeth sniffed back her tears. "He is in his chambers. He rarely leaves them."

"Bring him to me." Lord Winchester's tone brooked no argument.

Elizabeth silently welcomed the opportunity to escape her husband's wrath, even if only for a few moments. Hastily, she rose from the chair and bustled from the room. Beaufort didn't turn as the door shut behind him. He stood still, staring out of the window with narrowed eyes. The rolling green hills usually soothed his soul after the turmoil of London, but today he remained unmoved by their beauty. He knew what he must do, and he would be firm in his resolve.

Not for the first time, Beaufort regretted his marriage to

Elizabeth Charlesworth. It had seemed provident at the time. He needed money and a wife, she ably provided both. Her previous husband's strange disappearance had left Elizabeth with a daughter and a sizable estate to care for. For Beaufort Winchester I, it was less a marriage than a convenient arrangement. For some reason, he had assumed his new bride would feel the same. Her constant demands for attention surprised him not, for it was in her nature to seek flattery and reassurance. Her constant need for affection had surprised him. He had assumed she would be happy enough with vain compliments and gifts, and indeed, those things did delight her. However, she sought attention between the bed sheets more often than Beaufort would have liked. Her feminine curves no doubt enticed some men, but not he. The delights of female flesh held far less attraction for Lord Beaufort Winchester the First than the smooth, muscular bodies of the young men working the London docks or tending the gardens of his wealthy friends.

Initially, he had avoided her physical demands, pleading urgent business in London, but his subterfuge was but a reprieve. Eventually, he'd had no choice but to succumb to her desires. He'd entered her physical embrace fortified by a substantial amount of wine and thankfully, after a few repulsive encounters, had managed to impregnate her. Assured that Elizabeth was suitably occupied by motherhood, Beaufort had returned to London and his supple young men.

The click of the door handle snapped him from his thoughts. Lord Winchester kept his back to the door as the product of one of those distasteful intimate encounters entered the room. Beaufort Winchester II took after his father in nearly every aspect, a fact that had at first warmed Lord Winchester's heart. However, through Elizabeth's overindulgence, the boy had grown to show little or no aptitude for politics or even intelligent, committed thought. He had just managed to scrape through his expensive schooling and seemed to have little ambition for politics, business, or anything else useful, for that matter. Beaufort blamed his own frequent absence in part for his son's lack of business and political acumen, but he would not shoulder responsibility for the boy's often emotional behavior. On that level, father and son were entirely different, with the younger Beaufort's emotional outbursts proving tiresome to his father from an early age. Lord Beaufort Winchester the First prided himself on always being completely in control of his own emotions. His frustration with his passionless marriage and secret lifestyle remained well hidden behind a socially acceptable veneer of dignity and self-control.

He mustered that self-control now as he turned to face his son. Beau was much the worse for wear, no doubt due to one of his solitary drinking sessions. Lord Winchester had questioned the servants, always the best source of information. A few were reluctant to share details, but, ultimately, each one recounted the same story; his son, an alcoholic recluse, often gave into a dark melancholy which occasionally burst into explosive anger. Lord Winchester surveyed the pale, disheveled figure in front of him.

Beau felt like death. He squinted as the sunlight hit his eyes, recoiling instinctively. His father stepped forward, mercifully blocking its bright glare for a moment. Beau thought his father sought to embrace him, but Lord Winchester merely nodded towards a nearby chair. Awkwardly, Beau fumbled his way into the hard backed upholstery, sitting erect and uncomfortably. His head hurt from too many sweet wines the night before. It was a ritual that helped him sleep, only to seize him awake in a violent wrench of nausea, sweats, and headaches. It had vaguely occurred to Beau that he may be punishing himself, but he quickly drowned the thought in another glass of numbness. Any punishment owing, however, seemed to be imminent, judging by the look on his father's face. Well, not so much his face, which revealed only its usual cool demeanor. The eyes gave it away. His father's ice blue eyes were darker than usual. They scrutinized him to the core. Instantly, Beau felt transported back to his uneasy childhood. He squirmed like a guilty six-year-old beneath that disapproving gaze. His temples throbbed, and he lowered his head to escape both the pain and his father's eyes.

"You seem a little worse for wear, boy."

Beau winced inwardly. He hated it when his father called him "boy." It made him feel more vulnerable, more inadequate. He tried to muster an adult response but found himself muttering like a guilty child.

"I slept badly, Father. I have a splitting headache."

"Hmpf. Headaches seem to run in this family." The boy looked like he'd woken in an opium den. His hair resembled a rat's nest, his eyes red and bleary. He stank of stale sweet wine and sweat. Lord Winchester's nose gave an involuntary twitch of distaste.

"I do not suppose your current state would have been influenced by alcohol, perchance?"

Beau kept his head down. "I may have drunk a little last night."

"What is that boy? I cannot hear you! Raise your head and repeat yourself!" Lord Winchester's barked command jerked Beau's head up, an instant response.

"I...I had a nightcap." Oh, dear God, now he stuttered like a two-year-old. Any more of this and his responses would be infantile!

"Hmpf!"

Lord Winchester turned his back on his son, gazing at the rolling fields in silence for what seemed like an interminable amount of time. Beau waited, head bowed. Behind him, the mantel clock, a wedding present from Queen Victoria herself, ticked regally. It gave Beau something to focus on, but each resonant tick hurt his head, sending sharp shreds of pain between his eyes. Feeling like a prisoner facing execution, he readied himself for the next tirade. Finally, without turning, his father spoke.

"Beau, the recent scandals involving this household have led me to make some difficult decisions. One of these decisions, I am afraid, involves you."

Beau sat quietly, contemplating his father's rigid back. He wondered if he was expected to reply. There was nothing he could think of to say. His mouth was dry and his head hurt. It was less painful to remain silent.

"Have you nothing to say?" His father's voice snapped at him like a whip.

"I am not sure what to say, Father. I trust your judgment, of course." Beau's voice trailed off miserably. He longed for his darkened room, his comfortable bed. He longed for sleep, for blessed release from this parental nightmare. Instead, he struggled to focus on his father's words, all the while willing the pounding in his head to subside.

"I appreciate your trust. It is just as well, for the decision I have come to will involve substantial changes in your lifestyle."

Beau frowned. Even through the fog clouding his mind, his father's words carried an ominous tone.

"What changes?"

Now, Lord Winchester turned to look at his son.

"You have allowed yourself to go to ruin, Beaufort. Instead of facing the scandal of your missing friend like a man, you submerged yourself in an alcoholic well of self-pity and self-destruction. Look at yourself!" Suddenly, he leaped forward, yanking his son out of the chair and spinning him round to face the mirror above the mantelpiece. His well-manicured fingers dug sharply into Beau's arms, making him wince.

"Look in the mirror and tell me what you see! Tell me!"

Reluctantly, Beau raised his eyes. A blurry vision of wild hair and pale, sallow skin stared back hollowly.

"This! This is what you've become!" His father's voice lashed at him. He winced again. The verbal blow pained no less than the pinching. Without bothering to hide his disgust, Lord Winchester

84

pushed his son back down into the chair.

"You are a disgrace to the Winchester name. You are a drunk. You are indolent. You lack vision or self-control." Each word struck like a blow. Beau sat with his head bowed under the attack. There was nothing he could say or do. His father's words, brutal as they were, held the power of truth, and that made them so hard to bear.

"The sad state of your affairs and the scandal hanging over this household has led me to enlist you in the army." Beau's sat upright and stared at his father in shock and disbelief.

"The army?"

Lord Winchester regarded his son coldly. "The Boers need to be brought into line, and the discipline will do you good. You will dry out, regain your health. You will learn the value of comradeship and courage. And perhaps, if the gods are merciful, you will finally become a man!"

Those words delivered the last stinging blow. Defeated, Beau slumped back in the chair and stared at his father mutely. Taking his silence as acquiescence, Lord Winchester continued.

"You will pack your belongings and return to London with me immediately. Your mother will accompany us initially. It's imperative that we present a united front as a family. You have no idea the damage all this scandal has caused my political standing."

*Ah, there it was*, Beau thought. The real reason for his father's concern became evident. His son's health was secondary to the health of his own political career. Beau felt no surprise. Real concern on his father's part would have been far more surprising. Yet, perhaps he was right. A stint in the army may well be a good thing. He needed to get away from the family estate, from his mother's smothering presence and his father's lack of presence. He needed to escape from the memories, from the torment of loss, grief and the clinging sense of helplessness that ignited a simmering, frustrated anger within. Upon reflection, comparatively the army was quite an appealing prospect concerning his current situation.

Somehow, Beau managed to speak, in spite of his horribly dry mouth.

"As I said, Father, I trust your judgment."

Lord Winchester smiled thinly.

"Good! It is settled, then. We leave tomorrow morning at nine sharp. I expect your belongings to be gathered in the hallway ready to pack onto the coach. And I expect you to be ready to accompany me to London."

"What about the estate? Who will care for it?"

Lord Winchester glanced out the window at the rambling gardens.

"I have hired people from the village to care for the grounds. The house itself will be shut up completely and the furniture covered and stored. Some of it will be sent on later if needed."

Lord Winchester looked pointedly at his son before continuing.

"In any case, everything has been arranged, Beaufort. The only matter you need concern yourself with is having yourself ready to leave first thing tomorrow morning."

Beau responded with a nod, which his father returned stiffly. As he left the room, he sensed his father's eyes boring into his back. He knew he was a disappointment. It had become a familiar role, one he had apparently played quite well until now. He passed his mother on the stairs, ignoring her inquiring look. He felt strangely disconnected from events. Ironically, it was this creeping, emotional numbness that he had sought so desperately in alcohol, yet here, in the midst of turmoil, he found it. This presented a fresh start, an opportunity to break free of his demons, make his mark in the world. And perhaps, somewhere on his travels, he would find Margrethe. The thought gave him hope, and with unaccustomed enthusiasm, he headed for his chamber to pack.

LUCIUS slipped away at the first rays of dawn. He had finally regained consciousness and returned to his bedchamber, only to find it empty. Margrethe's clothes were gone, and after searching the darkened halls of the castle, he'd realized that she'd fled, leaving him no option but to pursue her and bring her home. She had a head start, but the forest, in its strangeness to her, confounded her, and he doubted she would have made much ground. He had to find her! He had to protect her from his mother. He wouldn't allow Claudia to overpower him again, nor would he allow her to destroy the one thing in his endless life that mattered. Pulling his hat firmly over his eyes, he guided his black steed silently out of the stables, through the gates, and into the shadowy forest, thankful for the thick cover of trees. The filtered rays of the weak sun had not yet caused him any pain or distracting discomfort. Once clear of the boundaries of the castle, Lucius spurred the horse on. It was a swift beast, sure-footed, and powerful. It responded to the sharp sting of the whip with a whinny of protest then sprinted forward. Lucius lowered his head against the cold air. He felt branches slice through the air above him. He hunched further forward, willing the beast on even harder.

Finally, when both horse and rider were breathless, they reached the deepest thicket of the forest. Here, he pulled up. Steam rose from the horse's flank. Lucius sat slightly bent forward, catching his breath in the morning stillness. Only when the pain in his lungs had eased did Lucius glance back in the direction of his family home. But for a distant turret that could be vaguely made out amongst the trees, the castle was shrouded in early morning mist and dense vegetation. He hoped he wouldn't be missed for at least a few hours yet. His mother, of course, clearly detested daylight, tending to keep herself hidden away in her darkened chambers during the day. For once, he could not curse the sun, for it delivered him as his savior.

Lucius thought momentarily of dismounting, but a gnawing desire to be as far away from his mother as possible changed his mind. With a solid kick, he swung the horse around and continued through the dense undergrowth of the forest. Beyond the trees, the world lay before him, vast and open. His beloved Margrethe had fled before him into that vast world, no doubt seeking the safety of her home in England. Perhaps she'd overheard the argument with his mother. He couldn't blame her for being frightened. Lucius knew better than anyone that Claudia's fury was enough to cause anyone to flee, let alone one whose death she sought. It did not occur to Lucius that Margrethe would run from him. Their shared passion had left him in no doubt of her love, her passion for him. He would not lose her, not for any reason. Mercilessly, he spurred his horse forward, cracking his whip hard against the hapless steed's rump. The horse whinnied in protest, responding with a huge leap. Rider and horse hurtled through the undergrowth. His destination remained uncertain, but his determination was sure: He would find Margrethe and bring her home.

*\*\**

# CHAPTER ELEVEN

MARGRETHE peered through window of the small room that had been her home for the past eight months. Below her vantage point, the streets of Windsor were filled with a sea of people gathering to watch Queen Victoria's funeral procession. The queen's death heralded the end of an era, the dawn of a new age. Margrethe watched the grieving throng with a growing sense of apprehension. This feeling wasn't new but had grown as steadily as her belly. She'd felt it from the moment she'd realized her pregnancy but had paid it little heed during her arduous journey home. Upon her escape from the castle, the couple in the forest had kindly taken her to Brasov. On the way to the medieval town, Margrethe discovered she'd been taken by Lucius to the Southern Carpathian Mountains, in the region of Wallachia. This, of course, seemed physically impossible at first, but Margrethe realized that in Lucius's realm of existence, anything was possible. He possessed a host of abilities and powers far beyond her imagining. Her knowledge of the world beyond the safe confines of her life and the family estate had left her unprepared for the vast breadth of the unknown world that lay before her, let alone the dark world from which she'd escaped. In the midst of that foreign environment, Margrethe had felt both awed and utterly alone. The woman who rescued her must have sensed her conflicting emotions. Before leaving, she'd pressed a pile of *lei* into Margrethe's hands, squeezing them with her own worn hands briefly as if to say, "I understand." Margrethe had closed her fingers around the cool, silver coins gratefully, holding that kindness close as she watched the woman climb back on the wagon next to her husband and rumble away toward the thriving town market.

The journey to London had been long and tiresome, but she had finally reached familiar ground. So blissfully relieved to be in England was she that even the potential anger of her stepfather couldn't daunt her. Her fears had been unfounded, for he had been more relieved than angry. Her mother hysterically welcomed her, awash with tears and self-recrimination. Margrethe endured her mother's dramatics for a short while, thankful her pregnancy remained disguised, but not for much longer.

Gathering her courage, Margrethe had drawn her stepfather aside to talk privately. Behind the closed oak doors of his library, she told him of the endless days of sickness that she had first presumed to be the result of her long travels. The absence of her monthly bleed had alerted her to the possibility that motion sickness may not be the cause of her malaise. By the time she had reached London, the second absence of her flow had confirmed her fears.

Her stepfather received the news with remarkable calm. He quickly made secret arrangements with trusted friends who were expecting their first child. Their assured discretion came with a generous payment that would cover all of Margrethe's expenses while leaving the couple a hefty bonus for their trouble. Officially she would hold the position of nanny until the birth of her own child, whereupon a speedy and very private adoption would be arranged. Margrethe would remain as a wet nurse to the couple's child until her return to London would elicit the least scandalous attention.

On the subject of Lucius, Lord Winchester had said little, save that Margrethe's suitor was a cad of the lowest order and she should have no further contact with him. Her stepfather's immediate concern seemed only to be for all details to be covered. His wife was to know nothing. Elizabeth's discretion most certainly could not be counted on and so would not be risked. He told his wife that her daughter had obtained a placement with a good family. There was no mention of Margrethe's delicate condition. With her social conscience thus reassured, Lady Elizabeth Winchester offered no argument and resumed her whirl of social engagements with little thought for the daughter who had brought such calamity to her life with her scandalous behavior.

If Margrethe were to be honest, this small, tidy room afforded her a welcome respite from the demands and cruel deceits of others. Beau had been sent away to the army, another development that had filled her with relief. Part of her wanted desperately to see her brother, but her shame in the face of her foolish elopement made it difficult to face him. Beau had desperately tried to warn her about Lucius. She had put it down to sheer jealousy and childish competition at the time. Beau's rantings had seemed outlandish, even a little insane. Margrethe, along with many others, had supposed that her brother's over indulgence of sweet wine had turned his mind to melancholy and paranoia. She knew better now, but perhaps it was as well that Beau had ventured into new horizons. She could not bear to think of his reaction to her pregnancy—in his absence, now a bridge she need not cross. At the same time, it would have been nice to be able to confide in someone who would believe her story.

Feeling the tears spring to her eyes, Margrethe shut Beau and Lucius out of her mind and turned her attention once again to the funeral spectacle unfolding before her. Suddenly, she felt an overwhelming urge to be among them, to melt into the anonymous outpouring of sadness. It was foolishness as her condition demanded rest, but Margrethe could not rest. Snatching a hat and a thick woolen wrap from a nearby chair, she quietly opened the door and peered into the hallway, knowing that she would be sternly admonished if her absence were discovered. Fortunately, the house appeared quiet. Her employers were attending the official service, and it seemed all but one or two staff had been given permission to watch the funeral procession. Closing the door behind her, Margrethe moved slowly and carefully down the stairs. The house proved indeed deserted, and she ably slipped into the crowded streets unobserved and unchastised.

HE watched the young woman slip out of the front door, taking a step back while looking around nervously about her, pulling her woolen shawl tight around her swollen belly as if to hide her condition from prying eyes.

She couldn't hide from his eyes, though; eyes that had seen everything and missed nothing. He hung back in the shadows. He blended well with this black-garbed crowd, his pale face and black cape not at all out of place amongst the seething sea of sadness. She was easy to follow, even without his extraordinary sensory abilities. She moved slowly, holding her hand protectively over her unborn child. It had taken him a while to find her, but when he finally succeeded, Claudia's evident glee had been reward enough for his efforts. Claudia, his weakness and his strength. If he had a heart, it most likely broke when she took that human to her bed. Fortunately, Valdymyr had realized many moons ago that the daughter of Nyx would never be his, so he had satisfied him with her friendship, devoting himself to her service. She had lost considerable influence among the Great Council and Elders with her foolish liaison, yet he alone had remained loyal, determined to see her restored to her rightful place. The House of Nyx had formed as the Earth itself had formed; in the belly of darkness and chaos. That which had such deep and ancient roots could not be easily destroyed and Valdymyr had decided it would be far more provident to remain in the service of the powerful family than to betray them. He knew Claudia, and he knew she always rewarded those close to her, be it for loyalty or betrayal.

He'd begun his search for the girl without his dear friend's consent or knowledge. He knew how the situation pressed upon Claudia, how she barely contained her anger, especially since Lucius too had fled the castle. He knew she wanted desperately to find the girl and the child before its birth. Of course, she would destroy them both, of that Valdymyr was more than certain. All necessary, of course. The line, already tainted enough by Claudia's own carnal mistake, now threatened to repeat itself through her son. The House of Nyx could endure no more scandal, real or imagined, in the eyes of the Great Council and the Elders. He'd heard murmurings, whisperings of assassination and had determined then and there to bring back to Nyx what was lost. When Claudia reclaimed her power, it would be he, Valdymyr, standing at her side, not that pathetic, weak, impotent human half-wit she called "husband."

He'd lost the girl's scent briefly in London, but furtive inquiry had revealed her whereabouts. Valdymyr had connections in high places and low places all throughout. There was nowhere to hide. The short trip to Berkshire taxed him not at all, nor did it take but a moment. It had been far easier to find the girl in Windsor. Rumors of a rarely seen, mysterious nanny had caught his ear. No one knew her name and no one had seen her for the past few months. His keen senses had sought her out, tracing her to an affluent townhouse just off High Street.

He watched the occupants, a young couple, come and go, noting that the wife showed signs of being heavy with child. He pondered this coincidence, certain that it was no coincidence at all. Were they going to pass off Margrethe's child as this woman's? He had waited three weeks for his first and, until today, only sighting of Margrethe. His initial impression was that of a fragile young woman of immense, haunting beauty. Valdymyr appreciated beauty in all its forms and, momentarily, he understood Lucius's loss of reason in the face of such temptation. Even now, amongst the funeral crowd, she stood out with her golden hair and startling dark eyes.

A sudden swell of the crowd jostled him forward, pushing him on top of his intended prey. She stumbled as his weight hit her full on, flinging her arms out in a vain attempt to regain her balance. Valdymyr leaped instantly upright, snatching her back with him just before she hit the cobbled street. She turned to better view her rescuer, her eyes wide with shock.

"I am terribly sorry, Madame, are you hurt?"

Margrethe smiled reassuringly at the older gentleman, his voice apologetic, his expression concerned.

"No, not at all, sir, just a little shaken. Thank you."

He held her arm as she steadied herself. The woolen shawl had dropped to the ground where it lay beyond rescue, trampled and soiled by many uncaring feet. Valdymyr removed his fine coat, draping it over her shoulders. He noticed her shivering, no doubt from the shock of her near fall as much as from the cold air. Keeping his arm around her, he guided her away from the melee to a nearby doorway.

"Perhaps I can be of some assistance, Madame, this crowd is a dangerous place to be for someone in your delicate condition."

Margrethe nodded.

"Yes, it was foolish of me to come out into the streets. It was a whim, a silly whim, dear sir and I am most grateful to you for rescuing me from my folly."

"A folly for which I am partly responsible, dear lady, given that I fell against you and caused you to fall."

Margrethe smiled. "It is all well. I am sorry sir, I...I do not know your name."

"Uh! How remiss of me! Petric Valdymyr, at your service, dear lady." Valdymyr bowed low, sweeping his hat aside in an extravagant gesture. Margrethe smiled at him, amused by the flourish and grateful for his intervention. He may well have saved her and the child from serious injury. She supposed his colorful behavior connected somehow with his obviously continental heritage. She felt at ease with those from other countries now. Her travels had brought her into contact with many people from all walks of life, high and low.

"Are you visiting Windsor for the funeral Master Valdymyr?"

"No, my lady, I am here on business, but detoured to view the funeral procession of your great queen. Such a sad and significant passing. My condolences to you and your countrymen."

Margrethe's curiosity was piqued. She wondered momentarily from whence this stranger came. She thought to ask but immediately dismissed the idea as rather rude.

"Thank you, sir. Yes, her passing has brought an end to a golden age."

A sudden wave of dizziness and nausea caught her unawares. She gripped the railing on the stairs next to her. Valdymyr saw the movement, immediately oozing concern.

"Please, dear lady, let me escort you to a tea house. I think a little refreshment and a rest would do us both the world of good." Gently, he took her arm and steered her around the outskirts of the crowd. By the time Queen Victoria's casket passed by, Margrethe and the stranger were watching the grand procession from the safety and comfort of a nearby tea house. Over a pot of the soothing, hot brew, Valdymyr told Margrethe he plied his living as a trade merchant dealing in tea and spices, traveling the continents in search of the finest blends. She listened to his tales of exotic destinations with interest as the hot tea gradually revived her senses. The dizziness subsided, the waves of nausea calmed. Margrethe felt herself relax in the company of this colorful and charming stranger. They waited until the crowds dispersed before leaving their sanctuary and walking slowly back to the townhouse, continuing their conversation as they strolled. By the time they'd reached the townhouse steps, Margrethe had promised her new friend to take greater care of herself and to keep in touch while he stayed at the local inn a few blocks down her street.

As the young woman made her way slowly up the stairs, Valdymyr watched her with an unfamiliar sadness. She had no idea of the dangers she faced or the obstacles before her. Claudia would happily see her dead if it meant ending the threat posed by the unborn child. He hoped he wouldn't be called upon for the task, for he liked the girl well enough. Nonetheless, if so tested, his loyalty remained with Claudia. His future and the future of the House of Nyx depended on it, and he, in turn, was dependent upon the House of Nyx. With a small shrug, Valdymyr pushed any petty sentimental thoughts aside and turned towards the Windsor Arms.

BEAU stared out over the Transvaal. The African plains seemed to stretch forever. Vast plains soaked in blood. It had been a long war. The British had made progress but were hampered by Boer attacks, causing enough casualties to persuade the British commanders to change their tactics. Beau had proven to be quite proficient at killing. He supposed his love of hunting helped his marksmanship, which in turn helped his survival. The Boers were farmers and hunters, and their rifle skills were extraordinary. The Boer marksmen would take their shot from a prone position, avoiding enemy fire while inflicting significant damage. Each bloody skirmish brought back painful memories of the last hunting trip with Freddie. Each memory would inflame Beau's senses, sending him into a killing frenzy that only subsided when the thundering of blood in his ears ceased. He had a reputation for fearlessness, but Beau knew this not to be so. His anger masqueraded as courage, and so far it had served him well, that explosive anger.

He was stationed at one of the many blockhouses that dotted

the South African landscape. The constant Boer raids had led to the British command bringing in thousands of troops to build and man the blockhouses, which were positioned at strategic points throughout the Transvaal. Beau had been one of those sent to such a garrison. He welcomed the respite. The fortifications were efficient. They now manned a circular structure of wood, corrugated iron, and steel designed to withstand wood rot and shelling, taking six men only six hours to construct. The men joked about its unusual shape, nicknaming it "The Pepperpot."

Having expended a great deal of his energy in the blockhouse's construction, Beau sat near the door of the completed structure, surveying the surrounding plains for any sign of a raiding party, occasionally taking an interest in the feeding of a white-necked raven as it dined on some unrecognizable carrion. He didn't speak much to the other men, only enough to maintain a degree of civility. Their uniform bonded them, and he saw no need to deepen any emotional ties beyond that. Life here on the Transvaal could be taken in an instant. He had no need of attachment or distraction. His purpose was to come out of this alive so he could find Margrethe.

His sister never drew far from his thoughts. He had written to his father a few times, asking if there were any news. Each time he responded with a short, perfunctory reply that bade Beau to fight for King and country, and to leave the domestic issues to those who remained at home. Beau had assumed from that response that there was no sign of his sister and that she was happily settled with Lord Lucius Ruthven. He still seethed at Ruthven's deception. Beau would find Margrethe or he would find Ruthven. Either way, he needed answers, and he would not rest until he had them.

"Oi, Winchester, weren't you asking about some chap by name of Ruthven?" A whiny, Cockney accent interrupted his thoughts. It wasn't so much the voice, but the name that drew Beau's attention. He turned to look at the private who had squatted down next to him.

"Yes," Beau replied shortly. "Why?"

"There's an officer in 4th Battalion named Ruthven. Thought he might be your man." The Cockney peered at him, head to one side. "Is there some kinda reward for this? I mean, if this fella's important…" His voice trailed off questioningly.

Beau fixed the Cockney with a hard look.

"If it is the fellow I'm looking for; I have access to some fine tobacco from the colonies. Would that be payment enough for your trouble?"

The Cockney looked pleased. "Oh, yes, indeed, it would. Indeed, it would!"

Beau rose to his feet, shouldering his rifle.

"Well then, I'll go and find out about this Ruthven fellow. Do you know anything about him?"

The Cockney shook his head.

"Not much. I've heard he fought with the 8th Mounted Infantry at Bothaville. Quite the hero they say, a bloody good fighter."

"Do they now?" Beau turned away from the Cockney, glancing over at the 4th Battalion encampment. There seemed to be some commotion over there. Wagons and men coming and going. The sound of shouts and the whinny of horses reached him over the plain. "If that is the case, I had best go and see if this hero is the man I am looking for."

"Don't forget the tobacco!" the Cockney lad called after him. Beau smiled to himself. If the boy had indeed found the vaunted Lord Lucius Ruthven, he would reward him with a mountain of fine tobacco.

***

# CHAPTER TWELVE

LUCIUS sat quietly in a corner, watching the general ruckus around him. Margrethe's mysterious disappearance and his mother's unrelenting fury had driven him from Europe. He'd found no sign of his beloved at her deserted family estate, but had managed to pick up the trail of her aggravating brother. Filled with a renewed sense of purpose, he'd his turned sights to the Transvaal and vengeance.

War had been good to Lucius. Exceptionally good. His cold nature made him a natural for warfare. Killing did not pose any problems for him and he relished combat, becoming well known for his ferocity in battle. He felt alive in the face of death, ever aware that his immortality enabled him to take risks other soldiers would dare not dream of. Yes, Lucius enjoyed the battles, but even more importantly, war afforded him a banquet of victims, hundreds of men cut down and left barely breathing, if at all, on the blood-soaked battlefield. He feasted on the fallen, alongside the kindred white-necked ravens, South African rooks, and white-bellied crows.

In the midst of chaos and bloodshed, Lucius would creep out at night, seeking out the shallow breaths of dying men. In a sense, he supposed putting them out of their misery had some merit to it.

Often they were unaware of his presence until his fangs tore into their flesh. Most were too weak to cry out. Feeding was a bloody affair, but no more so than war.

His battalion had arrived at their new post that day, tired, dusty, and dry. The other soldiers slaked their thirst from flagons of water. Lucius waved away a flask. He would have to wait until dark to quench his thirst. Yes, he would forgo on human refreshment and wait to feast on finer fare. The mood had lightened around him as water replaced ale, generously provided by command—a rare treat, and the weary men drank their fill. The inevitable fights broke out amongst choruses of bawdy ballads and rousing patriotic songs.

As dark fell, the songs trailed off as the battle-weary revelers dropped off into drunken slumber. It wasn't difficult for Lucius to steal away, seeking prey amongst the wounded in a nearby tent. He waited until the lone attendant left for a hard earned break. Slipping into the tent unnoticed and unchallenged, he found one potential victim clearly at death's door, a semi-comatose soldier with his upper body a mangled mess. Lucius sought the vein in the dying soldier's neck. Swiftly he swooped, sinking his fangs into the graying flesh. He drank thirstily, draining the nearly lifeless body. The sweet plasma coursed through his being, re-energizing him.

Finally satisfied, Lucius stepped back and examined the man, now drained of blood and life. The puncture wounds were barely visible amongst the other wounds. He doubted anyone would notice. This unfortunate lad would be quickly disposed of, like hundreds before him. His mother would receive a letter commending her dead son for his bravery and service. She would carry pride and sorrow together in her heart, a load she would never be able to lighten or lay aside. Lucius contemplated another victim, but the other patients were a little too healthy to expire unexpectedly. Perhaps tomorrow night.

He turned to leave, ducking through the flaps of the tent. Without warning, a figure stepped in front of him. Lucius stopped, peering into the darkness. A lamp from the hospital tent weakly illuminated the face of the man who stood in his way.

*Beaufort Winchester II.* Lucius smiled coldly.

"Well, if it is not my dear Margrethe's little brother! How are you, Beau? Are you finding this wonderful bloody war to your liking?"

Beau ignored his question, choosing instead to return the verbal attack. "Visiting the hospital in the dark hours, Lucius? How caring of you! How thoughtful!"

Lucius smiled thinly at the unmistakable facetious tone. "I have a friend who was injured today. I am merely concerned for his welfare." The lie slipped out easily.

Beau looked at him doubtfully. Lucius decided to get to the point.

"I am surprised you are not at home comforting your sister, Beau. I did not think you had heroics in you. War is a messy, dreadful business."

"Margrethe would have no need of comfort if not for your shameful behavior, Lucius. War is no more messy than the disaster you brought upon my family. How could I comfort her when she chose to elope with the man who has brought us so much misery?" Beau's eyes narrowed suspiciously. He fixed Lucius with a hard glare.

"Are you saying Margrethe did not elope with you?"

Lucius laughed harshly.

"We most certainly eloped, Beau. Your sister accompanied me most willingly. Unfortunately, she left for London shortly before I joined the war." He watched Beau's face carefully, hoping to elicit a reaction that might provide a clue to Margrethe's whereabouts, but Beau merely stared at him, dumbfounded. The man and the vampire regarded each other for a long, silent moment, neither trusting the other's words. The prize they sought eluded them both. Margrethe remained lost to them, hidden somewhere oceans away from the

Transvaal plains. When Beau finally spoke, his voice dropped low and shook with anger.

"If anything's happened to my sister, I swear I will kill you, Lucius. In fact, I should kill you now."

An amused smile crossed Lucius's face.

"And how will you kill me, Beau? Hm? Are you going to shoot me? Run me through with a bayonet? You know I am not like other men…" His voice trailed off, leaving his confession hanging tantalizingly between them. He watched the swift shadow of fear cross Beau's eyes. All the folk tales in the world couldn't prepare a mere human for the reality of dealing with the undead. Lucius smiled again, a humorless smile just wide enough to show his fangs, still stained with blood. "Perhaps I should make you one of us, Beau. Would you like that immortality?"

Beau's eyes widened, filled with fear mixed with disgust.

"I never want to be like you!" His voice, although small and brave, trembled with uncertainty.

"Really, Beau? Are you sure?" Lucius toyed with him now. "I think you would like it, very much. Just one small moment of pain, then you would be like me. You would be like Margrethe."

At the mention of his sister's name, fire leaped back into Beau's eyes. Lucius chuckled.

"Yes, that's right, Beau. Your sister is one of *us* now. Immortal and still beautiful."

Beau lunged, but Lucius saw it before he even moved. He stepped aside easily and Beau hit the ground with a thud, sprawling painfully on the hard dirt. He tried to roll over and regain his feet, but Lucius struck faster than lightning, grabbing him by the hair and yanking his head back without mercy.

He knelt on Beau's back, digging his knee hard into his spine, then whispered into his ear, "Don't suppose that I won't tear your heart out, Beaufort Winchester. Don't think for a moment that you can't disappear, just like your dear friend, poor Freddie."

102

He felt his enemy struggle beneath his restraining knee but to no avail. Lucius had the strength of ten men in his weakest moments. He lifted his knee and straightened up, dragging Beau to his feet, still tightly gripping his hair. Beau whimpered in pain and fear.

"This will be our little secret, Beau. Consider it a confidence between brothers. After all, I am almost family now." He loosened his grip and Beau broke away, turning to face him. He tried to stare Lucius down, but he proved no match for the unearthly eyes that bore into his soul. Struggling to maintain some sense of power, Beau managed to croak out a threat of sorts.

"I'll tell Margrethe you killed Freddie. I'll tell her the truth"

"Be my guest, Beau, when you find her, of course. She may believe you, she may not" Lucius shrugged. "Rest assured, no one else will believe your wild stories."

Beau knew he spoke the truth. He lowered his eyes, unable to endure the gaze of the undead any longer. He didn't know whether to believe Lucius about Margrethe. He couldn't bear to think of his sister's soul being as empty as this evil creature's. He would fight Lucius. He would think of a way but not now. He felt weak, disorientated. His legs began to buckle beneath him. Blackness washed over him, and he fell again to the ground.

Lucius stood over his inert form for a moment, barely resisting the temptation to finish the wretched creature off. The murderous urge almost overwhelmed him, but the sound of approaching footsteps and laughter stayed him. The hospital attendants were returning from their break. He knew Beau would remember little of their encounter when he woke. No doubt the attendants would think he'd been overcome by exhaustion or too much alcohol, perhaps both, when found. Satisfied that his presence would be neither detected nor reported, Lucius left Beau where he lay and melted into the dark arms of the night.

MARGRETHE leaned against a tree, breathing heavily. She laid a hand across her swollen belly. A contraction wracked her lower body, radiating sharp waves of pain from her back to her groin. She tried to breathe, to focus. The church was only a short distance away. It promised sweet sanctuary, if only her legs could carry her that far. She waited for the pain to subside. The contractions were much closer together now, and she sensed her time drew near. The baby strained and kicked her. He settled low in her pelvis, weighing her down like a rock.

She knew the child to be male. His strength consumed her at times, his hunger weakened her frequently. She could feel his demands upon her before he'd even taken a breath of air. Margrethe wondered, not for the first time, at her ability to carry this through. This child was not of her choice. Not now, knowing the true nature of her relationship with Lucius. Many times she'd wished the child away, but the child within defied her wishes, swelling her belly over the last nine months until she thought she'd burst.

She'd lived quietly with her stepfather's friends, rarely venturing out. She had intended to follow her stepfather's plan and adopt the boy out, but as the time for birth drew near, a dark sense foreboding overtook her. She'd formulated her own plan, suddenly reluctant to part with the child. No maternal instinct had changed her mind. Margrethe had realized, after much-anguished thought that she could not bring other people into this situation.

Lucius would look for his child. He would know. While she would never let Lucius find him, she could not entrust that task to anyone else or place them in danger. If the child were to be born with vampiric abilities, it would immediately draw attention and too many questions towards her. No, it was best if she kept the child. She would have to leave Windsor. She thought momentarily of returning to the family estate but knew Lucius surely would find her there. She would have to leave, perhaps even travel abroad again. She would lead the life of a peasant woman with her child. She would invent a story to explain her husband's absence. Her decision made in the throes of pain, Margrethe awaited the birth of her baby with a sense of purpose mixed with dread.

She'd decided to give birth in the Parish church, feeling the greatest safety lay within its sturdy holy walls. It was a small stone church dating back to the 1200's. Margrethe found its aged stone walls and stained glass windows oddly comforting. The church gave her a sense of light within her immeasurable darkness, bringing strength and hope where she saw only defeat and despair. She needed the protection of those holy walls. The Darkness wouldn't hunt her there in the realm of the Light.

The baby stirred inside her, bearing down on her pelvis. She didn't have much time. Gathering all her remaining strength and ignoring her pain, Margrethe staggered towards the church. She leaned against the wooden doors, willing them to give. They did, and she stumbled gratefully inside the cool silence of her sanctuary. Another wave of pain overwhelmed her and she gripped a pew, lowering herself down onto the hard wooden seat. It provided no relief, serving only to intensify her pain. An involuntary cry escaped her lips, echoing around the silent church like a banshee's wail. She felt the baby shift again and bear down. It felt as though her insides were being ripped out. She thought for a moment that she might pass out from the pain, but she steeled her mind. Carefully, she lowered herself from the pew. The baby sensed the opportunity and dropped deep between her legs. Water and blood gushed over the wooden floor, Margrethe gave a primal howl and pushed with all her might. The baby was eager to be born. With a few more excruciating pushes, new life slid into the world and onto the church floor. He emitted a guttural scream, inhuman and hungry. Margrethe reached down and gathered the bloody infant to her breast. A sudden contraction sucked out her breath. She pushed again, gripping the newborn tightly. As she bore down, Margrethe felt another sensation.

Another small body fell from between her legs like a bloody afterthought. It slid to the floor where its brother had been a couple of moments ago and lay, inert and silent. Another push and the afterbirth fell to the floor beside the second child, if indeed it could be called a child. Its head seemed huge for its body—tiny, thin, and transparently pale. The firstborn struggled against her breast, his sharp, little fingernails digging into her flesh. His mouth began to greedily search for her nipple. The baby's gums were hard and unforgiving in their quest for nourishment. Margrethe gave a small gasp of pain. She reached down and touched the motionless form on the floor. It didn't appear to be breathing. Kneeling down painfully, Margrethe broke the sac open. There came no lusty cry or any attempt to take the first breaths of air.

The child lay still, dead.

A sudden noise caught her attention. She stopped still and listened. *Footsteps?* She worked quickly, tying and severing the umbilical cord with her sharp teeth. She scooped up the lifeless form and, still clutching the firstborn to her breast, struggled to the altar. Waves of pain threatened to engulf her. She rested for a moment, leaning against the base of the gleaming cross. The lifeless child slid from her grasp. Wearily she looked down, trying to muster some semblance of grief or emotion. All she could feel was the cold need for survival. She made no attempt to retrieve the child. Let it stay beneath the cross. Perhaps it was the more fortunate one.

Silently, sorrowfully, Margrethe and her newborn son melted into the shadows and through the walls. Behind her, the wooden door of the church swung open. A young priest peered into the gloom, his eyes sweeping across the empty pews. All appeared quiet, yet he sensed something amiss. Unconvinced, he muttered a quick prayer before stepping over the threshold. He hesitated before walking slowly towards the altar. A trail of blood smeared along the aisle before him. Beneath the altar lay a small, bloody body. As he approached, the priest thought he saw movement. He hurried

106

forward and knelt beside the newborn child. He thought it to be dead at first, but the small, fluttering movement of breath caught his attention. He gathered the small and weak child gently into his arms. A prayer fell from his lips.

> *Oh Lord, please protect this child*
> *Let no evil befall him*
> *May your spirit strive with him*

Wrapping the child on his coat, the young priest hurried back to the rectory to the warmth of an open fire.

VALDYMYR heard the cry, like the howl of a banshee. He sat upright and alert, his keen senses searching the night. It was her, he knew it. The time had come. The ancient vampire focused on the source of the eerie cry. His mind sought through the streets, winding through the ether to her home. He picked up her scent quickly, following it to the Parish church. Now Valdymyr hesitated. He possessed no fondness for churches, they drained him of his energy. He would only enter a church under the more dire and desperate of circumstances. Valdymyr sighed. He supposed the situation dire as any. If he could take the baby and return it to Claudia, all disaster, real and imagined, would be averted. Claudia would have the child under her control, thus controlling both parents. Or, of course, if she wished it so, she could simply dispose of the child and its parents. Valdymyr suspected she would do the first to achieve the second, but for her to do that, he, Valdymyr, would have to retrieve the child. Resolutely, he moved towards the dreaded building.

The church doors were open when he reached them. Silently, he stepped inside. A familiar scent hit him. Blood! The tantalizing, fresh smell made his head reel. Valdymyr's eyes, already keenly attuned to the night, skimmed the confines of the church. The scent reeked strongest near the altar. As the vampire walked towards the center aisle, he made out smears of blood leading up the aisle to the gleaming gold cross. Valdymyr recoiled instinctively. The Cross of

Christ may bring comfort to thousands of humans, but it brought him none at all. Averting his eyes from the offensive cross, he sniffed the air. There, hidden beneath the sweet smell of blood, lay another scent. *Margrethe.* He caught her trail and followed, sidestepping the cross with a grimace. In his haste, even Valdymyr's keen eyes missed the human footprint faintly embedded in the bloodied floor. He stepped over it and, eyes fixed firmly on his prey, disappeared into the night.

***

# CHAPTER THIRTEEN

"RAFFY."

THE blonde haired boy stopped and looked back, his black eyes taking in the bustling crowds. The markets were exceptionally busy today, and he wished he'd left earlier to buy the ingredients for the Parish luncheon, a huge affair aimed as much at social chatter as for charity. Even with the help of three parishioners, much had to be done before the big event.

"Raphael, wait!"

The use of his full name caught his attention. He'd long ago shortened his angelic name to Raffy, which seemed much better suited to the rough and tumble of the street youths of Windsor. By sixteen years of age, it was the only name he went by.

Raised by kind strangers who'd taken him in as their own, Raphael wasn't even really his birth name. After many happy and peaceful years, an unfortunate accident had taken his adoptive parents. Raffy's world came tumbling down. He accepted the offer of lodging from the local priest and, at the age of twelve, went to live in the small, tidy rectory. It was still a peaceful existence, although at times punctuated by waves of inner doubt and anger. He would push these waves down by keeping busy. He helped with gardening and maintenance on the church. He learned the church rituals, yet believed in none of them. He didn't know what to believe. He had no sense of belonging, either with God or men. His benefactor, Father Johns, always referred to him by his full name. It was hardly surprising, as it was Father Johns who had originally found him and christened him Raphael, declaring him to be an angel from God. Many, many times Raffy had listened to the priest recount the story of his miraculous discovery and survival. It wasn't comfortable territory for him. The kindly old priest saw beauty in the memory of the small, inert child at the base of the cross. Raffy saw only abandonment.

Returning his thoughts to the present, he searched the crowd for the owner of the voice calling his name. His keen eyes focused on an agitated figure pushing through the crowd. He smiled as the figure drew near.

"Noah, I didn't recognize you!" The boy before him wasn't the pudgy boy he remembered from his youth. His childhood friend, a tall, strapping lad now, appeared solid but with not an inch of spare flesh. Two strong arms enveloped him in a mighty bear hug. Raffy felt his feet lift off the ground, swinging around in an arc. When his feet finally touched the ground again, the strong arms pushed him backward without releasing their grip.

"Look at you, Raffy! By God, if you haven't remained the small imp I used to know!" A large, familiar guffaw of laughter filled the air. The sound of his friend's laughter made Raffy smile. Some things didn't change.

They exchanged stories as they continued on through the market. Noah came visiting from London, where he apprenticed the butcher's trade, doing quite well for himself. His stories of London life, full of wine, women, and merriment made Raffy long for something more. Not necessarily drunken assignations in London alleyways, but something. His own quiet life suddenly seemed sadly empty and unappealing. Maybe one day he would live in London, too. Find a trade. Find a wife. Have children. Become a respectable member of the community and of his nation. He couldn't see the Church becoming his life. Oh no, the cloistered life did not suit him! Unlike Father Johns, Raffy had no confidence in an invisible God. The loss of his adoptive parents and his own fragile origins had convinced him of the impermanence of life and he assigned responsibility for that life only to himself. Quietly, Raffy determined that one way or another, he would find his way to London.

BEAU looked at the man through a drunken haze. The Great War had finally come to an end. Soldiers danced in the streets with civilians, choosing the prettiest girls to twirl in their arms. The war was over! Peace reigned! It had been his second war, this war to end all wars. Raising a toast to the Empire, he threw back his head and drained the last of the sweet wine, slamming the empty cup drunkenly onto the wooden table. He leaned towards the man, trying not to slur his words.

"So, let me get this right, good fellow: You know Lord Lucius Ruthven?"

The man smiled and nodded.

"Personally?"

"Yes."

"And you say you can help me defeat him?"

Again, the man nodded. He didn't smile this time.

Beau sat back in his chair. The old man didn't look as if he could do much at all. He appeared frail physically, with almost translucent, deathly pale skin. At least, it looked to be so in the dull light of the tavern. Beau's eyes blurred, and he struggled again to focus. The man's face wavered in front of him. Not so old maybe but not young either, an ageless face with strange yellow eyes that looked straight through him.

"What do I have to do?"

The man smiled again. Beau could have sworn he saw a glint of a fang.

"All you have to do is trust me and follow my instructions to the letter."

Beau scowled at the stranger.

"How can I trust someone I do not know?"

The man gave a low chuckle. "You cannot, my friend. You must trust your instincts."

Beau's only instinct concerned revenge. Cold, dark, and bloody. He decided to trust his instinct.

"Very well, then, I accept your offer. Show me how to defeat Lucius Ruthven."

The man stood up. "Follow me." And at that he went through the tavern door and into the street.

Beau followed the man into a dark alley. This small Hungarian village thrived on a maze of dark, oppressive alleyways and back streets, now further compounded by a moonless night. The houses were black silhouettes lit by the occasional candle. All remained quiet.

They came to a two story house. The man opened the door and ushered him inside. Beau hesitated for a moment before stepping over the threshold into the darkened hall. He heard the door close behind him with a small whoosh. A lamp illuminated the narrow hallway. To his left lay a room that looked like the parlor. His new friend motioned him inside the room. Beau obeyed, as though directed by the hand of another. The drink had clouded his thinking. Everything felt strange, stifling. He groped his way to a lounging chair and sank into it gratefully. He raised his bleary eyes. His host stood before him, a glass of wine proffered in his outstretched hand. Out of habit, Beau accepted the wine.

"Nice place you have here, my friend. I am sorry, I have forgotten your name, most ungracious of me."

"Valdymyr." The man's voice cloaked itself around him sleepily, soft as silk. Beau took a sip of wine in the hope it would revive him. If anything, it relaxed his senses to the point he could no longer hold the glass. Unsteadily, he found a small side table to rest the unfinished drink upon. His hand trembled, his head spun and he slumped back in the chair as he fell into dark oblivion.

He awoke screaming. Unearthly pain assailed his body, His head reeled, rainbows of pain shot behind his eyes. He felt something splashing into his mouth, a vaguely familiar, metallic taste. It poured down his throat. He gagged at first then suddenly had a thirst for the sticky liquid. It no longer tasted metallic, but sweet, like the nectar of the gods. As he drank, the pain eased from his body. He felt energized, made anew. He struggled to sit up, blinking as his eyes adjusted to the gloom. He wiped his mouth. Red, sticky liquid smeared his hand. Whose blood? His blood? He felt fine, apart from a persistent pain in the side of his neck. He touched the area with a fingertip and gingerly prodded at the raised, angry lump that seemed to be caked in dried blood. The skin around it felt fiery to the touch. Beau dropped his hand and raised his eyes. Valdymyr stood above him. His strange eyes regarded Beau coldly, his mouth stained with blood.

"Welcome to the Kingdom of Nyx, soldier boy. You have joined us. You are now, eternally, one of us."

"Us?"

"The Undead." Valdymyr smiled mirthlessly.

Beau sat for a moment, taking in his words. His body felt different, teeming with a new sense of heightened reality. He could feel every cell, read every thought. His eyes could see worlds hitherto invisible to him. He felt immortal and lost. Understanding burst in his mind. Valdymyr had made good on Lucius's offer of immortality.

He looked at his new friend questioningly.

"And now?"

This time, Valdymyr's smile held genuine warmth.

"Now we will find Lucius."

"And Margrethe. You said you could find Margrethe."

Valdymyr raised a hand as though to stay his words.

"Dear boy, you do understand, do you not, that if we are to find one, we must find the other?"

Beau nodded but truthfully, he didn't understand. He just knew he needed to find Margrethe. He would follow this undead creature into the bowels of Hell if it meant being reunited with his sister.

Valdymyr smiled at his guest.

"I saw your sister many years ago in Windsor."

"England? She is in England?" Beau barely contained his excitement—the first stirring of happiness he could recall since Margrethe's disappearance.

Valdymyr raised a restraining hand.

"Now calm down, soldier. There has been a war and many years between. Your sister could be anywhere." He did not mention the child. He hadn't actually seen a live child. He'd smelled it, though, the stench of a new birth. He'd pursued her through the trees, only to lose her in Windsor's maze of winding streets. Thwarted, he'd vowed to find Margrethe and her child, and return them to Claudia, no matter how long it took. Time was of little consequence to him. Most importantly, he would find the child and bring the offensive blood line to an end.

Claudia's gratitude would convey upon him the richest of rewards.

Snapping himself from his reverie, Valdymyr turned his attention to Beau, who clearly still adjusted to his newly acquired, heightened senses.

"We'll travel to England soon. You can search for your sister from there."

Beau nodded. He felt alive, ready to take on the world.

"Yes, we can stay at the family estate. It has been shut up for years now. I am sure my parents would be happy for us to give it a new lease of life." The irony of his words hit him, and he chuckled.

They would bring a new lease of eternal life, he and his vampire friend. And he would meet Lord Lucius Ruthven on his own terms, and he would win.

He had to win. He had to bring Margrethe home.

LUCIUS smirked at his mother. The Great War that ravaged Europe hadn't been good for her or Edmund. His father had retreated even further into his inner world. He rarely spoke, or even looked at anyone. His mother had fared little better. Impossibly, she seemed to have aged. She still maintained her eternally youthful looks, but an unfamiliar fragility shrouded her now though her eyes were still sharp as was her tongue.

"I suppose you are still looking for your whore."

Lucius answered her calmly.

"Well, yes, Mother. As a matter of fact, I am still searching for my fiancée."

"Pffft! Your fiancée! The woman who ran from you! Did you know she gave birth to your bastard, Lucius? Did you know she is hiding your own monstrous child from you?" She spat the words at him like venom.

A child? He had a child? Lucius stared at his mother incredulously. She saw his confusion and laughed.

"So much for her love for you, Lucius. She hides from you! She hides from the monstrous father of her equally monstrous child!" She cackled with wild laughter. "Such a legacy! A monster's legacy!"

"You are the monster, Mother. It is your legacy," Lucius snapped at her.

"Mine? Did I bed my own sister?" Claudia rounded on him viciously.

Lucius scowled. "Half-sister," he snarled, daring his mother to challenge him. "Where is Margrethe? Where is my child?" He didn't even know if he could believe her about the child, but if all were true, it changed everything. With a son and heir, he would rule not only the world of the Undead but the world of the living as well.

Claudia gave a derisive snort.

"I do not know where your whore is, or the spawn of your incestuous union. The gods only know what creature of diluted blood you have bred between you! If I knew where to find them, I would have destroyed them both long ago! Unfortunately, loyal Valdymyr lost their scent in Windsor."

"Windsor?" Lucius's ears pricked up. "You mean Windsor in England?"

"Yes, Windsor. Valdymyr followed her scent to the Parish church. She had obviously just given birth. She fled not long before he reached the church." Claudia's eyes narrowed. "If you wish to find your whore and your spawn, I suggest you start there."

"Why are you helping me?" Lucius asked. Knowing his mother as he did, it was reasonable to be suspicious.

"I think it's time for a family reunion, Lucius. My child, your child..." Her voice trailed away. She looked out the window, and he knew he'd lost her attention. He was unsure whether or not to take her seriously. Perhaps the war had changed her, but her apparent loathing for Margrethe told him otherwise. He decided it would be prudent to withhold his trust for now. Silently, he withdrew from the room, leaving his mother to sit agelessly by the flickering fire. He finally had a destination, a newfound purpose in his undead life.

Windsor.

He would find Margrethe, and he would find his child. His instincts told him it was a son. A strong, handsome boy with blonde hair and impossibly dark eyes. A boy through whom ancient blood flowed.

His blood.

His son.

Claudia heard him leave. She smiled to herself. Soon Valdymyr would have them all together. Then she would strike. Her son, his whore and their spawn would plague her no longer.

THE war had ended. Margrethe let the thought wash over her as she watched the boy chop wood. He was vital and beautiful in his sixteenth year. After fleeing England, she had made her way to Hungary and settled in a small village, making a quiet life for herself and Ari by finding work as a laundress. People were happy to accept the young, hardworking widow and her child into their community. At first, Margrethe had managed to keep her bloodlust to a minimum, feeding on deer and other local fauna running wild in the forests. She may have been satisfied with animals, but she knew, sooner or later, Ari would not be.

And she proved correct.

In one way, Margrethe had been grateful for the wave of destruction that engulfed the world and stole away everyone's attention. It covered the strange disappearances as Ari's appetite increased with his height. They easily slipped under that wave, for the most part, but there were some difficulties. She sheltered with him in a succession of small villages, somehow remaining invisible to the soldiers who invaded the small streets and shops. Her son was not so inconspicuous, however, and a few unsavory incidents had forced them to flee in the dead of night, one time with hounds and angry torch-wielding villagers in hot pursuit.

His bloodlust had started early, much earlier than she had anticipated. As a young child, he would capture rodents and drain their small corpses of blood. She tried to discourage it, fearing both contamination and discovery of their dark secret. She easily contained the boy at an early age, but now, on the verge of manhood, he had become a force to be reckoned with. A very dark force, Margrethe thought. She sighed and wondered at the fate of her

117

twins. If the other had lived, would he have been like his brother, steeped in vampire blood? Or would there have been some thread of humanity, some memory of compassion, in that tiny, lifeless body? She sighed again. She would never know her other son, now reduced to a memory she left at the base of a cross.

Sadly, she leaned out of the window. The cool night air stung her skin.

"Ari, come inside now."

Her surviving boy stopped chopping and looked back at his mother. Well-built and strong for his age, his physique was more a man's than a boy's, his face equally chiseled and handsome, with black eyes framed by a shock of dark hair. He was his father's child, as dark as Margrethe was fair. Apart from the eyes, of course. Black as coals. Like her eyes. Like his father's eyes. There was no going back now. She knew that this was no ordinary boy. Her hopes that she might raise him with some semblance of humanity were dashed with his first taste of rodent blood. Not surprisingly, he grew up with a great love of hunting. This was something of a blessing as it provided regular food for a pot that might otherwise be empty. However, Ariel's love of the hunt went beyond necessity. It appealed to his thirst for blood. Margrethe knew that not all kills made it to her kitchen. She chose to ignore this aberration. As long as Ari had access to blood, he would be happy enough to leave domestic animals and small children alone. She had to admit to many moments where her maternal instincts all but vanished. Her son frightened her, as though he had taken all the strength of his twin in the womb and devoured it. He was larger than life, without conscience and with an insatiable hunger.

Sadness washed over her. At least the other child had mercifully died at birth. Margrethe suspected her visions of her oldest son draining his brother were closer to the truth than she cared to admit. If she'd only known what manner of creature she would bear, she might well have done away with him before birth. It was a hard thing for any mother to admit, but she was not just any mother. She was a vampire and so was her son. That was his heritage, to be born of a darkened womb like his father before him, a legacy of darkness, handed down through eternity. She'd been foolish to think she could escape it, or help her son to escape. And now, he was a monster, this beautiful boy of hers. She heard his footfall on the stone step. Margrethe bit back her tears and smiled as her beautiful monster stepped inside from the chill night air.

"Ari, I have wonderful news. The war is over." The boy looked at his mother, his eyes unfathomable pools of darkness. Slowly, a look of comprehension crossed his young face.

"We can go back to England now?"

Margrethe smiled at her emotionally vacant son, searching in vain for a glimmer of joy or excitement on his expressionless face. She sighed.

"Yes, Ari, now we can go back home."

***

# CHAPTER FOURTEEN

LORD Beaufort Winchester the First died in most ungentlemanly circumstances that left those close to him in no doubt as to his sexual preferences. Money was paid out to the good-looking young man found in the Minister's company at the time of his death. The possibility of sudden ill health should he ever breathe a word of this scandal ensured that the young man slipped quietly back to the London back streets from whence he sprang, never to be heard of again. The cause of death was officially noted as a heart attack, and funeral invitations went out to family, friends, and politicians alike.

Beau stared at his invitation with mixed feelings. He wouldn't have thought his father's enforced absence in death would affect him any more than his father's preferred absence in life. However, it slowly sank in that his father was, in fact, irretrievably gone. Unlike Beau, who now enjoyed immunity to death and other such ills, Lord Beaufort Winchester the First had finally lived out his human existence and breathed his last. Beau's mother was beside herself with grief. Another husband gone, another abandonment. Fortunately for Lady Elizabeth Winchester, she remained blissfully unaware of the true circumstances of her poor, late husband's death.

She wept into her fine linen handkerchiefs for the hard-working Minister of Parliament who had died at his desk, eliciting clucking sympathy from the other parliamentary wives. It would be a large funeral, attended mainly by politicians and diplomats. Lord Beaufort Winchester the First's friends were exceptionally few and exceptionally private.

Valdymyr peered over his shoulder at the invitation.

"Ah, my sympathies, soldier. A sad passing, but good fortune for us, nonetheless."

Beau stared at his companion pointedly. "My father's passing is *good fortune*?"

"Your father's passing is very sad, I'm sure. But let us be honest, you were hardly close to him. His passing gives you a certain amount of freedom. It is also a good reason for your sister to return home."

*Of course! Surely Margrethe would not miss Father's funeral.* The thought momentarily overrode his sorrow. He longed to see her again, to be certain she was alive and well. The Great War had been hellish, the carnage widespread. Throughout the bombing and shooting, Beau had been tormented by the thought that his sister could be anywhere and that he could, once again, do nothing to protect her. Just as he had in the Boer War, Beau had decided to focus on his own survival. He kept himself alive, but he felt lifeless until he met Valdymyr. Now, he enjoyed his newfound vampiric abilities. The extra strength and vitality were the perfect antidote to war weariness. His increased senses were hard to adjust to at first, but gradually Beau became used to seeing things at great distances or hearing whispered conversations through stone walls. He could move swiftly and silently. His strength had increased tenfold, yet with all this, nothing filled the empty space deep within him.

Upon his return to England, Beau had found his father in failing health. Their relationship was as strained and distant as ever. Lord Winchester had wearily agreed to let Beau and his foreign friend stay at the family estate, which had been entirely closed up throughout the war. Valdymyr seemed to take gleeful enjoyment in ripping the covers off the furniture. The heavy French doors were thrown open in the late afternoons and evenings, allowing the fresh country air to chase out the mustiness of years of hibernation. It was a relief to be home where his surroundings were comforting and familiar. Beau watched as Valdymyr bustled about his family home, rearranging chairs and covering the brighter windows with heavy drapes that obscured the light. The older vampire seemed to have greater photosensitivity than Beau, whose eyes still seemed to adjust to daylight as well as when he'd been human.

Beau's debt to Valdymyr weighed heavily upon him at times. There was no doubt that the older vampire had been considerably helpful in the early days of his transformation. Valdymyr had nurtured his creation, reveling in his Svengali-like status. Gradually, though, as Beau's abilities increased, so did the realization of his predicament. He was indebted to Valdymyr until death. Of course, death was not a common occurrence in the society of the undead, save that it often only came by another vampire's clawed hand. It didn't occur to Beau for a moment to kill his mentor. The older vampire's power frightened him, and his ruthless nature chilled Beau to his already cold bones. But Beau had learned quite a bit from his undead mentor and master and felt beholden to him just the same. He wouldn't dare cross Valdymyr. He'd made his choice. An eternity of bondage in return for the chance to vanquish his enemy and see his sister again, that sufficed for him. Now that both goals seemed tantalizingly close, he could afford to allow Valdymyr a sense of entitlement in his family home. That was the price. Eternal debt. Beau sighed, folding the invitation in half and placing it gently on the desk. Somehow he would escape the inescapable. For now, his only eternal desire was to see Margrethe again.

And then utterly destroy Lord Lucius Ruthven.

LUCIUS stood outside the tiny Parish rectory. A warm light filtered out from a window, breaking through the cold shadows of dusk. Its brightness hurt his eyes momentarily. He averted his gaze from the house, staring instead at the cemetery beyond. He wondered briefly what it would be like to taste death. That which humans accepted as inevitable was as foreign to him as love. He thought he'd known love with Margrethe. He realized now that he'd just mesmerized her. He'd taken her in the only way he'd ever known, possessively, like a predator taking down his prey. She'd inflamed his senses, and he'd poured all his energy into his pursuit of her, eliminating all opposition.

All opposition, that is, except Beau.

He wondered if Beau had survived two wars. He hadn't seen him since their last encounter outside the medical tent in Africa. Perhaps the Great War had accomplished what he could not. Perhaps Beau was dead, torn apart on a distant battlefield. Or, of course, he could be safely at home, minding the family estate. Perhaps Margrethe was with him. Lucius entertained the thought for a moment before dismissing it with a derisive snort. She'd know it would be the first place he would look, and she would be right, had he not detoured to Windsor to retrieve his son.

If this boy *was* his son.

A sudden noise snapped his attention back to the house. The door swung open and light poured out into the neat garden. Lucius shrank back into the shadows and watched as a boy who appeared to be in his late teens stepped outside. He held two bowls. From out of nowhere, four cats gathered around the boy's feet, their hungry yowls chorusing through the silent evening. He watched as the boy spoke to them softly, bending down and placing the bowls a couple of feet apart. The cats dove into them hungrily. The boy straightened and looked around. The glow of the window lantern caught his face. His hair was blonde, like his mother's, framing an elfin-like face that brought Margrethe back to him for an instant, swimming before his eyes like a siren. He focused his gaze more keenly on the boy. The eyes sealed it for Lucius. Dark, black eyes that burned like coals in that pale, youthful face. They burned through the encroaching darkness, boring through the branches that covered his hiding spot. Lucius shrank back even further, cloaking himself in the gathering night. He could feel the intensity of the boy's searching gaze. It alighted on the huge oak that covered his presence and lingered for a moment before slowly moving on. He waited, barely breathing. There was silence for a moment, then footsteps, followed by the clatter of dishes and some rather ungodly cursing. Lucius waited until he heard the door close before emerging from the undergrowth.

Even if the boy's strong resemblance to Margrethe hadn't convinced him, he'd felt the boy's intense power, and that left Lucius in no doubt. He'd found his son.

MARGRETHE heard the news the minute she stepped foot in England. Her stepfather's face, made famous in death, stared at her from an obituary in the newspaper. Next to her, Ari slaked his thirst with a glass of milk laced with honey and cinnamon. The fragrant aroma wafted towards her like a comforting blanket. On the few occasions she'd spent time with Lord Beaufort Winchester the First, they'd shared cups of cinnamon milk beside the fire. He would regale her with tales of London, reducing her to shrieks of laughter with his imitations of fellow politicians and their wives. Those were rare moments when she'd seen him happy and relaxed. Smiling at the memory, Margrethe gazed down at her son. After so many years in Europe, she had hoped for her stepfather's help in quietly resettling in England. Now dead, her plans, or what there were of them, were gone with him. The smile faded. Absently, she stroked Ari's dark hair. Thick black hair, so like his father's.

So much about him reminded her of Lucius. The same black eyes, the same arrogant saunter, as though Lucius haunted her through their son. Of course, he couldn't possibly know about Ari's existence. When she'd fled the castle, she'd known it would be impossible for her to return to England. Lucius would look there first and possibly stalk the family estate.

One of Margrethe's greatest agonies throughout the war had been the uncertainty of her family's fate. The small villages in which they'd hidden had been largely without communication, save for occasional news from straggling lines of refugees that passed through. One night, driven by desperation and hunger, Margrethe dragged one of those refugees into the woods and fed greedily on the girl's warm blood. She'd turned from her bloody feast to see Ari watching her, his eyes dark and dead. From that point on, she and Ari hunted together. They had to move regularly. She'd lost contact with her stepfather very early on. Now the Great War had ended and Lord Beaufort Winchester the First was dead. Suddenly she felt vulnerable, without cover. She would have to throw herself on the mercies of fate and family. She had more faith in the former. Her mother no doubt observed a self-absorbed grieving period before hunting down her next husband. And her brother.

*Beau.*

She knew he'd returned to England safely after the Boer War. Her stepfather had been most happy to tell her about Beau's decision to continue his military career. Margrethe found it hard to imagine Beau in the military at all, much less choosing to remain in service. She'd hoped he'd changed his mind, given the last three years of carnage. If he had emerged from the Great War alive and well, she knew he'd be at his father's funeral, in spite of their fierce differences and estrangements. Beau might be hot-headed, but he wasn't callous unless war had made him so. It was a possibility, of course. The war had changed many people. Beau had seemed callous to her on his last visit home. When she left, she believed him to be heartless. She knew better now. Beau had only been trying to protect her. If only she'd listened instead of falling under the dark spell of Lord Lucius

Ruthven. Margrethe shuddered. Some mistakes could not be undone.　　　　Unfortunately, this mistake would stay with her for eternity.

Difficult though it may be, she knew she would have to attend the funeral. She needed her family, especially her brother. She grew tired of facing the world alone. She had kept herself and her son alive, stealing food and preying on refugees and the half dead for their precious blood. She'd spent years running, protecting her son from the war and from himself. That last battle had been the most taxing of all, leaving her worn out and tired of running. They needed a home. Ari needed a family.

*Express to London now boarding!* The guard's cry rang out across the concourse.

"Ari, it's time to catch our train." The boy drained the last of his hot brewed milk and shrugged his arms into his coat. A dark lock of hair fell across his eyes, and he brushed it away impatiently. He smiled at his mother and lifted up the two bags sitting at her feet.

"I will carry these, Mother."

Margrethe smiled back, noting the endearment. She loved small moments like this where the light shone through. They were few, but in those moments he was almost like any other boy faced with a life full of possibilities. He was, for those moments, free of the stain of his legacy. He was, for a brief breath of time, human.

"I PROMISE you that he will be well taken care of, Father Johns." Lucius smiled the warmest smile he could muster in the presence of the sacred cross. The priest smiled back a little uncertainly before turning to the blonde haired boy standing next to him.

"You're certain about this, Raphael?"

Raffy nodded. He didn't want to hurt this man who'd been, to the utmost of his ability, a father figure towards him. If not for Father John's kindness and devout guidance, Raffy had no doubt he would be living a far more troubled life by now. Sadly, Raffy had lately found this sheltered existence to be more claustrophobic than comfortable. He wanted to get out into the world, to explore new possibilities, make new friends, the only thing he prayed for. Finally, this invisible God in whom he didn't believe answered his fervent prayer in the form of Lucius Ruthven. He'd appeared on their doorstep, tall and resplendent in well-tailored clothing. He had a compelling air about him, no doubt from his considerable military background. Raffy had seen a few soldiers on their return. They were broken men, sad shells driven mad by shelling. This man proved different. He was strong and vital, as though war had been a tonic for him, planning on traveling to his family home in Europe. There would be many opportunities in the aftermath of the war. He needed someone to travel with him. He needed Raffy.

Father Johns had been hesitant. Raffy could see it hurt him to think the boy might leave, but even with that, he gave Raffy the choice, so in deference to Father John's feelings, the boy merely nodded his assent. They set out for London in a black Renault that made Raffy's eyes light up. An ancient man named Silas drove the car. Raffy sat in the back seat with Lucius. He felt a strange sense of belonging with this dark, handsome officer who had requisitioned him. It wasn't that Lucius had a particularly friendly air. He was polite and attentive, but there was an unsettling coldness about him, too. In spite of this, Raffy was happy to entrust himself to his new benefactor. Smiling at his incredible luck, Raffy sat back in the leather seat and watched the English countryside speed by. The cold air stung his face, and he wrapped the scarf Lucius had provided even more tightly around his neck. Traveling with a European aristocrat would open doors for Raffy that he'd only dreamed about. The entire world lay before him, a brave new world emerging from the ashes of war.

They stopped for lunch at a small Inn. The harried innkeeper brought ale for Raffy and red wine for Lucius and Silas. Lucius poured the wine gratefully and sat back, regarding Raffy with a quizzical look.

"So, Raphael, tell me, have you ever felt different?"

Raffy gazed at the dark-haired man, uncertain of his meaning. Yes, in a way he'd always felt different. Being found half dead at birth at the base of a cross was different. But apart from his remarkable birth and piously sheltered upbringing, Raffy didn't feel any different to the other boys he knew.

"I...I...well, sometimes, I suppose I do." He felt foolish, stammering like a baby.

Lucius looked at him for a long moment before waving a hand at him lightheartedly.

"Never mind, Raphael. T'was just a silly thought." Lucius swirled the wine in his cup, watching the ruby liquid glint in the lamp light. So like blood. He wondered if the boy had the hunger. Had he already made his first kill? Were there drained bodies of nameless victims buried in the cemetery behind the rectory? Lucius had tried to read him, but the boy's thoughts were unreachable, as though locked behind an invisible stone wall. Lucius had experienced a similar situation with Valdymyr, an expected result due to the ancient vampire's age and power. This boy though was still young, yet easily kept Lucius out of his head.

*His boy.*

Lucius quickly guarded the thought, unsure if the boy could read minds. If so, then Lucius didn't want Raffy discovering the true nature of their relationship. Not yet. The time for that revelation would come. For now, Lucius remained interested in getting to know this elfin-faced boy with the powerful presence. This boy, who may be his son.

Lucius called the bar wench over and ordered more ale. Their journey would be a long one, and he preferred it not to be silent as well. Ale might loosen Raphael's tongue. Lucius wanted to know as much as possible about the boy. He had to be absolutely certain this was indeed his son. He could imagine his triumphant return to his mother's castle, Raphael beside him. He still didn't trust his mother, in spite of her conciliatory words. He would indeed bring her grandson to her. She would kneel before the fruit of her womb and acknowledge the Lord of Nyx and his heir. Lucius would accept no less.

***

# CHAPTER FIFTEEN

MARGRETHE didn't attend the funeral service. She hadn't been inside a church since giving birth, and she now found herself unable to enter one at all. She preferred the cemetery, with its comforting oaks and silent headstones. She stood at the back of the crowd of somberly dressed mourners. Ari stood quietly beside her, his dark eyes taking in everything and giving away nothing. The priest's strong voice reverberated across the distance, both solemn and mournful.

"And so we commit the Lord's servant, Lord Beaufort Winchester the First, to his place of eternal rest."

Margrethe pushed apologetically forward, pulling Ari with her. She wanted to see these last moments. She needed to see the casket lowered into the Earth. Ashes to ashes, dust to dust. She needed to remember mortality, if only for a moment. She needed to say goodbye.

The casket hit the bottom of the grave with a small thud, followed by another thud as the first shovelful of dirt hit the polished lid of the coffin.

*"Our Father, who art in Heaven."*

The mourners joined the priest in the familiar prayer. Their voices hummed like bees. Margrethe glanced at Ari. He stared at the grave with an air of bewilderment. The concept of death was foreign to him. He had tried to understand when his mother told him his grandfather had died. He'd witnessed death many times, but never quite understood it. She often saw him look into the eyes of his victims as they died in his arms. She asked him once what he sought.

"Death."

"Did you find it?"

"No."

"What did you find?"

"Fear."

"Humans fear death, Ari."

"Why?"

"Because it is the unknown from which they never return."

Two attendants continued to shovel dirt onto the casket. The mourners began to drift away, back to the land of the living. Margrethe raised a gloved hand to her eyes and wiped away her tears. She glanced at a group of people on the opposite side of the grave, and her heart stood still.

*Beau.*

Resplendent in full military uniform, he looked healthy and strong. A little pale, but that was to be expected at such an emotionally strenuous time. As though he felt her eyes upon him, he suddenly looked straight at her. Involuntarily, Margrethe gripped Ari's arm.

"Look, Ari! Your Uncle! That man there in uniform is your Uncle Beau." Margrethe couldn't contain the excitement in her voice.

Ari squinted at the man in uniform. He had blond hair like his mother's, but his eyes were blue to her brown. He looked somewhat shocked to see them, then nodded at his mother. Her eyes were bright, gleaming with happiness. He'd never seen her eyes like that. They'd always been dark, empty, and sad. Perhaps humans died so that other humans could remember how to live. In any case, death seemed to be an incredibly powerful thing.

THE last rites were given, and the mourners began to disperse. Beau pushed his way slowly through the sea of black, stopping regularly to shake hands and receive condolences. He wanted to push them all aside so he could reach Margrethe. He must see her, talk to her. Finally, he made his way through the crowd. He walked up behind her, tapping her lightly on the shoulder. She turned and upon seeing him, an expression of pure joy crossed her face. She threw herself into his arms, which were already waiting outstretched. Years of estrangement melted away as brother and sister embraced. Margrethe sobbed into his shoulder, clinging to him in a mixture of grief and joy. Beside her, a dark-haired boy watched silently.

"Margrethe." His voice was soft. He stroked her hair, soft to his touch.

"Beau." She released her hold on him and stepped back. "Thank God you are all right."

"Yes, I am fine, Margrethe," Beau chuckled. "Although I would thank my excellent survival skills first and foremost before I thanked God."

"Well, by whatever means you are safe, and I am thankful for it!"

"And likewise, Margrethe, I had no idea if you had survived or where you were. I thought you were with…?"

"No!" She spat the word out like an alley cat before glancing at the boy beside her. He followed her look and raised a questioning eyebrow.

"And who is this young gentleman?"

Margrethe seemed unable to speak.

"I am Ariel, sir, but most people call me Ari." The boy held out his hand confidently. Beau took it in a firm handshake.

"Good to meet you, Ariel. That is a most unusual name." Beau directed this observation more at his sister than the boy.

Margrethe finally found her voice.

"Ariel is my son, Beau."

Beau felt his grip tighten involuntarily. He released the boy's hand quickly, as though burnt by hot coals. The boy didn't seem to notice his reaction. If he did, he gave no indication of it but continued to smile politely at Beau. The smile didn't reach the boy's eyes. They remained cold and dark.

Quickly, Beau recovered his senses. He took another closer look at the boy. He couldn't see much of Margrethe in Ari, but there was no mistaking his father in the dark eyes, the black hair, and the finely chiseled features. Beau plastered a smile on his face.

"He is a fine looking boy, Margrethe." His voice gave away nothing of his inner anguish.

"Thank you, Beau." She seemed a little awkward, but greatly relieved. He should have known, of course. If he'd been more observant, he would have recognized Lucius in the boy straight away.

"Do you wish to speak to Mother? She's over there receiving condolences and dry sherries." Beau smiled at his sister wryly.

Margrethe glanced over at Lady Elizabeth Winchester, clearly pressed by a sense of obligation.

"Yes, I should talk to Mother, of course. But in good time."

"Does she know…?" Beau cast a meaningful look towards Ari.

Margrethe shook her head.

"No, I do not think so."

Beau thought for a moment. "Well, perhaps it would better to introduce her to her grandson later."

Margrethe nodded.

"Where are you staying?

Margrethe couldn't meet his gaze.

"You do have somewhere to stay, do you not?"

She shook her head.

"We only arrived today." her voice trailed off wearily.

Clearly, he couldn't leave his sister and her son at the mercy of London's streets. Beau took her arm gently, steering her towards a row of automobiles parked near the cemetery gates. Ari followed closely behind them, his eyes lighting up at the sight of the black sedan waiting for them.

"You and Ari shall go ahead to the estate in my car. I will requisition one of Mother's cars and follow." He clasped her hands in his. They felt small and fragile. Her skin was rougher than he remembered. "Winchester House is your home, Margrethe. We have missed you. I have missed you." Those last words caught in his throat. He'd missed her more than he could say. He'd carried the loss of her like a stone in his heart. For years, he'd felt the loss of her. Not just the loss of her presence, but of her essence. She'd left hating him. Not trusting him. That had hurt him more than anything.

It was as though she could read his mind.

"I should have listened to you, Beau. I should never have left."

He hushed her with a finger to his lips.

"You are here now. You are safe. You and Ari. That is all that matters."

She nodded again, tears welling up in her eyes. He helped her up into the car. Ari bounded in beside her, his excitement stirred by this new adventure.

Beau leaned down against the car, peering in at the darkened interior.

"I'll see you soon Margrethe. Oh, I forgot to mention, I have a friend staying with me. I'm sure he'll make you most welcome until I get there."

He banged the roof of the car and strode off before she at least asked his friend's name. Never mind, they would just have to introduce themselves. The car started with a jolt. She smiled over at Ari. He smiled back. His eyes were gleaming with anticipation. It would be good for him to be with family, to know the security of blood kin. Blood. A dark cloud descended upon her. She would still have to deal with the dark legacy that now engulfed their lives, but it hopefully would be easier to contain the situation if she were living on the Estate. The memory of Freddie's disappearance gnawed at her mind. She tried to push it away. That situation had hardly been contained. It had been the beginning of the end of her family as she knew it. And now they were returning to the family estate where it all happened. She would have to be careful and watch Ari like a hawk.

The boy stared out the car window, watching the passersby with an air of cold detachment. Her boy, she reminded herself. Margrethe sighed. She loved her son, but she could never forget what he was. Or what she'd become. She couldn't blame this dark-haired, dark-eyed youth sitting beside her for their predicament. She had made the choices, and she had to bear responsibility for the consequences. That didn't make it easier, of course, but there it was. Her son was now a young man with ideas of his own. He wouldn't be under her care and guidance for much longer. The thought filled her with both dread and relief. She was relieved to be soon free of the burden of his welfare, and the well-being of those he came into contact with. And the dread? She had no idea what Ari would turn into without her constraining hand. She sensed the deep darkness in him. His remote aloofness greatly resembled his father's cold arrogance, but even Lucius had been far more given to emotional displays than his son. Lucius had been more prey to anger than anything else, but Ari never allowed himself overwhelming emotions, not even anger. Always temperate, he seemed never to fight himself, except, perhaps when his frustration at times overcame him. Trying to understand the world and one's place in it proved a difficult and common occurrence for all youth, but for Ari,

135

his difficulties were further complicated by his vampiric heritage. Margrethe often wondered if Ari even loved her, or if he just tolerated her presence until free to make his own choices.

Casting her doubt aside, more from discomfort than any sense of peace, Margrethe set her thoughts to the journey home with forced optimism. Things would be better this time. She would make them better.

VALDYMYR watched the car pull into the driveway from his bedroom window. The first to alight was Margrethe. She looked as beautiful as ever, but there resonated a weariness in her movements that hadn't been there before, even in pregnancy. Behind her, a dark-haired youth stepped out of the car, tall and strongly built. The boy looked around for a moment then raised his gaze to Valdymyr's window as if sensing him there. The ancient vampire stepped back quickly. There'd been no mistaking the finely chiseled features on that young face. This had to be Lucius's son. He crept back to the window and peered out carefully. Margrethe and the boy stood at the base of the stone steps. The driver unloaded a few small bags, carried them to the door, and knocked sharply. Valdymyr keen ears heard the maid's footsteps scurry across the grand entrance as she hurried to answer it. He smiled. The mice had entered the cat's lair. How surprised Margrethe would be to find him here, with her brother. Still smiling, he rose to his feet. He should greet their guests. Perhaps he could offer them some refreshment. He'd often wondered how the young maid's blood would taste.

Voices echoed up the staircase, reaching his finely tuned ears.

"Lord Winchester sent us ahead in his car. He will be following shortly." Margrethe's voice lilted up to his ears.

"Yes, Lady Margrethe. Please come in, I will show you to the drawing-room."

He heard the door close, followed by a clatter of footsteps

across the tiled entrance hall. A squeak emitted as another door opened.

"Please take a seat, Lady Margrethe."

Even with his finely tuned ears, Valdymyr could barely hear the maid's timid words. Refreshment was about all she was good for. Smiling again, he straightened his day coat. He looked forward to seeing Margrethe again and making her son's acquaintance.

MARGRETHE sank gratefully into the comfortable chaise. Ari sat in a chair beside her, perching tensely on the edge of its plump cushion. She raised her head and looked around the room. Everything looked so different. The furniture, which she noted had been rearranged, had a stored, musty smell, in spite of the open windows. The mantel was dusty. Her old home had clearly suffered for lack of a woman's touch. Ari kept his gaze on the French windows. The trees that shaded the room from the afternoon sun moved in the gentle breeze, casting dancing shadows on the walls. The light skipped across the boy's face, highlighting the straight nose and strong jaw. His eyes, as always, were unreadable.

Margrethe sighed and sat back in the chaise, relishing the opportunity to rest.

The squeak of the door stirred her from her reverie. Standing up, she turned and stopped, her words caught in her throat.

*Valdymyr!*

What a strange coincidence that Beau should know this man. She smiled, glad of a familiar face.

"Dear Valdymyr, how lovely and unexpected to see you."

Valdymyr bowed and took her extended hand, brushing it with dry lips.

"Greetings, Lady Margrethe. You look well." He turned towards Ari.

"And this young man is?"

For some reason, Margrethe hesitated for a moment, then

smiled.

"This is my son, Ariel. He prefers to be addressed as Ari."

Valdymyr chuckled, a dry, raspy sound. He extended his hand to Ari, who clasped it firmly.

"It is an honor to meet the son of the lovely Lady Margrethe." He smiled ingratiatingly. Ari smiled back, but his smile lacked warmth. He dropped the older man's hand and took a step back, regarding Valdymyr silently. Valdymyr returned his gaze, squinting at the youth with a strange, searching intensity that made Margrethe a little uncomfortable. She put her arm around Ari and pulled him close. Valdymyr smiled thinly, sensing the defensiveness of the gesture.

"You must be tired and thirsty. I will hunt down this maid and have her fetch you some refreshments."

His choice of words put Margrethe even more on edge. *Hunt down?* She squeezed her eyes shut for a moment. She must be tired, terribly tired. At least Beau wouldn't be far behind them. She relaxed a little at the thought.

"That would be lovely, Valdymyr. Thank you." She sank back onto the couch again, motioning Ari back into the chair. The boy still seemed tense. His eyes hadn't left Valdymyr. She turned to him when the older man had left the room.

"Are you feeling unwell, Ari?"

"No, Mother, why?"

"You just seem unwell."

He turned his black eyes towards her and smiled without warmth.

"I am fine, Mother."

She wasn't satisfied but sensed she would get nothing more from him, so she sank back into the soft cushions and closed her eyes.

ARI sat in the fancy chair, watching his mother dispassionately as she drifted into sleep. She still seemed to bear the marks of her humanity. She felt weariness, she felt emotion. He, on the other hand, had no human traits to show, being of the undead, the Immortal Ones. His mother had told him the truth on his sixteenth birthday. He'd been relieved to know. He'd been killing for over a year by then. Not animals. Humans. The animals had ceased to satisfy him by the time he had turned fourteen. Puberty had increased his appetite. He'd always chosen homeless children. There were plenty of them, war orphans begging on the streets, sweeping out shops just to earn a coin. They were never missed.

He'd honed his survival instincts and his strength in those hard years of war. He trusted his instincts and right now, his instincts told him not to trust this man, Valdymyr. He'd felt a little uncomfortable with Beau. Perhaps it had been the uniform. Ari wasn't comfortable with anything to do with the military, but he didn't dislike his Uncle.

Valdymyr, however, proved different.

Something about the man reeked predator. Ari might not be emotionally competent, but he sensed danger like a wild animal. It pervaded his senses and tensed his body in readiness. He sat perched on the edge of his chair, muscles tensed, jaw set, his ears alert to every sound, his eyes to every movement. Outside in the trees, some sparrows settled for the evening. Their noisy chorus invaded the room. Ari became aware of a creeping thirst, but he'd already decided to refuse any refreshments Valdymyr may offer. He didn't trust this man. He would follow his instincts. He was nearly a man now himself. He'd soon need to look not only after himself but his mother, too. Her human taint made her weak. He would be careful of this man Valdymyr, even though his mother seemed to know him. And yes, he would even be wary of his uncle. He knew neither of them and neither one had his trust.

Alert and quiet, Ari continued to wait, listening for the sound of returning footsteps. Watching, waiting.

\*\*\*

# CHAPTER SIXTEEN

RAFFY watched as Lucius crouched behind the bushes. His mentor scanned the driveway of the mansion with an intensity that made Raffy feel somewhat intrusive and uncomfortable. He sat on the kickboard of the car, making circles in the dirt and leaves with his foot, bored. They'd come to this same spot for two days now, and Lucius had done the same thing. Watched and waited. For what, Raffy did not know. Lucius hadn't been forthcoming on the subject, save it being of the utmost importance to them both. His mood hadn't invited further questioning, and Silas provided no interesting conversation or insights, so Raffy had simply sat quietly for two days in this secluded spot, waiting for some life changing event currently kept secret from him.

A sudden rustle of bushes made him look up. He jumped as a raven burst from the dense foliage, its mournful cry echoing through the trees. With a flutter of its ebony wings, it perched on a branch above them and eyed them inquisitively. Lucius rose from his crouched position and stared at the driveway, his body tense and unmoving. The rumble of a car engine reached Raffy's ears. Curiously, he stood up, straining to see over the bushes. He spotted

141

the top of a car making its way down the driveway of the dilapidated mansion. He moved forward quietly, standing behind Lucius, who remained motionless. The two watched as a woman and a boy alighted from the car. The boy appeared to be about his age, only with dark hair cropped short, just above his collar. A thick fringe fell over his eyes, shielding his face even from Raffy's keen eyes. The woman, blonde and slender, possessed an elfin face and large dark eyes. Raffy thought she was quite beautiful. She stopped as the driver unloaded their bags and stood hands on hips, looking at the mansion in front of her. A strange expression settled on her face, sort of happy but wistful, even a little sad. She seemed familiar for some reason. Strange really, as Raffy was sure he'd never seen her before. He'd certainly never seen the other boy. He continued to watch from the shadows as they mounted the stone steps and disappeared into the once stately home.

Lucius finally moved. He turned to Raffy, a small smile of satisfaction playing on his mouth.

"Raphael, there is much I have to tell you. There's no time now, but you must trust me and know that I act in your best interests."

Raffy nodded. He had no choice but to trust his new benefactor.

"Good." Lucius pushed him gently towards the car. He nodded at Silas. The old man climbed silently back into the driver's seat. Raffy followed Lucius into the back seat and slammed the door behind them. The car sputtered to life and began to make its way down the winding dirt road towards the mysterious mansion and its occupants. The silence in the car was pregnant with expectation. It filled the air with its heady, adventurous scent. Raffy sensed that something important drew near. Unable to contain his curiosity, he ventured a question.

"Are these people family, Lord Ruthven? Friends?"

Lucius looked at him with unfathomable black eyes. For the

first time, Raffy noticed how like his own eyes they were, a fleeting thought.

"You will find out soon, Raphael. Just be patient a little while longer."

Raffy remained silent, but his curiosity grew undiminished. Was it some kind of family feud? Would they even be welcome at this run down mansion, or would there be a confrontation of some sort? Raffy hoped not. He was handy with his fists when he needed to be, but he wasn't a fighter, preferring words and humor as a means of escaping awkward situations. He stole a sly glance at Lucius. His benefactor's finely chiseled face looked relaxed, but an air of anticipation clung about him. He seemed sure of himself, certainly not nervous or afraid. Raffy doubted that Lord Lucius Ruthven feared anything. If the medals in his top drawer didn't attest to that fact, the man's confident manner most certainly did.

The car tires crunched on the white gravel driveway as they passed through the entrance gates. The gardens were overgrown, with moss-covered statues peeping up over the wild sprays of blackberry bush that dotted the grounds. Raffy made a mental note to steal away and pick some of the ripened fruit. He often would search the fields near the rectory for blackberry bushes, stripping them of their bounty and feasting upon the sweet sticky berries, his mouth and fingers stained deep red with the juice.

An ornately carved stone doorway loomed above them as the car pulled up to the main entrance. An ominous feeling washed over Raffy. He shrank back in the seat and shivered a little. Lucius seemed to have no such hesitancy. Without even a glance in Raffy's direction, he leaped out of the car and, bidding Raffy and Silas to wait for him, walked straight up the stone steps and knocked on the door. The authoritative rap of the heavy brass knocker broke the silence with the sharpness of an arrow. Raffy picked up the sound of light footsteps, followed by the sound of bolts being drawn back. The door swung open, and a maid peered out nervously.

"I am here to see Lady Margrethe Charlesworth-Winchester." Lucius's voice echoed boldly over the driveway. The girl seemed a little taken aback by his request. She looked back over her shoulder uncertainly before turning her attention back to Lucius.

"Well, she's only arrived a short time ago, sir. She's with Lord Valdymyr right now..."

"Valdymyr?"

Lucius spat the name like venom. Raffy sat up straight, startled by the tone of his benefactor's voice, the first time he'd seen Lucius Ruthven's composure ruffled in any way. This Valdymyr was clearly no stranger and by the sound of it, no beloved friend, either. The ominous feeling returned, stronger than before. Lucius's next move took him completely by surprise. He pushed the door aside, sweeping the hapless maid backward with it. She fell back into the hallway with a thump and a whelp of pain. Lucius stepped over her without care and strode into the gloomy depths of the mansion. Raffy felt compelled to follow but Silas's restraining hand pushed him back.

"No, boy. Do as he says."

And so, against his better judgment, Raffy sat in the car with Silas and, once again, waited.

THE girl's frail body hurtled backward as he pushed the door open. Lucius stepped over her, then hesitated. Harnessing his anger for a moment, he turned and helped the wretched creature to her feet. She opened her mouth as if to speak, but he shushed her with a finger to her lips.

"There is no further need for your assistance, thank you. I know the way."

She bobbed a hurried curtsey, all the while staring at him with huge, terrified eyes. Lucius could see she wanted to flee, but her fear held her fast. He broke the spell.

"Go!"

His barked command jolted her from her paralysis. She turned and scurried across the stone floor and up the winding staircase, hesitating only once to glance back at him. He wondered momentarily if he should have disposed of her, but a soft murmur reached his ears. He turned his attention to the drawing-room across the hallway. Beyond the partially closed door, he could hear two voices. One belonged to Valdymyr, and the other unmistakably belonged to Margrethe. His anger dissipated for a moment at the melodic sound of her voice. Caught off guard, he shook his head, reminding himself that she loved him so little as to flee from him and hide their son. The thought brought the anger flooding back. Fired by his pain, Lucius strode across the hall and flung the door open. The three occupants turned to stare at him, eyes wide with surprise.

Margrethe looked as beautiful as ever. She hadn't aged. Her delicate face was a little gaunter than he remembered, but she'd remained over the years, radiantly beautiful. He didn't even glance at the boy who sat in a chair with his back to the door. Instead, he turned to face Valdymyr, who had stepped forward challengingly. It may have looked like a protective gesture to Margrethe and her companion, but to Lucius, clearly a threat.

"Lucius, what a pleasant surprise! Do join us for some refreshments. You know Margrethe, of course."

Lucius wanted to tear his heart out. Valdymyr ignored his guest's thunderous expression and continued with his pleasantries.

"I don't believe you've met young Ariel yet." The old vampire gestured to the person sitting in the chair. A dark-haired youth rose and turned to greet him. Lucius stared at him, his thoughts and words frozen. That face, those eyes. The boy bore an uncanny resemblance to himself. He blinked and looked more closely, as though adjusting his vision might somehow alter the boy's features. There was no mistaking it. The boy looked exactly like him. The young man seemed to have been struck by the same thought as he returned Lucius's stare with equal intensity.

"Lucius, this is Ariel. Apparently he prefers to be addressed as Ari." The boy held out his hand politely. Lucius raised his hand to return the greeting.

"Ariel, this is your father, Lord Lucius Ruthven."

Valdymyr's words exploded in his brain, confirming what his own instincts had told him. Lucius dropped his hand and stared at the boy numbly. His *son*. Even as he knew in his heart the truth, Lucius told himself it was impossible! His son waited out in the car with Silas. Yet, looking at the young man before him, there was no denying it. The boy carried his genes to such a degree as to be a mirror image of him. Had he been mistaken? Was Raphael not his son after all? He looked over at Margrethe. What little color she'd had in her cheeks had drained from her face. She gazed at Valdymyr with a mixture of horror and fury. Her lithe body coiled like a cobra about to strike. When she spoke, it dripped with the venom of a snake.

"How dare you! What right do you have to interfere in matters of family? You may be staying with my brother, but I would remind you that you are most certainly not family!"

Valdymyr inclined his head, polite in the face of her anger.

"My apologies, Lady Margrethe. You are quite right, it is not my place to announce such sensitive information."

With a snort, Margrethe turned to face Lucius, pulling the boy close to her.

"Yes, Lucius, this is your son. Ari." She cradled the boy's head to her shoulder and whispered into his hair. The youth stood quite a bit taller than Margrethe, so she had to pull his head down to her, bending him awkwardly. He looked uncomfortable, and his mother's soothing words didn't seem to be helping.

"I am sorry, Ari. I did not mean for you to find out this way." Margrethe's voice quivered with desperation, begging her son's

146

forgiveness for this terrible truth.

The boy remained motionless in his awkward position. His eyes were dark and unfathomable. Lucius couldn't see past their black emptiness. He turned his gaze to Valdymyr, now leaning against the mantelpiece with a knowing, smug look. Valdymyr smiled.

"Is this not what you have wanted, Lucius?"

Lucius kept his voice low and even.

"What are you doing here, Valdymyr? Did my mother send you?"

Out of the corner of his eye, he saw Margrethe's head snap around at his words.

"Lucius, what do you mean? What does this man have to do with your mother?"

Lucius gave a mirthless laugh.

"Clearly, you do not know your friend here very well, Margrethe. Lord Valdymyr has been a close friend of my mother's for many centuries."

Margrethe turned to stare at the man she'd thought to be her friend. She fell silent for a moment, taking in this new information.

"So, you are a vampire? Like Lucius."

Valdymyr inclined his head.

"Yes, Lady Margrethe, I am a vampire like Lucius. Like you. Like your son."

Ari looked up at the ancient vampire, a spark of interest entering his eyes. Lucius caught the look. So the boy knew of his heritage? The boy's mouth curled in a smile. The news of his long-lost father had elicited little or no response, but the fact he was a vampire seemed to please him greatly. There was little doubt in his mind now. Ari was indeed his son and Ari belonged with him.

Lucius stepped forward so quickly that the motion was a blur. He grabbed Valdymyr by the throat and held him fast against the mantelpiece. His words were for Margrethe, but his black eyes bored into the ancient vampire as he spoke.

"Valdymyr has been working for my mother. It was his avowed mission to find our son and return him to the castle. He seems to think he will receive some manner of favor from my mother for doing so, eh, Valdymyr?" His eyes were barely an inch away from the older vampire's face. Valdymyr tried to speak but found it impossible with Lucius's fingers clamped around his throat. He made a small grunting noise and struggled again, but to no avail. Lucius's anger seethed, and his grip like unto iron. He lifted Valdymyr off the floor and threw him headlong against the opposite wall. Valdymyr sank down the floral wallpaper, slumping to the floor in a daze.

Lucius turned towards Margrethe, who held Ari protectively.

"Ari must come with me."

"He's going nowhere with you!" Margrethe's voice reached a hysterical pitch.

Lucius turned his attention to the boy, holding out his hand in invitation.

"Ari, come with me now. I can protect you."

Ari looked at him with those empty black eyes. He took a step forward then hesitated, glancing back at his mother.

Lucius was about to step forward and grab the boy when a sharp blow sent him reeling. In an instant, he felt Valdymyr upon him. The elder's teeth and talons tore at his flesh, sending searing pain across his arms and face. He recovered quickly, pushing his attacker off with all his strength. Valdymyr flew backward again, but this time Lucius reversed upon him, ripping and tearing without mercy. A high-pitched wail of pain burst from the ancient vampire as blood spurted from his wounds, spraying the wall in delicate, crimson arcs. Somewhere in the distance Lucius heard Margrethe's screams, but he didn't stop. He attacked with years of pent up fury until he felt the older vampire's strength wilt beneath him. With one last swipe of his hand, he reached into Valdymyr's exposed chest

148

cavity and ripped out his heart. It throbbed weakly in his hand as he held it aloft. A look of horror filled Valdymyr's dying eyes. Blood spilled from his open mouth. It flowed down his chin and his neck, staining his fine shirt a deep, dark red.

Lucius reveled in the beautiful, glorious sight. He stood up, flinging the dripping heart aside. Smiling, he turned back to Margrethe, now cowering in shock beside the chaise. The boy stood in front of her, unmoving. His dark eyes glinted at Lucius. Was he trying to protect his mother? Again, Lucius appealed to his son.

"Ari, you must come with me. Your mother, too, if she wishes." He added that offer as an afterthought. He didn't trust Margrethe, but if she chose to come with him, he would be happy enough to keep her close.

The boy looked back at his mother questioningly. She shook her head and held out her hand to him. The boy ignored it and turned back to Lucius.

"If I come with you, will you promise not to hurt my mother?"

"No, Ari!" Margrethe's cry rang with despair.

Lucius smiled at the boy. He doubted if it reassured him any with Valdymyr's blood still smeared all over his mouth. Strangely, the boy didn't seem to mind. He smiled back.

"I have no wish to hurt your mother, Ari. I think, however, that it would be best for you to return with me. Your mother loves you, but she cannot keep you safe in this world. I can."

"It's not true, Ari, don't listen to him. Look at him, he's a killer! A murderer!"

"He is my father." The boy's voice sounded old for one so young. "He is a vampire, like you. Like me. As for that man he killed, I did not like him. Or trust him."

Margrethe stood forward now.

"Yet you trust the man who killed him? Ari, I have kept you safe all these years. Please, do not doubt me now."

149

Tears began to spill down her face. Although beaten, empty, she yet determined not to let Lucius win. She moved towards the door as though to bar their exit, then stopped abruptly as a huge figure loomed in the doorway.

"Beau! Thank God!"

Lucius gave a cynical laugh.

"Ah, Beau, come to save the day. Tch. Sadly, you have just missed the excitement."

"What in God's name?" Beau stood for a few moments, taking in the bloody chaos. He looked at Valdymyr's motionless, disfigured remains then at his sworn foe.

"Well, Lucius, it seems you have a rather nasty habit of mauling my friends."

Lucius gave a short laugh.

"Since when has Valdymyr been your friend, Beau?"

"Since he turned me, Lucius."

A deadly silence fell upon the room. Margrethe stared at her brother, open-mouthed. Lucius eyed Beau suspiciously. Could he believe him? Would Valdymyr have turned Margrethe's brother? A distinct possibility he supposed. He decided to exercise caution.

Beau seemed to share no thoughts of caution. He leaped forward, shouting at Margrethe and Ari to run. Lucius wasn't taken completely off guard. He met Beau in mid-air. Their bodies slammed against each other with a force that sent them both hurtling across the room. They fell heavily against the door, slamming it shut and blocking Margrethe and Ari's escape. She screamed again, pulling Ari away from his father and uncle as they leaped upon each other in bloody fury. Ari tried to shake her off, but remained in her grip, now made stronger by fear. She dragged herself and her son to the farthest corner of the room and cowered there with her trembling arms around him.

Lucius didn't see her move, his attention focused solely on his adversary. He recovered quickly from the fall, pouncing on top of Beau in an instant, surprised by Beau's strength as he fought back. Perhaps he told the truth after all. If so, Lucius would have little choice but to rip his heart out as he'd done with Valdymyr. If Beau was a vampire, he was a far greater threat than before. Lucius felt a blow hit the side of his head. It wasn't too strong, but strong enough to daze him for a few seconds, enough time for Beau to push him aside and regain his feet. A blow from Beau's boot hit his temple. Lucius screamed in pain and rage. He looked up at Beau's now bloodied face.

"Let me take the boy now, Beau. There is no need for further bloodshed."

"Since when has the spilling of blood bothered you, Lucius? The boy goes nowhere against his mother's wishes."

Beau turned to Margrethe, who still cowered in the corner.

"Margrethe, do you wish Ari to go with Lucius?"

She shook her head, unable to speak.

Lucius quickly took advantage of the distraction. In a blink, he sank his talons deep into Beau's neck, pulling him towards him with such force that Beau's feet lifted off the ground. Blood spurted from the arteries like fountains, spraying Lucius's face in a sweet, red shower. Beau looked at him in shock and surprise.

"Never give your adversary a chance, Beaufort. He may just take it and rip your heart out."

With that, he pulled out his hawk-like nails and drove them in again. This time, they tore into Beau's chest, ripping through muscle and bone. Beau had no time to scream. His mouth gaped in mute agony as gouts of blood and bits of flesh flew into the air, covering their faces with a gruesome veil of death. Lucius felt the throbbing heart beneath his hand and pulled with all his strength. The life-giving organ burst out of Beau's chest in a cascade of bloodied flesh and shredded bone. Lucius howled victoriously, throwing the heart against a nearby bookcase. It splattered against the sharp edges of the shelves, spewing a bloody mess over Plato and

Jane Austen. Beau finally released his pain in a loud, piercing scream and fell to the floor. He lay there motionless, his sightless eyes staring at the ceiling. A pool of blood began to seep out beneath him, forming a red lake that spread across the floor. Lucius stood above the body of his enemy, breathing hard. There was no time to relish his victory. Lucius raised his eyes and looked around the room, smiling as his gaze came to rest on Ari and his mother.

\*\*\*

# CHAPTER SEVENTEEN

THE room grew eerily silent. Margrethe rose shakily from her crouched position, staring in horror at her brother's bloodied remains. A scream rose inside her, but no sound came out. Her mouth became dry, her throat constricted with shock and fear. She tried to move but remained in one spot, paralyzed. Ari stood beside her, looking mutely at the remains of his uncle.

"It is time for Ari to leave, Margrethe."

"No!" Somehow, she managed to croak the word out.

"He wants to go with me, Margrethe. It is no use trying to stop him."

Anger helped her speak.

"No, he doesn't, Lucius. You-you have mesmerized him, just as you did me! You destroyed my life, and I will not let you destroy his."

"I am his father, Margrethe. I will not destroy him."

"You are a monster, Lucius! You do nothing *but* destroy. It is in your nature!"

"Ari, there is a car outside. Go straight to it. Wait for me."

Ari glanced at his mother, then back at Lucius.

"You said you would not hurt her."

"No, I will not. On my honor."

"Honor? You have no honor!" Margrethe's voice grew shrill with rage.

Ari looked at his mother and hesitated, then shook his head resolutely.

"No, I will come with you now. We will leave together. She will not try to stop us, will you Mother?"

Margrethe sank to her knees, mentally begging her son to change his mind.

"Ari, why are you doing this? Why are you going with him?" She didn't understand. He had to be mesmerized in some way.

"I am nearly a man now, Mother. The bloodlust is overwhelming, almost beyond my control. My father knows the way of darkness. He is not afraid of his nature as you plainly are. He revels in it. He understands it."

Tears started rolling down her cheeks. *No, no, no!* She'd fought so hard to save her son from his dark inheritance, yet here it was, ingrained in his nature, apparently immovable. Ari knelt beside her and whispered in her ear.

"If I go with him, he will leave you alone. It is me he wants."

"No, Ari, I don't want you to go." She began to sob, grief already wracking her body. She couldn't lose them both. Not Beau, not her son.

"I must go. It is my heritage. I have never belonged, no matter where we have been, and now I understand why. I belong with him. I belong with my father."

His words cut her to the bone. Unable to speak, she shook her head helplessly. Tears streamed down her face. She had no fight left in her. Her son wanted to leave, and she couldn't stop him. Lucius had won.

Through her tears, she looked over at the bloody mess that had once been her brother. Part of her longed to crawl over there

154

and cradle him in her arms, another part repulsed. Ari gave her a short hug and rose slowly to his feet. She watched in anguish as he walked across the room. Lucius held the door open for him. Ari turned once more to look at her, then disappeared through it.

Lucius gave her a cold smile. "It has been a day of loss for you, Margrethe. My condolences on your brother's untimely demise, but, unfortunately, he left me little choice. Perhaps he thought he could fight a vampire by becoming one. He, like you, seems to have been brought undone by a sad lack of good judgment." He nodded towards the broken body of Valdymyr.

"Your choice of friends, for example, leaves much to be desired. Not only did your chum, Valdymyr, turn your brother, but he did so purely for the opportunity to deliver both you and our son to my mother. You know, of course, she would have killed you both, without mercy, without hesitation."

"Where are you taking him?" Her heart was breaking.

"It is better that you know nothing of his whereabouts. If he wishes to contact you, he will be more than free to do so."

With a curt nod, Lucius turned and left the room, leaving Margrethe behind with the body of her brother and a vast feeling of emptiness that threatened to engulf her.


RAFFY was about to disobey orders and go into the mansion when the door suddenly burst open. A dark-haired boy emerged and hurried down the stairs, followed closely by Lucius wiping at himself with a large cloth. Raffy caught sight of a red stain on it before Lucius tossed it away hastily. They were both breathless. Raffy wondered if his ominous feeling had been right and there'd been some sort of fight or upheaval.

He leaned across and pushed the door open. The boy climbed in first, then Lucius, who hastily slammed the door shut. He sensed that now was not the time to ask questions, so as the car took off, Raffy sat back quietly in his seat, slyly observing the boy seated next to him. He was a good-looking fellow, with one of those faces carved out of stone; solid and manly, yet beautiful, like a Michelangelo statue. He had dark hair that fell across his handsome face. He looked to be about Raffy's age, although Raffy couldn't see his face properly. The boy stared straight ahead as though in shock. Lucius shifted about next to him, fumbling with his kerchief and wiping at his face. He shifted again as he shrugged off his coat and folded it hastily. He threw it onto the floor and leaned forward, whispering in Silas's ear. Raffy tried unsuccessfully to hear what he said. He wondered what had happened. The boy seemed remarkably calm, but Lucius seemed somewhat shaken. And, of course, there was the blood. Had there been a fight? And who was the boy? He thought maybe he would introduce himself. He turned to his new traveling companion and held out his hand.

"I'm Raffy."

The boy looked down at his hand then up at him with dark, black eyes just like his own. A glimmer of recognition sparked between them. The boy took Raffy's hand. His touch was cold and smooth.

"Ari."

Raffy felt a jolt of recognition. He didn't know this boy Ari, yet he felt a connection with him that one would not normally feel with a stranger. It was an odd sensation and one he wasn't used to, although, on reflection, he remembered experiencing a similar feeling of belonging when Lucius Ruthven had turned up at the rectory door.

He had hoped that an introduction would start a conversation, but Ari fell quiet, staring blankly at the road ahead. They drove for what seemed like hours in silence, each immersed in their own thoughts. Finally, Lucius leaned forward and whispered again to Silas, who pulled the car over at a small country inn. They all climbed from the car, stretching gratefully after the long, silent journey. Wordlessly, Lucius strode to a nearby water trough, washed his face and hands. When he'd finished his ablution, he straightened, shrugging on a clean coat that Silas handed to him. He turned to the two boys, still buttoning the stylish jacket. As he fastened the final pearl button, Raffy thought he caught sight of a blood stain on the white shirt beneath. Lucius caught his stare and frowned. Raffy looked down at the ground quickly, guilt inexplicably shaming him as though he'd stumbled upon some secret, private moment. If Lucius was aware of his discomfort, he gave no sign of it.

"We will take some refreshment. It will give me a chance to talk to you both. I have much to tell you and a few questions of my own."

Raffy's curiosity was aroused. Perhaps now he would finally find out about the mansion and the mysterious boy, Ari, who stood quietly beside him. Lucius motioned the boys forward, and they followed his direction. He walked behind them, shepherding them into the Inn. Silas, who never seemed in need of nourishment, remained with the car. The innkeeper, a portly, red-nosed man with impossibly bloodshot eyes, directed them to a bench in the corner. They sat on the hard seats, waiting for their cool ales to be delivered.

Lucius sat opposite the two boys. He regarded them both with strange intensity, looking from one to the other as though assessing them in some way. Raffy shifted uncomfortably under the penetrating gaze. Lucius's eyes finally came to rest on him.

"Raphael, I had intended to introduce you to someone in the mansion. I need answers to some questions and only that person could give them to me, but some things eventuated that prevented me from doing so."

Raffy listened intently. Lucius's words were clear enough, but his meaning remained frustratingly obscure. Whom did he speak of? Did he mean the boy, Ari? He glanced over at the dark-haired, black-eyed youth. Lucius followed his gaze.

"Ari, has your mother ever spoken to you about the circumstances of your birth?"

Ari looked over at Lucius calmly.

"Yes, she has told me a little."

Lucius smiled at him encouragingly.

"Would you mind sharing it with me?"

Ari shrugged.

"I was born in a church. That's why she named me after an angel. She says the angel was my protector." Raffy pricked up his ears. The story of Ari's beginnings sounded something like his own. He sifted through his accumulated knowledge of angels and devils. Ariel, the third archon of the winds, the wielder of fire. Lion of God. Angel and devil, darkness and light.

Lucius continued his gentle but persistent interrogation. "Is there anything else? Did she mention Valdymyr?"

Ari seemed surprised by the question. He shook his head.

"Nooo. Not Valdymyr." He frowned. "The only one she ever mentioned was my brother."

Lucius sat up straight, his eyes more intense.

"Your brother?"

Ari nodded. "Yes, he would have been my brother if he had lived. He was stillborn. My mother left him behind in the church." His black eyes stared blankly at Lucius. "She was frightened and alone. She did what she could." To Raffy's ears, the other boy sounded almost apologetic. It was a fleeting observation as the significance of Ari's words began to dawn on him. His gaze shifted from Lucius to Ari, trying to understand the enormity of this new information.

Lucius also seemed to absorb Ari's words for a moment, his brow creased in thought. He looked over at Raffy, the frown still marring his forehead.

"And you, Raphael, were also born in a church?"

"Found." Against his good sense, Raffy corrected his benefactor.

Lucius shook his head.

"No, Raffy, not found. Born." He leaned across the table, grasping Raffy's hands in his.

"Raffy, this boy, Ari, is your brother. The woman who was with him, Lady Margrethe Charlesworth-Winchester, is your mother."

Raffy's head reeled as the missing pieces of the puzzle that had been his life suddenly came together. He glanced again at Ari, who returned his look of confusion. Raffy tried to find his voice. He had a hundred questions to ask, but Ari spoke first.

"So Raphael is the baby my mother left for dead? How can that be?"

At last, Raffy could offer something constructive to the conversation. Shakily, he recounted the story of his miraculous discovery and rescue, his pious upbringing, first with the kindly parishioners then with Father Johns. This seemed to encourage Ari to open up. He had stories of his own, war-torn memories spent running from village to village, feeding where they could.

At the mention of feeding, Lucius raised a finger to his lips, hushing Ari mid-sentence.

"Boys, we have to leave. We have a ship to catch. I know you have more questions, but the most important ones have already been answered. I have searched for years for my son, never knowing that your mother had given birth to twins, much less that they both lived. I cannot begin to tell you how happy I am." He reached across, this time gripping both the boys' hands in his. He squeezed them and smiled. Ari remained stone-faced. Raffy smiled numbly back. It was all too much to take in. Yesterday he'd had no family. Now he had a father, a brother, and a mother he'd never met, and who even now had abandoned him. He was overwhelmed, unsure of how or what to feel. Ari, on the other hand, remained calm, taking the news in his stride as though it was as important as the weather. Raffy wished he had Ari's, his brother's, air of self-possession.

Raffy felt no such composure. Waves of emotions battered

him. He felt adrift, yet anchored, bound, yet free. Once again, he decided he would have to trust in fate, for he seemed to have no control over the circumstances of his own life. Still numb, he followed Lucius and Ari out of the inn. Lucius seemed eager to be on his way. Raffy had to hurry to keep up with his long strides. He hung back for a moment and watched as his father and brother climbed into the car. He couldn't make the shift in his mind from benefactor to father, but this news did explain the feeling of connection he'd felt with both Lucius and Ari. He thought for a moment about the woman who'd remained behind at the mansion, then pushed the thought away. She hadn't come with Ari, who'd been with her from birth. If she didn't care about the son she'd nursed at her breast, why would she care about the baby she'd abandoned? His place was with his father and his brother, they were his family. His mother remained a stranger and even Ari's protestations of her helplessness hadn't softened Raffy's heart towards her. With a heavy sigh, he climbed into the automobile behind Lucius and Ari. The sedan door slammed shut behind him, closing the door on the life he'd known and the innocent he'd once been.

MARGRETHE had no idea how long she'd knelt in the sticky blood and shattered remains of her brother. Sobs had wracked her body uncontrollably, and even hours later, she still shuddered with grief and horror. There was nothing she could do for Beau now. She was heartbroken, but he was beyond saving.

Her son, however, was a different matter. Even in the midst of her shock and confusion, Margrethe knew she couldn't lose both Beau and Ari. She would find Lucius and take her son back. Still sobbing, Margrethe reached down to close her brother's eyes, but they remained stubbornly open. Avoiding his lifeless gaze, she straightened and turned away, leaving Beau to stare endlessly into oblivion. With a deep breath, she stepped out into the hallway. All was silent and deathly still. A wave of nausea and dizziness overtook her, and she leaned against the wall. She couldn't sense Ari's presence anywhere and was sure he was gone, spirited away by his father as she had been so many years before.

The thought of her son spurred her on. Steadying herself, she made her way to the kitchen. She needed water to refresh her, to help clear her head. She probably needed something stronger, but water would do for now. She remembered the way easily. The kitchen was in darkness. From memory, she made her way through the gloom, feeling her way along the cold stone bench. She hadn't spent much time in the kitchen, but she remembered there being water stored near the huge open stove. The cook used to keep it handy for cooking and refreshment.

Her eyes began to adjust to the dark, and she could make out the water container. Letting go of the bench, she stepped towards it and recoiled as her foot connected with something soft. Peering down, she stared into the face of the young maid who'd let her into the mansion.

She crouched down to examine the body more closely. The girl's eyes were closed as though asleep, her face pale and moon-like in the dark. On her neck, trickles of dried blood had caked around two small puncture holes. Margrethe stood up. No wonder the girl hadn't returned with refreshments. With a sad sigh, Margrethe moved the girl's body out of the way and leaned over the water vat, scooping some water into her hands. It proved cold and refreshing, reviving her senses and sharpening her thoughts. Ari may have thought he was doing the right thing in going with his father, but she knew better. The proof laid sprawled and lifeless unblinking at her feet. Lucius was without care or conscience. She had to find Ari. She wouldn't rest until she did.

ARI laid his head on the feather pillow, luxuriating in its softness. Pillows had been scarce during the war, and he had become thankful for such small comforts. They'd boarded the ship at noon. Lucius had seemed grateful to retreat to the dark comfort of his cabin. The boys shared a cabin between them while ancient Silas was assigned a smaller cabin next door. The constant motion of the waves soothed Ari. He thought of his mother and wondered where she was. She'd been hysterical, well to be expected under the circumstances. The ferocity with which Lucius had attacked first Valdymyr, then his Uncle Beau, had left even Ari breathless. He understood why his father did it. He had no choice. He did it to protect Ari.

Ari felt something with his father that he'd never felt with his mother. Kinship. His mother loved him, of that he had no doubt, but it was love mixed with fear. His father had no such fear. His father lived the life Ari had only dreamed of, reveling in his vampiric heritage and the supernatural life that came with it. Ari wanted that for himself. He knew it, felt it deep inside. It was where he belonged, this world of the undead. He had become tired of hiding amongst the living, pretending to be what he was not—tired of restraining his thirst, taking only enough to sustain him for a couple of days. He wanted to feast, to revel in the pursuit and kill. His mother would never let him do that. His father would.

He wondered if his brother felt the same way, remembering how Lucius hushed him when he went to speak of feeding. Perhaps Raffy knew nothing of bloodlust or vampires, or anything of darkness for that matter. Ari saw a weakness in Raffy nowhere to be seen in his father. Perhaps it was due to the years of pious upbringing, or perhaps the weakness stemmed from the shaky circumstances of his birth. Raffy lacked the dark power of Lucius Ruthven or even, indeed, of himself. Aside from his coal black eyes, nothing distinguished his brother as his father's son. Of course, Raffy's likeness to their mother left Ari in no doubt that he was his brother. Clearly, Margrethe's bloodline was foremost in Raffy. The last strands of humanity wound their way through his brother, robbing him of the strength of his dark heritage. Ari considered himself to be the heir apparent to the House of Nyx, he who carried his father's bloodline. He was the firstborn, the true heir. To him belonged all that his father's house contained. He liked Raffy well enough, and he was prepared to treat him with brotherly respect, but if Raffy threatened his rightful inheritance, Ari would take whatever measures were necessary to stop him.

A deep snore jolted him from his thoughts. Ari pulled the covers over his head and turned his back to his brother. With Raffy's noisy slumber happily muffled, Ari closed his eyes and let the waves soothe him to sleep.

***

# CHAPTER EIGHTEEN

CLAUDIA sensed his approach long before he arrived. He was, after all, the fruit of her bitter womb, and by that they were bonded, no matter how unhappily. She had always known Lucius would return. She knew he would not return alone and she sat now, awaiting the arrival of her son and her grandchild with the patience born of an eternity of waiting.

Beyond her bedroom window, the forest began to emerge from the white blanket of winter, the same view that she'd looked at for centuries. It changed only with the seasons, and this winter had been particularly harsh. The trees were only now regaining their dense foliage, their naked branches bursting into bud, heralding the season of renewal.

In the bleak, foreboding sky above the budding trees, three ravens restlessly circled the castle, their keen eyes watchful, expectant.

Claudia didn't see the trees or the ravens. Her eyes were fixed upon the black automobile winding its way up the steep, narrow road leading to her castle. She watched as it climbed, the motor laboring under the strain. Occasionally disappearing as it passed between the trees and outcroppings, she easily followed its progress by its desperate mechanical chug. Even during the war, the Romanian troops had found it difficult to transport supplies when they'd taken over her castle.

Those had been hard days. The Great War had ended, and the collapse of the Austro-Hungarian Empire had led to even more bloodshed. The Romanian army crossed the Carpathians on their way to occupy Budapest, invading the dark sanctuary of Nyx with their raucous jokes and heavy boots.

Claudia had considered their presence a minor annoyance. She'd kept mainly to her rooms, consigning the west wing of the castle to the troops.

The few faithful servants that remained with them hunted down vagrants and refugees, providing a steady stream of victims for Claudia's hunger. Edmund, as always, drained the blood of animals. She no longer tried to persuade her husband to sample the sweet delicacy of human blood, concentrating instead on her own comfort and survival, living on her wits and her strength.

Even the soldiers who commandeered her castle treated her with respect. They hadn't stayed long, only a matter of weeks really; enough to see out winter before taking the great city of Budapest. When they left, the household had settled back comfortably into its routine.

Edmund had become even more withdrawn after the war, rarely communicating with her at all. On the few occasions they had any contact, he would just stare at her with cold, dead eyes. At least he seemed finally free of the terrible affliction of human emotion.

Claudia gave a small shrug and turned her attention back to the car, which had now reached the gates. Edmund's condition concerned her little. She'd long ceased to have any care whatsoever for his well-being.

Her last contact with Lucius had been at the end of the war when he'd come to the castle in search of Margrethe. When news of

Valdymyr's destruction had reached her, Claudia knew that Lucius had finally found his whore and their monstrous child. It was only a matter of time before he returned to challenge her, with his son beside him.

She smiled as the black car pulled up in the driveway beneath her window. It seemed that time was finally at hand. Claudia continued to sit, calm and still. Let him bring his spawn. She'd been waiting for this moment. She was ready.

THE castle loomed above them as the evening mist began to roll in. The winding mountain road had been improved since the war, but it still remained difficult for the car to negotiate the steep slope. Lucius got out first, followed by the boys.

"Silas, you know what to do. Wait with the car, but be ready to leave at a moment's notice. No matter what happens, keep the boys safe."

Silas nodded solemnly. Lucius looked across at his sons; Ari, tall, strong, silent and emotionally detached. Raffy, small and slender, full of chatter and curiosity, but watchful, insightful. He'd observed them closely during their travels, noting their strengths and weaknesses. Clearly, Ari's greatest asset was his size and strength, enhanced, of course, by his vampiric heritage. Ari's lack of emotion occasionally proved advantageous, leaving him unmoved under any circumstances, be they good or bad. Unfortunately, it also hindered him. Ari was unable to read men's minds or predict their actions. This total lack of emotional attachment was a severe disadvantage for his eldest son. Ari simply had no interest in anyone except for any immediate benefit they may afford him.

Raffy's perception, on the other hand, was razor sharp. He could read human minds as though their thoughts were spoken out loud. He took an interest in humans and could predict their actions with keen accuracy. Sometimes Lucius could feel Raffy trying to enter his mind. It took considerable effort to keep him out, so great

166

was the boy's mental strength. The combined strength and abilities of his two sons, together with his own, would be more than enough to vanquish his mother and reclaim his rightful inheritance. As to Edmund, it would suit Lucius quite well to destroy his father, despite the fact his hermit-like presence would pose no threat whatsoever. Nonetheless, Lucius was not about to take any chances. Claudia and Edmund must be destroyed. The ancient heritage of Nyx would belong to Lucius and his boys. With grim determination, Lucius set his collar against the chill wind and ascended the stone steps of the castle entrance. He banged the bronze gargoyle knocker with authority. A scuffle of footsteps came from behind the aged oak and the door swung slowly open. The manservant, a long-serving member of the household, recognized him immediately.

"Master Lucius!"

Lucius swept past him with a nod, beckoning the boys to follow him. Raffy paused and smiled at the servant as they entered. Ari merely glanced at the man and moved on, following his father up the stone staircase. They were moving so quickly that Raffy had to follow them at a run.

They reached the top of the stairs and Lucius paused, waiting for Raffy to breathlessly catch up. It was a pity the boy took after his mother physically. Margrethe's delicate beauty was an ill-suited inheritance for a male child. Raffy's weak disposition caused Lucius the greatest concern. He had no doubt that Ari would handle the bloody battle that might ensue, but Raffy didn't seem given to either bloodlust or battle. Lucius just hoped that Raffy's ability to sense and avoid danger would serve him well should this become a fight for survival, which he had no doubt it would. His mother wouldn't give in easily. He still didn't trust her and suspected she'd as soon kill her grandsons as embrace them. He had no wish to kill his mother. The penalty for killing another vampire was severe if it were not proved to be in self-defense, but Lucius knew Claudia would attack him as she had on many previous occasions. For a moment, Lucius regressed to being a mere boy again, cowering before his mother's blows. He shook his head to dislodge the memories. He had his own sons with him now. Together, they were invincible. He turned to them, his voice calm and authoritative.

"Boys, you are about to meet your grandmother. Stay next to me at all times and do as I say."

They nodded. Motioning them to follow him, Lucius walked up to his mother's chamber door. He raised his hand to knock, but her voice stilled him.

"Come in, Lucius."

Of course, she'd seen him coming. Her powers were as attuned and keen as ever. He opened the door and stepped inside. The boys followed and stood, one on either side of him. The woman in front of them had her head turned to the window. She didn't turn to face them, even when she spoke.

"I knew you would return, Lucius. News of your unsavory activities has preceded you."

Lucius raised an eyebrow. How typical of his mother to greet him with an accusation.

"Hello, Mother, lovely to see you, too. And, pray tell, exactly what activities are you referring to?"

She turned to look at him now. Her eyes were cold.

"You know what I am referring to, Lucius. Valdymyr was a close friend for many years."

"He attacked me, Mother. It was self-defense."

Claudia fixed him with that cold stare.

"Tell that to the Council of Elders!" Her gaze shifted to the two boys, lighting first on Ari then on Raffy.

"And who are these two young men?"

Lucius straightened to his full height.

"These are my sons, Mother. Your grandsons, Ariel and Raphael."

Claudia raised an eyebrow, pinning the boys with her sharp

eyes.

"Two sons, Lucius? She gave a low chuckle. "Ariel and Raphael. Monsters with angels' names."

Lucius ignored her comment, hoping the boys would do the same. Ari seemed not to notice the insult, but Raffy frowned at Claudia's words.

"Boys, this is your grandmother." It was a curt introduction. Claudia held out her arms to embrace them, but they remained motionless, standing beside their father. Claudia dropped her arms, threw back her head, and laughed again.

"Ah! Such a warm family reunion." Her words were heavy with irony.

"You know why I am here, Mother."

"Of course I do, Lucius. And you know I will not give in."

"It is my time, Mother. I am here to claim what is rightfully mine."

"Nothing is yours!" She aimed her words like arrows. "This is my castle, my home, and you, Lucius, are nothing but a mistake!" She looked at each of the boys contemptuously. "And now, as if your own presence were not insult enough, you dare to bring your own mistakes to my door and claim your rights!" Claudia rose from her chair, her attention fully on him. Lucius tensed. The boys felt it and tensed with him.

Lucius gave a harsh laugh.

"You are right, Mother. I am *your* greatest mistake. I am the reminder of your own weakness. The daughter of Nyx, impregnated by a mere human, a weak excuse for a man who even now cowers in his chambers?"

His words stung her. Claudia's pale cheeks colored in fury, her eyes grew dark and dangerous. Lucius readied himself. Baring her fangs, she flung herself across the room, knocking Raffy to the floor. Terrified, the boy crawled away as his grandmother leaped on his father, digging ferocious nails into his chest. Lucius staggered,

169

backward then managed to regain his balance. Gripping his mother's arms, he pushed her away, gritting his teeth against the pain as her claws tore out of his flesh. She staggered, hitting the wall behind her but managed to stay on her feet. Her strength was still formidable, even after years of hardship.

War hadn't weakened Lucius, either. If anything, it had strengthened him and he gathered all that strength now, hurling himself at his mother with a roar of rage. She managed to duck, and he hit the wall, hard. Pain shot through his shoulder, leaving him momentarily breathless. Claudia quickly saw her advantage and flung herself on him again, mindless of the dark-haired boy who'd crept up behind her. She pushed Lucius to the floor, raking at his face with her talons. He swiped back at her, ripping desperately at her arms. Over her shoulder, Lucius caught sight of Ari. He tried desperately to cry out, but Claudia's hands were around his throat now. As he stared helplessly, he saw the boy raise a heavy crystal vase and bring it down on Claudia's head. It smashed into her skull, tearing her skin with jagged shards of finely cut Bohemian workmanship. She toppled sideways, enabling Lucius to slip out from under her. He wasted no time. As his mother opened her eyes, he fell upon her, pinning her arms with his knees. A still dazed Claudia blinked at him in confusion.

"Lucius, my son."

"You have no son!" The words spilled from him in a howl. Consumed by years of hatred, Lucius plunged his nails into her chest, extending his talons to their sharpest point. The breast upon which he'd suckled burst open like a ripe peach, spewing ribbons of flesh and blood through the broken bones. Claudia let out an unearthly scream, her eyes filling with horror and pain. When his fingers touched her heart, he felt mild surprise. He'd always supposed his mother had no heart. He curled his fingers around it and pulled hard, tearing it from its cavity. Claudia's blood-curdling scream echoed through the ancient stone walls of the castle.

It was the last sound she ever made.

Lucius stood, victorious, his mother's heart pumping its last beats in his hand. Ari stood on the other side of Claudia's body, looking at his father with something like excitement in his eyes. Lucius had never seen him so animated and alive. Ari knelt and dipped a finger in his grandmother's blood. He raised it to his lips and tasted the sticky, red fluid then looked up at Lucius and smiled. Lucius smiled back, lowering the bloody heart and dropping it to the floor. He looked around the room for Raffy. There was no sign of him.

"Ari, where is your brother?"

Ari shrugged. "I am not my brother's keeper."

Lucius grabbed him roughly by the shoulder.

"Yes, you *are* your brother's keeper, Ari. It is called loyalty, and for once, this family will show a great deal of it. If we are to survive, Ari, we must look out for each other. Do I make myself perfectly clear?"

Ari shrugged Lucius's hand away and nodded. Lucius softened his tone.

"Good. Now come and help me find your brother."

Still savoring the taste of Claudia's blood, Ari obediently followed his father out into the dark hallway.


RAFFY crouched in a small alcove, thankful to be small enough to squeeze into the cramped space. The hallway was lined with alcoves, some of them containing statues that were eerily lifelike. Shivering in the darkness, Raffy wished fervently that he could be safely transported back to the rectory. At the moment, he would give anything to reclaim his mundane life with the parish priest. The dream he thought he'd stepped into was quickly becoming a nightmare. He'd fled his grandmother's room in terror, horrified at the bloodbath that had unfolded before his eyes. His grandmother's attack had been instant and vicious. Raffy had been

171

paralyzed by fear, unable to help his father. He'd watched helplessly as Ari had snatched a vase from an oak sideboard and brought it down on their grandmother's head with a sickening crunch. It was then that Raffy had fled the room, driven by terror and shame at his own lack of courage. He'd run along the shadowy corridors before stopping to rest in the alcove, breathless and confused.

His eyes searched the gloom of the darkened hallway. Further on, the flickering light of an oil lantern glowed through the darkness, urging him on. He took a moment to catch his breath then walked quickly towards it, moving quietly, listening carefully. The lantern hung outside a solid oak door. Raffy pushed the door a little. It gave under his touch, creaking open a few inches. He pushed again and peered into the room. At first he thought it empty, but as soon as he stepped inside he spied the man, sitting quietly in a chair by the fireplace, covered in woolen rugs piled high over his legs. He turned to look at Raffy with dark, sad eyes.

"I'm sorry to intrude, sir." Raffy tried to sound apologetic but even to his own ears, he just sounded frightened. The man in the chair seemed to hear the fear in his voice. He held out a hand, beckoning him forward. Raffy took a couple of steps towards him and stopped warily.

He had no idea if this man was friend or foe, and after the bloody scene he'd just witnessed, he dared not take any chances.

The man saw his hesitation.

"Do not be afraid, boy. There are those who will hurt you, but I am not one of them. You are right to be wary, though. What is your name?"

"Raphael, sir." Raffy wanted to tell him about the bloody fight but thought better of it. He just needed to find a way out of this place.

"Hmm, Raphael. An angelic name. Are you an angel, young Raphael?"

"My guardian believed me to be so."

"Your guardian?" The man peered closely at Raffy's face. "Who are your parents, boy?"

Raffy avoided the question. "If you would be so good as to help me, sir, I am looking for the way out of here."

The man gave a mirthless chuckle.

"Aren't we all lad, aren't we all?" Slowly, he raised himself out of the chair. The pile of blankets fell to the ground. He pushed them aside with one foot and motioned Raffy to follow him. Again, Raffy hesitated.

"Come now, Raphael, how can I help you if you do not trust me?" He squinted at Raffy. "You look familiar. Come closer into the full of the light where I can see you."

Against his better judgment, Raffy moved closer. The man fell silent for a moment. The warm glow from the fire drained from his cheeks.

"Margrethe!"

Raffy started in surprise at the familiar name.

"My mother's name is Margrethe, sir."

The man raised his hand and gently touched the boy's cheek. "And you are the very image of her!"

Raffy shied away from the touch, still uncertain.

"Your mother is my daughter, Raphael. I am Edmund Charlesworth, your grandfather."

Raffy took an involuntary step backward, remembering his grandmother's greeting and the glint of her fangs as she'd attacked his father. The man shook his head.

"No, I am not like them, Raphael. I am one of them, but it is a prison from which I cannot break free. I assure you, I don't share their nature."

"Why have you never escaped?" He couldn't imagine why anyone would choose to remain in this horrid place.

"Where would I go?" the man asked quietly.

Raffy frowned. "During the Great War you could have gone

anywhere. You could have disappeared in all the chaos. They would never have found you."

"Why would I escape into more bloodshed and carnage? God knows, I have already seen enough of both."

"You could leave with me now." The words were out of his mouth before he could stop them. Perhaps pity moved him. Perhaps a modicum of self-preservation, too. Somehow, Raffy knew he would feel safer if this man went with him. He didn't want to be alone in this strange place. It would be far better being with someone who knew their way around. The man seemed to consider his offer for a moment, before replying.

"Is your mother with you?"

Raffy shook his head.

"Pity." The old man's attention seemed to drift away.

"The last time I saw her was at her family home."

That caught his grandfather's attention again. "Charlesworth House?"

Raffy thought for a moment. "I believe they called it the Winchester Estate."

The man looked sad. "I will take you as far as the outskirts of the forest. I cannot take you further."

Raffy wanted to ask why, but he knew his father and brother would come looking for him soon. A sense of urgency overtook him. They'd want him to stay. Lucius might even keep him against his will, as he did with this poor man standing before him. So he kept his silence, nodding before glancing over his shoulder, half expecting Lucius and Ari to come crashing through the door. Sensing his urgency, Edmund beckoned him over to the door. They peered out into the empty hallway.

"Hurry, come this way!"

Raffy followed his grandfather, keeping to the shadows. They hurried down three winding corridors, barely wide enough to accommodate them both, before finally reaching a small wooden door. It opened into an obscure corner of the garden, overgrown with weeds and rambling rose bushes. Their thorns scratched at Raffy's arms as he pushed his way past. A tiny wooden gate, barely discernible through the undergrowth, creaked open under Edmund's hand, revealing a vast expanse of dense forest. Panicked, Raffy looked at his grandfather with beseeching eyes.

"You're not leaving me here are you?"

Edmund shook his head. "No, I will go a little way further with you."

The forest yawned before them. A mist began to form in the cold evening air, its ghostly fingers winding between the thick tree trunks.

"Take my hand, young Raphael. We do not want to lose each other." Raffy did as bidden. He certainly did not want to be lost in the vast expanse of dark, gloomy forest. Together, hand in hand, their ghostly figures left no imprint as they melted into the mist.

***

# CHAPTER NINETEEN

THEY'D searched a large part of the mansion before Lucius thought of his stepfather's chambers. The hallway to Edmund's room, usually illuminated by lamplight, was in darkness, the door to the bedchamber already ajar. Lucius quietly pushed it open. No one occupied the room. Edmund's chair was empty, the blankets he usually piled upon himself cast hastily aside on the floor. Lucius turned to Ari.

"Go and fetch Silas. We will search the grounds. Hopefully, they have not gone far." *Damn that old man!* He doubted Raphael would risk fleeing at night by himself, but if Edmund accompanied him, they were likely halfway across the forest by now. Lucius had intended to dispose of Edmund when he'd finished with his mother, and now he wished he'd had the opportunity. It was bad enough that Raffy had fled, terrified by the events that had unfolded in his mother's room. Now Edmund would be filling the boy's head with tales of fear and blood, poisoning his own son against him. Lucius thought hard. Where would they go? Probably to Budapest. It was dangerous, but Edmund would be desperate to get back to England. The chicken always returned to the coop.

Filled with fury, Lucius followed Edmund's scent down the winding corridors and out into the overgrown rose garden. He scaled the castle wall in an instant and stood atop of the gray stones, scanning the dense forest undergrowth. His eyes peered past the evening gloom, tuning themselves to every sound and movement. He sensed nothing of the boy. No doubt, Raphael had sealed his thoughts away behind an impenetrable mental wall. Lucius focused on Edmund, hoping to pick up his scent. It didn't take long. He faintly sensed his father's movements near the outer edges of the forest. They'd managed to move quite quickly. With no time to summon Ari or Silas, Lucius leaped from the wall, landing with a soft thud on the leaves beneath. He crouched for a moment, listening intently, before leaping across a thick copse of bushes into the arms of the forest.

RAFFY'S feet gave way beneath him. He slipped down the moss-covered stones, sliding down painfully through the thick undergrowth. Covered in scratches, he regained his feet. Edmund stopped and doubled back, grabbing Raffy's arm. He winced.

"Ow, that hurt!"

"Are you bleeding?"

"Yes, I'm bleeding and it hurts! Now let me go." Wincing again, Raffy snatched his arm back.

Edmund shook his head. "Cover your arms, or they will smell your blood."

Raffy hastily pulled down the remnants of his coat sleeves over his shredded shirt. The last thing he wanted was to be found and returned to the castle.

"I'm fine, let's keep going."

Without another word, Edmund nodded and turned, continuing to wind his way through the forest. Raffy followed, amazed at how quickly the old man could move. He sometimes had trouble keeping up with him.

"Have you spent much time in the forest, Grandfather?"

"A little."

Raffy felt a wave of doubt. "Enough time to know the way out?"

"I hope so. Now hush boy, or they will hear us."

Raffy hushed. He wished to be as far away as possible from that dark castle drenched in blood. He still had doubts he could trust this man who claimed to be his grandfather, but he knew that, once again, he had no choice.

Edmund began to move far ahead of him, stopping every now and then to wave him on. Beyond the old man, Raffy could see light filtering through the trees. His faith restored a little. They'd finally reached the edge of the forest. Invigorated by the thought of escape, he pushed forward through the dense undergrowth until he stood, breathless, beside his grandfather. Before them lay a small village consisting of a few houses thrown haphazardly together on either side of a rough dirt road. Raffy stepped forward, eager to reach any form of civilization. Edmund stayed him with a hand.

"Dacians."

Raffy looked at him questioningly. Edmund continued, his voice low.

"People of the Wolf God. Enemies of the Clan of Nyx since time immemorial."

Raffy hesitated. Suddenly, the village didn't seem so welcoming.

"What will we do? Is there another way past?"

Edmund shook his head. Raffy gripped his grandfather's arm.

"Come with me. Please! I can't do this alone."

Edmund glanced back in the direction of the castle, then again at the small village. Raffy could see the longing on his face. The old man sighed.

"Very well, Raphael, I can't abandon you. We can hire a cart and horse here. Hopefully, they will be more interested in our money than our business. If not, we will tell them we are joining the Romanian troops. Under no circumstances must you mention or indicate that we have come from the castle. Do you understand?"

Raffy nodded. His heart pounded in his mouth, and he hoped he could remain calm. Their lives may well depend upon it.

Together, they made their way down through the trees to the village. There was no sign of life, but Raffy could feel many eyes upon them, watching their every move. They came to a particularly run down house with a cart in front of the door. Edmund looked relieved.

"This will do. Now, we must appeal to their pocket." Resolutely he strode to the door and knocked firmly. There was a moment of silence, followed by the sound of a latch being lifted. The door slowly creaked open and wild yellow eyes peered out, regarding Edmund with a hostile stare. His grandfather seemed undaunted by this cold examination.

"I would like to buy your cart and a good horse. I have enough money here to compensate you most generously." He opened his hand, revealing several gleaming gold coins. The wild eyes stared at the gold for a moment before studying Edmund again. This time, the eyes held a gleam of interest. The door swung open, and a man stepped out. Well, a man, yes, but a giant of a man with long, wild hair framing a fierce, bearded face. Raffy took an involuntary step backward. Edmund stood his ground, his hand still extended. The man closed his huge hand over Edmund's.

"Where are you from? Why do you want my cart and my horse?" The wild man's voice rumbled deep and guttural, his accent harsh, reminding Raffy of a wolf. People of the Wolf God, his grandfather had called them. A cold shiver ran through his body. He wished this business of buying the cart would be over and done with quickly, and they could be safely on their way. The wolfman glanced over at him, sniffing the air as though for a scent. Raffy closed off his thoughts, struggling to keep his composure under the primal scrutiny. Deeming him to be of little importance, the wolfman turned his attention back to Edmund. His hand had closed on the coins now but still remained on top of Edmund's hand.

"We are traveling to join the Romanian liberators. We have urgent business in Budapest." Edmund kept his voice even, sounding believable to Raffy's ears, although he did not know how to speak Hungarian—somehow he understood most of it, another strange developing ability of his.

A long pause filled the air. Finally, the wild man grunted, scooped the extended money into his huge hand and stepped back towards the doorway, clutching his newfound wealth tightly.

"The horse is around the back, in the small barn. Don't be taking all the hay, we've barely enough for our stock." Raffy glanced over at a small field nearby. It had been hastily fenced to house three sad, skinny cows, and a lone ragged goat. These people clearly had little wealth or comfort. The wild man choosing the gold over further questions now didn't surprise him. Casting them one last, suspicious look, the strange man closed the door firmly. Raffy heard a heavy bolt slide into place and click. Dismissed, they traipsed through the mud to the barn, where they found a sorry looking horse stabled as promised. Raffy scraped out the remains of some hay and carried it to the cart while Edmund led the horse behind him. With the poor beast hitched unhappily to its load, they started off down the dirt road through the last winding miles of forest. Before them lay Budapest, a city waiting for the cloud of war that followed close behind the man and the boy in their cart. Behind them, hidden by the dark trees of the forest, Lucius helplessly watched them depart.

He couldn't follow. The Dacian village stood between himself and his prey. Lucius cast his mind back to the stories he'd read in his mother's ancient books. The Dacians and the vampire clans had clashed many times over many centuries, and the battles were always bloody. Lone vampires were known to have been ambushed by packs of Dacians and mercilessly torn to pieces. What Dacians lacked in grace they made up for in ferocity, and even the most powerful vampires respected the strength and savagery of the wolf people. Lucius knew that, given the opportunity, the Dacians would tear him apart in an instant. Frustrated, he could only watch as the cart grew smaller and smaller until it vanished altogether into the other side of the forest. Lucius's mind raced. Maybe, if quick enough, he could skirt around the village, heading the cart off further down the road. Determined his prey wouldn't escape, Lucius turned and began to double back around the village. He moved swiftly through the trees, a shadowy, blurry figure that blended into the gloom like a trick of the light. He reached the back of the village in no time and stopped for a moment, listening intently. He could hear faintly hear the clip-clop of the horse's hooves and the clatter of the cart wheels. They sounded closer now.

Satisfied he'd gained ground, Lucius prepared to launch himself into the forest again when a small movement caught his eye. He quickly dropped to his knees behind a tree and, while holding his breath, peered out into the undergrowth. He couldn't see anything at first then his keen eyes picked up a dark figure a few yards away. As Lucius watched, the figure began to move slowly towards him. A sliver of light hit the shadowy form as it reached a small clearing. Lucius drew a sharp breath as the most powerful Dacian he'd ever seen stopped and sniffed the air searchingly. He was a monster of a man, with a powerful body and a wild tangle of black hair. His thick, dark eyebrows framed primal yellow eyes that gleamed in the pale sunlight as they scoured the forest. He looked like a wolf. He moved like a wolf. Offensively, he even smelled like a wolf.

Lucius shrank back into the shadows. Had the Dacian seen him? As the cart's wheels clattered further and further into the distance, Lucius realized that his pursuit of Edmund and the boy would have to wait. He had to escape before the Dacian picked up his scent. A sharp crack of a tree branch caught the wolfman's attention. He turned to follow the sound and Lucius seized upon the opportunity gratefully, sprinting from behind the tree in a dark blur. The air shimmered behind him as he darted through the shadows. Sensing the movement, the Dacian turned back again, spinning on his heel and piercing the forest with his ancient, yellow gaze. He was too late. Lucius had already fled the nightmarish vision from his mother's tales and melted quickly and silently back into the protective arms of the forest.

\*\*\*

# CHAPTER TWENTY

A YEAR passed by like a moment. Margrethe had spent many days as she did now, gazing emptily into the overgrown grounds of the Winchester Estate. The wild allure of the garden held no beauty for her now. She'd taken no pleasure in the estate since the loss of her son and her brother.

On that bloody night, Margrethe had retired to her room, unable to face the ghastly carnage in the drawing-room. There she'd remained for two nights, drawing the heavy curtains tight against the slightest intrusion of light.

By the third night, she felt she'd steeled herself enough to dispose of the bodies. She'd decided on burning their remains, intending far less ceremony for Valdymyr than for Beau, whose death she still could not come to terms with. She'd thought of alerting someone, but what would she say? In the end, she'd come to the heartbreaking conclusion that her beloved brother's body must join Valdymyr's and the maid's on the funeral pyre.

She disposed of the maid first, bowing her head in respect for the unfortunate girl as her dead flesh roasted in the flames like a suckling pig. The sweet smell of burning flesh turned her stomach at first, but she became used to it, standing by the fire until her senses were dulled by heat and grief.

Resolutely, she'd ventured down to the drawing-room, opening the door with a hesitancy that belied her outer calm. Beau lay where he had fallen, eyes staring lifelessly at the ceiling. Valdymyr's bloodied corpse lay near the fireplace where Lucius had left it, ravaged and torn. Taking a deep breath, Margrethe steeled herself, dragging the older vampire's body to the fire first, a surprisingly easy task. Margrethe's strength had increased significantly since she'd joined the ranks of the undead. She tossed Valdymyr's body into the fire as if it were a rag doll. The flames licked at the vampire eagerly, blackening flesh until it melted from his bones. Margrethe watched with grim satisfaction until heat and flames consumed him.

Beau had been more difficult. She carried him easily and tenderly, the heaviness of her heart slowing her steps. She'd laid him gently next to the raging fire before gathering blooms from her beloved rose garden, placing them over his breast where his heart had been. She told him once more how much she loved him and how sorry she was, then, choking back her tears, she lifted him to the fire and laid him on the flames. The heat scorched at her arms, burning her dress and blistering her flesh. She felt no pain other than the overwhelming pang in her heart. Stepping back from the heat of the flames, she'd turned away, unable to watch her brother's final journey. Only then did she allow her tears to flow freely. She could feel the heat on her back and the sharp sting of the burns on her arms, but she paid no heed. Her heart was in the fires of hell itself, where the flame never extinguished. By the time she reached the sanctuary of her bed chamber, all that remained of her broken heart was a pile of ash.

After the funeral pyre, grief had overwhelmed her. She ached to find Ari and bring him home, but the journey to the castle was long and hazardous. Even if she made the journey, she couldn't be sure that Ari would want to return with her. Sorrow and lack of sustenance weakened her. She had no appetite, no will to live. This last proved the greatest torture to one who could not die. Margrethe wished it had been her heart that had been ripped out. Willingly, she would have endured the pain to escape the misery that had become her existence. Sadly, her heart remained beating in her chest, chaining her in her immortal prison.

Her misery had deepened with the news of her mother's sudden death. Lady Elizabeth Winchester had died of complications brought on by an aneurysm while en route to the estate. The news devastated her, yet Margrethe couldn't deny a sense of relief. If the aneurysm hadn't killed her mother, the news of Beau's death would certainly have done so, for Margrethe surely could not have hidden her grief or the dreadful tidings from her mother. Now, that problem was gone, along with her family. Margrethe was left truly alone, adrift in an ocean of dark, dangerous depths. Beaten and bowed, she remained hidden away in Winchester House, in the place that had once felt like home, paralyzed by grief, uncertainty and loss.

Blinded by the visions of memory's ghosts, her sightless eyes missed the cab that pulled up unceremoniously in the drive. Only the putter of its engine alerted her to its presence. Shaking away the painful memories, Margrethe stood up and leaned her face against the cold glass. Just beneath her window, a young man alighted from a cab. Margrethe's heart leaped. She craned her neck, peering intently at the boy. A wave of disappointment crashed over her. His hair was fair under his cap, not black like Ari's.

A man climbed out behind the boy. This time, she recognized the occupant as the familiar figure of Edmund Charlesworth stepped from the cab. The sight of her father brought her instantly to life. Unable to contain her excitement, she shrugged a shawl around her shoulders and hurried downstairs to greet her guests.

A YEAR had passed since Lucius had fruitlessly pursued his wretched father and his equally wretched son. His father had been no sad loss, but Raffy was a different matter.

Lucius returned to the castle in a black mood. Overwhelmed by anger and frustration, he turned his mind to Ari's instruction in the dark delights of vampiric existence. Ari had proved to be a willing student in all areas. His ferocious appetite for blood made him formidable in battle, and his loyalty unquestionable. Ari worshiped Lucius and strove to emulate him in every way.

Under his father's tutelage, the boy grew rapidly in strength and abilities. His eyes were sharp, his hearing acute. He had the strength of twenty men as well as being lightning fast and stealthily quiet. His prowess at hunting outstripped his father's and his thirst for blood nearly did the same, which gave even Lucius pause.

As he watched Ari train, Lucius realized he had been far too limited in his vision. With his powerful son beside him, Lucius would rule not only the realm of the Undead but the world of the living as well. The boy lacked only one quality: Ari had no psychic gift whatsoever. None. He showed no ability to mesmerize his prey, choosing instead to use his superior physical attributes to overpower his victims. The result often proved needlessly bloody, although that seemed to be the thing the boy enjoyed most—the carnage.

He seemed unaware of the thoughts of others, even humans. He didn't seem to read them or be remotely interested in doing so, taking his cues from their body language and base instinct. When they were at their most vulnerable, he struck.

Raphael, on the other hand, had little physical strength or ability but exhibited acute mental abilities far beyond his brother's. Lucius had been unable to track his youngest son through the forest, having to rely instead on Edmund's imprints. He remembered observing the boy looking at a person, his gaze both distant and intent as though he were trying to read their mind. A few times, Lucius even wondered if Raphael had tried to enter his own thoughts. If Ari had Raphael's psychic abilities as well as his superior strength, he would be unstoppable. As it was, Ari had the empathy of a deranged killer, barely containable.

Word of Claudia's demise had spread throughout the underworld. The shock of her death, combined with rumors of the bloodthirsty nature of the newest member of the House of Nyx, kept most of the clan away. Emboldened by curiosity, some Elders finally broke the solitude, calling by to pay their respects to the son of Lucius of the House of Nyx. They left impressed by the boy's strength and power and subdued by the combined threat of both father and son. For the first time in his life, Lucius felt that he could hold his head high as the ruler of the Clan of Nyx, his loyal son beside him.

Raphael, the only fly in the ointment due to his existence, also had a rightful claim to the same inheritance as his brother. In spite of his undeniable connection with the boy, Lucius had no wish for his younger son to lay claim to anything. Raphael had betrayed him and thus, had betrayed his heritage. A year of bitterness at his son's escape had turned Lucius's heart to stone concerning his youngest "lost" son. No doubt the traitor cowered with his mother and grandfather in England. His wish to find Raphael didn't spring from paternal love. Lucius's motives were far less pure. The only interest his youngest son held for him now was his superior psychic ability; the one thing Ari lacked. If Lucius could persuade Raphael to transfer his psychic abilities to his brother, Ari would be fully endowed with every vampiric power needed to help him rule both the vampire world and the human world. Lucius had devoted many sleepless hours to this idea. He doubted Raphael would relinquish his abilities willingly or succumb to force. Raphael's strength of will would be more than enough to resist any attempt to wrest his ability from him. No, he would need persuasion of a less gentle kind. Perhaps his morally superior son would trade his abilities for the life of his grandfather, or even for that of his mother. The plan formulated over many brooding months and now, as winter closed in, Lucius finally chose to put his scheme into action.

He called Ari to him. His son was no longer a youth, but a strapping man in his prime, built strong by the air of the Carpathians and the seemingly endless amount of hunting and feasting in which he indulged.

Lucius would have to keep a tight rein on his son's appetite when they reached England. Once they'd accomplished their mission, Ari would have the means to restrain his appetite and hunt his prey with less chance of detection. His son's animalistic instincts had held Lucius back from implementing his plan earlier. Finally, after many harsh reprimands, Ari seemed obedient to his father's wishes over his voracious appetite.

Lucius smiled now at his son. "Ari, we are leaving for England. There, we will find your brother and grandfather. I expect they have fled to your mother's ancestral home."

Ari nodded agreeably. His expression remained blank, disinterested. No doubt the boy was not overjoyed at the thought of leaving his hunting grounds and unrestrained lifestyle to reunite with the mother he'd abandoned, nor with his younger, weaker sibling. That was of little concern to Lucius. There were greater things at stake than Ari's mere, trifling happiness.

"Go now and pack only what you need, nothing extra. We leave this evening."

Again, Ari nodded and turned to the door. He paused at the threshold and turned to his father.

"Are we bringing them back to the castle?"

Lucius hesitated. He didn't want to give away too much at this stage.

"No, we will stay a while with them in England. I am sure you would like to see your brother and mother again?"

"Of course, Father, as you wish."

Lucius looked at his handsome son. Ari's eyes were dead, his voice cold and distant. Without another word, the boy turned and left the room, leaving Lucius to ponder his plan with a new sense of urgency. It wouldn't be long now until he would accomplish all he had hoped for. With Ari at his side, the Lord of Nyx would have the respect he deserved, the loyalty he commanded, and the power he'd always craved.

But to do that, he needed Raffy.

RAFFY sat on the stone wall, surveying the seemingly endless grounds of the Winchester Estate. Over the past three months, he'd come to feel at home in this stately mansion with its faded grandeur and hidden secrets. The air of sadness that hung over the estate didn't subdue the beauty of the roses that rambled through the overgrown garden, robust even after years of neglect. It was amongst those blooms that he and his mother had often strolled, awkwardly at first, but with growing ease as they shared their stories. All those years of feeling abandoned and unloved melted away at the realization that his mother had only left him behind in the belief that he had left this earthly realm shortly after he'd entered it. It had taken Margrethe some time to adjust to the fact that her youngest son survived. Gradually, it became a gentle journey of discovery for both of them, with each step bringing new understanding and insight. The awkwardness between them gave way to the warmth of bonding. They were alike, his mother and he. Their gentle souls were so easily bruised by the cruelty of the world, their memories scarred by atrocities both rather would forget. Bound together by the blood that flowed through their veins and the blood spilled before their eyes, mother and son found comfort and solace in each other.

Their walks in the garden were the only time his mother could be persuaded to venture outside. She spent most of her time in the vast rooms of the mansion, shunting herself away from the prying eyes of the rest of society, genteel or otherwise. The need for hospitality had encouraged Margrethe to busy herself in a flurry of house cleaning. Her fine hands were unused to the harsh soaps and scrubbing and were often left red raw. Raffy admired her gentle strength and determination. Edmund remained quiet but seemed content. He appeared to relish the sense of family that now surrounded him and Raffy would often catch his grandfather watching Margrethe with a small, sad smile. Despite the melancholy air that hung over them, these were peaceful times and slowly, Raffy found himself putting the past scenes of bloody violence behind him. The ever present dark legacy shadowed him, but for now, the forbidding castle and its horrors seemed far away from the serenity of the rose garden. Raffy closed his eyes and breathed in the sweet perfume that filled the spring air, grateful for the semblance of normality he had thought lost to him forever. The warmth of the sun caressed his bare, thin arms, and the birds sang a merry chorus. Raffy let himself drift.

As he began to cross the border of wakefulness and sleep, a sharp sense of foreboding cut into his blissful reverie. He jolted upright, nearly losing his balance on the garden wall. Gripping the stones, he steadied himself and took in his surroundings. The birds, full of song a moment ago, had fallen silent. A sheen of sweat broke out on his brow as a wave of nausea washed over him. The moment of peace he relished before had fled, replaced by an all-consuming feeling of approaching doom.

His body stiffened as a bewailing, dark cry broke the uncanny silence. It wafted through the trees, wrapping the garden in a thick, looming shroud. Squinting against the glare of the sun, Raffy peered up into the sky. Three ravens wheeled and swooped above his head, encircling him with their mournful calls. Their song traveled upon the breeze, covering the fields and trees with a veil of sorrow. The horrible feeling grew stronger. Raffy's heart began to race. Something was wrong; very wrong.

He turned towards the mansion, eager to reach the safety of the open French doors. A movement caught his eye, just beyond a copse of trees near the driveway.

*Visitors!*

Stealthily, Raffy crept up to the thick bushes, shielding himself behind their sharp branches. He had acquired some physical skills since they'd arrived. He particularly enjoyed traipsing through the woods—on the estate and beyond—"hunting" he called it, seeing how close he could get to a flock of birds or an unsuspecting rabbit. Once, he even found himself able to sneak up on a skittish doe. He tried to touch her, but she sensed his presence at the last moment, making her bound off in surprise.

Raffy peered through the bushes, parting the leaves as quietly as possible. He found it difficult to make out the identity of the new arrivals. From his secure hiding spot, he could only see their shoes, two stylish pairs of men's boots, and one pair of more serviceable footwear, also masculine. Again, Raffy felt a rush of foreboding, stronger than before. *Three men!* He prayed silently to the non-existent God that it could not be his father and brother. Even as he prayed, he knew with a sinking heart that his prayer would go unanswered. He shut his eyes, straining to hear a voice by which he could confirm his fears. The visitors didn't speak. Only the crunch of their footsteps on the gravel entrance announced their arrival. Raffy held his breath, listening for the thud of the heavy brass door knocker. Then, only silence. Still with bated breath, he crept slowly around the bushes, crouching low to the ground. An empty driveway greeted him with no automobile and no visitors. Nothing.

Raffy blinked, shook his head, and rubbed his eyes. Did he hear things? *Seeing things?* No sound could be heard now. No movement. Everything was as it had been before, peaceful and serene.

For a moment, he contemplated returning to the rose garden but decided against it, preferring to allay the gnawing anxiety that still pressed upon him. He'd just go inside for a moment and check on his mother and grandfather, just to be certain.

The cool gloom of the hallway enveloped him as he pushed against the front door. It swung open easily, and he tried to remember if he'd left it ajar. He heard no sound in the house. His grandfather often napped through the day while his mother would be awake and busy, sorting and tidying the house with her usual industrious air. He made his way to the drawing-room, only to find it empty, freshly tidied, and aired, so he knew his mother had been there. He tried the kitchen, then the formal lounge. Nothing. No one. The house remained eerily quiet. A wave of fear engulfed him. There rose around him another presence, dark, malevolent. He could feel its tendrils wind their way through the hall and around his body, raising the hairs on his skin. Carefully, silently, he padded across the hallway, making his way up the stairs.

His mother's bedchamber was closed, same as his grandfather's. He was about to knock on Edmund's door when something stayed his hand. He turned his attention to his own bedroom at the end of the hall. His door was open, and this time he was certain he'd closed it. He always closed it to keep the warmth of the fire in the room. Even in the early days of spring, the morning air carried a slight chill.

The chill Raffy felt now had nothing to do with the weather. His heart pounded in his ears as he stepped slowly towards the open door. The hallway seemed to stretch further than usual. He walked for a dreadful eternity. Reaching the door, he felt an impulse to turn and run from whatever lay within. Steadying his resolve, he stepped inside the room.

His mother sat in a straight-backed wooden chair. Her hands were tied behind her, her feet bound to the legs of the chair. A torn strip of silk had been wound hard around her mouth. Her eyes were wide with terror as she stared at Raffy. Beside her, Edmund was similarly bound, unsilenced by any piece of cloth. Upon seeing his grandson enter the room, he cried out, his voice harsh with fear.

"Raphael, run!"

A figure stepped forward and in a swift movement, silenced his grandfather with a blow that nearly knocked him unconscious with its force. Edmund slumped in his chair, and the figure stepped forward into the light. Raffy retreated in horror.

"Ari!"

Accompanied by a quiet chuckle, another figure stepped forward from the shadows. Even if the imposing stature and cold black eyes had not been enough, Raffy recognized the laughter instantly. Lucius. His worst nightmare had come true. His father and brother had returned.

He watched mutely as his father stepped into the lamplight, his face gaunt and harsh, his eyes dark and unfathomable. Raffy glanced helplessly back at his mother and grandfather. Even if he'd heeded his sense of impending doom, it hadn't been enough to warn him of this horror. He'd truly thought they'd never pursue them. Of what use was he, the weakest son? What threat could his mother or grandfather possibly pose, so far away from the dark castle of Nyx? These past few months had lulled him into a false sense of security, now cruelly shattered.

He swallowed, feeling the need to say something. Anything.

"Lucius, Father."

Lucius cut him off sharply. "Do not call me Father. Do not speak. Your only concern right now is to listen if you value the life of your mother and grandfather."

Raffy swallowed again, remaining silent. He felt Ari move behind him, blocking the doorway. His only chance of escape gone, Raffy decided to listen.

"You chose to betray me, Raphael," Lucius continued, his voice cold and void of emotion. "You chose to flee with a half-witted excuse for a vampire and a woman ruled by her emotions and little good sense. You chose to pledge your loyalty to them and now it is that loyalty you shall prove."

Raffy nodded dumbly, too frightened to speak. No mercy

resonated in his father's voice, nothing to soften his harsh words of condemnation. His heart sank. What sacrifice would Lucius demand to prove his loyalty? Lucius seemed to read his thoughts.

"Rest easy, Raphael, there is no great sacrifice to be made. All I ask is that you give your brother a gift. In return, I will give you the precious gift of your mother's life."

"And my grandfather?" The question slipped out before he could stop it.

Lucius smiled coldly and shook his head.

"Your brother has a ferocious appetite and an even greater sense of entitlement. I had to promise him a reward in order to preserve your mother's life."

It took a moment for Raffy to understand what he meant. The awful realization dawned on him but before he could move, Ari pounced. Edmund's agonized scream rent the air as Ari's fangs tore into his flesh. A spray of blood showered Raffy's cheek as he backed away from the terrible frenzy of gore and pain. He watched horrified as Ari continued his onslaught, using not only his fangs but his talons in a deadly assault on their grandfather—like a wild animal. No, worse than an animal. An animal killed out of necessity. Ari killed for sheer enjoyment. The thrill of death shone in his brother's dark eyes as he slashed and tore at Edmund's flailing body. Seated helplessly beside this bloody spectacle, Margrethe struggled in her chair, straining against her bonds as her father's blood rained over her. Her eyes were upon Raffy, imploring him to do something, but he couldn't move. Transfixed with horror, he could only watch as Ari tore out Edmund's heart and held it aloft, dripping and glistening in the lamplight. Lucius smiled at his blood-soaked son with visible pride before turning to Raffy, who now trembled uncontrollably.

"As you can see, Raphael, your brother has grown considerably in strength. Sadly, he has also grown considerably in his thirst for blood, which seems to know no bounds. I must be

194

honest; I find it impossible to control him. He seems to have no sense of proper conduct, even in the finest of social company." Lucius inclined his head towards Raffy. "You, on the other hand, Raphael, have an innate ability to read people. It has served you well until now, this ability to infiltrate the minds of others. It gives you the insight your brother sadly lacks."

Raffy felt exposed, vulnerable. True, his uncanny ability to read people's thoughts and hearts had saved him from many a beating or altercation. Unfortunately, this catastrophe had crept up upon him in spite of his abilities, finding him blissfully unaware. He'd felt nothing until danger threw done upon them. His mother had tried to warn him of his father's persistence, but he'd dismissed her fears, supposing their existence to be of little importance or threat to Lord Lucius of Nyx.

He was wrong.

He should have listened to his mother. He should have been more vigilant. He should have been prepared for this.

A sudden calm enveloped him, as though the cloak of destiny had draped itself over his shoulders. Perhaps he was prepared. The inevitability of his situation convinced him that he was called upon to use his gift for something other than his own immediate benefit. He looked over at his mother and gave a faint nod as if to quiet her distress. She stopped struggling and stared at him with huge, tear-filled eyes. Feeling strangely in control of himself, Raffy turned to his father. No, not father, he reminded himself. He had to stop thinking of this cold, undead creature as his father.

"What do you want me to do?" Raffy asked, his voice steady. Lucius gazed at him for a long moment before replying.

"I need you to enter your brother's mind, just as you have with so many others."

Raffy knew there was more. He waited, barely breathing.

"When you are deep within his mind, relinquish your power. Release it all into your brother. Let your conscience become his. Give him the gift of empathy, Raphael. It is the only hope we have of restraining him." Lucius's voice was mesmerizing as he drew nearer. Raffy could feel the vampire's cold breath on his face as he leaned towards him. "Give back to your brother what you took from him, Raphael. If you do not, he will have no conscience when he rips your mother's heart from her breast."

Raffy thought quickly. If he could do this, if he could journey inside the blood filled mind of his brother, perhaps he could remain there long enough to draw on Ari's physical strength and absorb it into himself. He knew this to be possible somehow, if only he could harness the strength of mind to achieve it. He had to hope that the power of his will proved greater than his brother's physical strength. If not, he would be pulled into Ari's powerful body and consumed forever by its darkness.

"Well?" Lucius's voice barked at him, startling him back to his present dilemma.

"I'll do it," Raffy replied, hoping and praying he had made the right decision. It occurred to him that really, once again, he had little choice in the matter. If he refused, they would kill Margrethe and then kill him. He couldn't fight his brother, let alone both of them. This was his only hope. In saving his mother, he would also save himself. Taking a deep breath, he turned to face Ari, forcing himself to ignore the sight of his grandfather's blood smeared over his brother's handsome face. Ari stared at him with cold, black eyes so like their father's. Raffy focused his thoughts, delving into those dark depths, finding no resistance. Raffy slipped inside his brother's mind as easily as slipping into a bath.

A wall of red greeted him, writhing with violence and bloodlust. Visions assailed him, scenes of carnage as bloody and horrible as the one he'd just witnessed. Men, women, even children, all torn apart with gleeful abandon. He felt a gluttonous hunger rise in him. It made him sick, and he gagged. The words of an old Romanian song rang in his ears.

*Beware, my child, lest you become one of them*
*To dwell in history's darkest shadows*
*Never resting or appeasing your hunger*
*Nor finding the peace that haunts your immortal soul*

The nausea passed. He tried to block the visions, tried not to feel the pain of the victims as they died their horrible deaths. He resisted the taste for blood that suddenly flowed through his veins, dulling his conscience and sharpening his darkest instincts. Desperately he sought the memory of his mother and her large, fearful eyes. He found her there and fed upon her fear, reveling in the sense of power that surged through him. He saw the pulse on her neck, he smelt her fear and the acrid scent of her blood. The hunger rose again, insistent, unrelenting. It pounded him in angry waves, wearing down his resolve, engulfing him in a sea of violence. With the last of his strength, Raffy mustered up the only prayer he could remember.

*Our Father, who art in Heaven,*
*Hallowed be thy name.*

He wasn't sure if he'd spoken the words aloud, but miraculously, he felt the hunger subside, as though the power of those words had pushed it back into the dark pit from whence it sprang.

*Thy kingdom come, thy will be done*
*On Earth as it is in Heaven.*

A huge shudder rattled his brain. His body felt compressed. He couldn't breathe. Raffy struggled to focus on the prayer, but it was ripped from him as Ari's muscles contracted. He felt their iron grip on him, squeezing his mind and body until he thought he would pass out. Somewhere just beyond consciousness, he heard his mother call his name. He struggled against the powerful force pressing around him, willing it to release its deathly hold. It did for a moment and he thought himself free. He started to withdraw, unraveling his mind from the bloody thoughts of his brother. The

197

screams of the dying rang in his ears as he passed, their desperate cries imprinted on the ether as he pulled himself back towards his own body. He knew he had only a little time to drain his brother's strength. It would mean opening up again, just enough to open the inner portals.

With a deep breath, Raffy plunged back into the darkness of his brother's soul. He could feel Ari's strength tighten again around him, muscles pulsating with the fire of battle. Raffy opened his mind fully, drinking in as much of that strength as he could take. It overwhelmed him, pulling him inward relentlessly. He focused his thoughts, forming a mental net to capture his brother's might. He felt the sharp, violent onslaught of Ari's anger as he resisted the unfamiliar feeling of weakness. Raffy struggled to maintain the mental web he'd constructed. He imagined himself as a spider, sucking the strength from his brother. Ari's body shuddered, and Raffy felt his mind rip away from him. The net disintegrated and the spider fell from the web, tumbling, falling into the darkness below.

\*\*\*

# CHAPTER TWENTY-ONE

ARI opened his eyes and stared in confusion at the ornate ceiling. He couldn't remember having ever seen it before. Painted cherubs danced across it on gleaming white clouds. The cherubs wore wreaths of pink roses on their heads, their plump cheeks rosy and their teeth pearly white, their eyes blue pools of innocence.

It was a horrible, garish painting.

Ari lifted himself groggily on one elbow and looked around him, his gaze falling on the solitary figure seated at a simply carved desk in the far corner of the room. His father occupied himself with the task at hand. His pen moved rapidly, scratching the parchment beneath it. He paused for a moment, finally sensing his son's movement. Slowly, Lucius lowered his pen and turned to look at Ari.

"Ah, you are awake. Good. How are you feeling?"

It was a good question. Ari felt rather strange. The fact he felt anything at all proved strange in itself. He studied his father, his brow creased in confusion.

"I am not sure, Father. I feel different."

Lucius rose from his chair, crossing slowly and deliberately across the room. His eyes never once left his son. Ari shifted a little under the intense gaze, feeling uncomfortable. He'd never felt that before.

He'd never felt anything before.

The realization hit him hard. That's what was different. He could *feel*. His senses, for so long held prisoner to his basest instincts, had been set free. Overwhelmed by this inner transformation, Ari gazed up at his father.

"I can feel. I have feelings. Not just hunger, but feelings." The sense of amazement trembled in his voice. Lucius smiled.

"What of the hunger, Ari? Do you still feel the hunger?"

Ari thought for a moment, searching himself for the familiar bloodlust that had always ruled him. He found it, coursing through him as always, but more gently now, as though somehow contained.

"It is still there, Father. It just..." He hesitated, looking for the right words. "I feel like I can control it now, that it will not overtake me."

His father's smile grew wider.

"Good. Rest now Ari, you need to regain your strength before our journey home."

Ari frowned. He still wasn't sure where he was. Nothing in the room seemed familiar.

"Where are we?"

"We are in a hotel in London. Your mother and brother are in the room next door with Silas. We will all be returning to Castle Nyx as soon as you and your brother are well enough to travel."

"Raffy is ill?" Ari surprised himself with his concern. It gave him a strange, warm feeling to care about his brother's welfare. He remembered caring little about Raffy before this amazing transformation.

"You have both been terribly ill. Even the doctors had no clue as to what ailed you. Thankfully, you seem to be well on the way to recovery. Your brother has been less fortunate, no doubt due to his more fragile physical condition."

"And Mother?" The concern for his mother's welfare was even stronger than for his brother. It unsettled him, as though her pain was his.

Lucius gave him a cursory pat on the shoulder. Ari thought it probably meant to reassure him.

"Your mother is fine, Ari. She is caring for your unfortunate invalid brother night and day." He paused. "I am afraid Raphael may never be the same."

Ari opened his mouth to inquire further, but Lucius interrupted him mid-sentence.

"No questions for now. You need your rest, Ari. We need to return to the Carpathians as soon as possible." Squeezing his son's shoulder, Lucius turned and strode back to the desk. He shuffled a pile of papers together and with one last glance at Ari, he left the room.

Alone with his thoughts, Ari strained to remember recent events. He had no recollection of falling ill. In fact, he had little recollection from the time they'd reached his mother's home.

He supposed they'd fallen ill there. He wished he knew the nature of this illness that had left him not just well again, but far better than he'd been previously while taking the scant good health his younger brother had. He supposed his father was correct and that it was his physical strength and constitution that had given him the edge on recovery. A new feeling rose up within him. Fear gripped his heart with cold fingers, momentarily freezing the warm feelings he'd been experiencing. Ultimately, the strongest and fittest were the ones who survived. Ari would not allow these newfound feelings to be his weakness as they had been his mother's and brother's. No, he would train them as he'd trained his body. He would bring them under his control and maintain his mastery over them. He would never end up like his brother, broken and destroyed.

Never.

MARGRETHE cradled Raffy's head in her arms. She wasn't sure if he was even aware of her. Her youngest son remained an empty shell. His eyes stared unseeingly. He never blinked. He never slept. It was a living death in which he breathed, but nothing more. She rather would have seen him dead; at least then he would have been released from this bitter existence.

Lucius had released her bonds after the boys battled. Raffy had lain at her feet, crumpled and lifeless as the day he'd been born. The sight of him lying like a helpless husk on the floor tore her heart to pieces more surely than any vampire's fang or talons. If Lucius sought to punish her, he had surely succeeded.

She'd agreed to go with them. She knew she had no choice. Lucius would not leave her or Raffy alive. She had no idea why he had bothered to keep them alive, anyway. Perhaps it was some perverse attempt at wit, or a dark, misguided attempt to reunite their family. The Clan of Nyx, never ending and ever cursed. She had no wish to be a part of their wretched lineage, yet the children who shared her blood and her heart decreed it so.

Her other reason for agreeing to return to the Carpathians was her oldest son. Raffy's essence lay deep within Ari, where their souls intertwined. She only could protect Raffy by protecting Ari. Margrethe supposed she shouldn't be surprised at the outcome of their battle, but Raffy had been her last hope. That hope lay in ashes now. She would care for one son and try to protect them both. She had yet to see Ari for herself. Lucius assured her that he was more than well, but she couldn't trust Lucius. She wanted to see her son with her own eyes.

Lucius finally granted her wish when he entered the room, tickets in hand.

"We leave for France tomorrow. Ari is well enough to travel, and Raffy is as well as he will ever be." A heartless thing to say, to be sure, but it was foolishness to expect any different from someone with no heart. Silently, she took the ticket he handed to her. Her heart leaped, not at the prospect of travel, but at the knowledge that she would see her eldest son.

The ship sailed in the early hours. The morning was unseasonably cool, and the sight of Ari, strong and handsome in a well-tailored coat, warmed Margrethe's cold bones. She held out her arms to him, hoping fervently that he would accept her gesture. He did, wrapping his powerful arms around her, holding her close. She sensed a genuine warmth in his embrace that she'd never felt before, even as a small child. Stepping back, she examined him closely. An unaccustomed glimmer of light flickered in his dark eyes. His jawline appeared more relaxed than she remembered, retaining his powerful masculinity, but now tempered by a new sensitivity. The raw, animalistic instincts no longer claimed dominance.

Margrethe thought back to the night of the battle. She knew not what to call it, for she'd never seen the likes of it, but battle would suffice. Never would she have believed that a war of minds could be as painful and devastating as a physical battle. She knew better now. She'd watched helplessly as her sons had embarked on their own inner war, tearing at each other in the deepest realms of their beings. For once there was no blood. Indeed, there had been nothing to show the violence of warfare except the empty husk of her younger son that had remained when all was done. Yet something told Margrethe that Raffy, or at least his essence, remained alive and well within his brother. She could sense Raffy's presence in Ari's eyes, in the warmth of his hug. She tried to comfort herself with the thought that her youngest son lived on inside the elder. An empty comfort, to be sure, but it would have to do. Resolved to be there for her sons as best she could, Margrethe followed Ari onto the gangplank. Ancient Silas walked ahead of them, carrying Raffy's inert form as easily as a sack of potatoes. Lucius walked behind her, pushing his hand into the small of her back to urge her on. She needed no urging. She had made up her mind. She would be there for her sons, to nurse one and protect the other. This thought, and this thought alone, gave her the will and perseverance to go on.

She needed to draw upon that will many times during that arduous journey. After many long weeks, they finally reached the castle in the Carpathians. The sight of its gloomy walls filled Margrethe with dread. She was thankful that Raffy was in no state to share her fear. He stared at the place he'd once fled in terror with no hint of recognition in his empty eyes, no creeping realization that he'd returned to the dark place of his nightmares. Beside him, Ari's eyes lit up at the sight of the ancestral family home.

Many times during their travels, Margrethe had seen instances of genuine warmth and empathy in Ari's words and actions, interspersed with moments of cold objectivity and cautious withdrawal. It seemed at times as though her eldest son remained embroiled in his inner battles. In the end, she still felt somewhat estranged from him, uncertain as to which way his mood would swing from one moment to the next. Lucius, of course, did not bother to hide his delight at having returned to his ancestral home. Lucius ruled the Clan of Nyx now, all in accordance to his birthright. With Ari by his side, Margrethe knew his claim would be accepted without challenge. Father and son made a formidable team, not to be taken lightly by even the most powerful of vampires. Throughout the journey, Lucius had often drawn his eldest son aside, spending hours in deep conversations to which she was never privy. After each of these meetings, Ari would emerge with his jaw set, his eyes hard. With each father and son talk, her eldest boy became colder, more distant. Even before they reached the castle, Margrethe had already realized her hopes of protecting Ari from his father's influence were most likely in vain. With a sinking heart, she followed Lucius and Silas, still carrying Raffy, up the moss-covered entrance steps. Ari stopped for a moment, raising his face to the highest tower. She followed his gaze and shuddered uncontrollably. Whatever lay before them, she knew certain the future boded to be cloaked in darkness and soaked in blood.

LUCIUS wasted no time in organizing the household of Nyx to his specifications. He consigned Margrethe and Raffy to Edmund's old chambers. It seemed fitting, after all, that Margrethe should be as close to her father's memory as possible. Lucius allowed himself a small, cold smile. Let her live out her days with her shell of a son and her father's ghosts. She'd betrayed him, and her punishment proved just. He locked the heavy door himself and handed the key to his faithful servant.

"Silas, see to it that Raphael and his mother receive sufficient nourishment. Under no circumstances, however, are they to leave their room unless I say so. Ever." Silas nodded in his usual inscrutable fashion. He pocketed the old iron key and with a small, practiced bow, retreated into the shadows.

He installed Ari on the floor below, very close to his own chambers. He'd considered giving the boy an entire wing to himself but decided that, for now, the boy should best kept close. Likewise, he decided to keep Margrethe and what remained of Raphael close as well. He believed Margrethe to be of little threat to him, now so broken and disillusioned. There had been no light of hope in her eyes when they'd reached the castle's shadowy gates. Her spirit was crushed; her dreams were dust. Nearly as much a shell as her son, she differed only with more awareness of her tragic, doomed predicament. Nonetheless, Lucius felt it wise to err on the side of caution. Nothing ever remained certain in the realm of the undead. The phoenix may yet rise from the ashes of Margrethe's dreams, and if it did, he was not going to be taken unawares.

Not again.

Later that night, when the dusk had long settled its debt to the day, Lucius knocked on Ari's door. It creaked open slowly. Ari peered out, cautiously at first, before opening the door wide at the sight of his father. He stepped back and Lucius strode into the room, filling it with his commanding presence. Lucius's power seemed to have increased with his influence among the clans. The Elders deferred to him now and it bode well that it would be only a matter of time before he claimed his rightful place on the Council of the Undead. His mother's foolishness had lost that precious position, but his determination would take it back.

Lucius focused on the young man in front of him. He'd noticed the change in Ari since the battle with his brother. He'd been worried at first that he may have miscalculated. Initially, Ari had seemed confused by his newfound sensitivity. He'd clumsily made his way through the bombardment of joy, fear, and sadness that assailed him, often swinging from elated, nearly drunken happiness to deep gut wrenching despair in a matter of moments. Ari had been caught off balance by such an emotional onslaught. Lucius had watched carefully for moments of vulnerability and softness, taking Ari aside often to remind him of his filial loyalty and the inherent duties that came with it. Patiently, over and over, Lucius would define Ari's purpose with calm intensity. The boy drank in his words and, after a few of these discussions, began to respond, regaining the single-mindedness that had made him a brilliant and bloody hunter.

On one occasion, when they had reached the lower slopes of the Carpathians, Lucius had decided to test Ari's battle skills— worried that his son had lost his taste for violence, although his hunger seemed as strong as always. Thankfully Ari had learned to restrain his bloodlust, but Lucius needed to be sure that his skills as a warrior remained formidable and able to tear a man apart at his father's command. He took Ari deep into the forest, away from prying eyes, and goaded him to battle. Ari had been hesitant at first, but at Lucius's insistence he'd attacked, leaping with agile ease between tree and bush, ducking in and out of the shadows with a speed that defied even Lucius's keen eye. No longer did he seek to subdue his prey by sheer brute force. Now he foresaw each move, read each thought. He even played with Lucius a little, seeming to enjoy the mental game. His final attack, however, came swift and hard. In less than the blink of an eye, Lucius found himself crushed beneath his son's strong hand. He stared into those black eyes so like his own and for a moment felt fear, mixed with relief. The boy's ferocity still flowed. The call of battle seemed to draw out Ari's warrior instincts, filling him with a deadly strength that left even his father entirely at his mercy. Grateful for the hold he had on his son's mind, Lucius knew he would not have the strength or ability to defeat him in a real battle, at least not in a fair fight. Lucius motioned Ari to a chair but remained standing, choosing to retain the advantage of height over his powerful son.

"I have been observing your progress, Ari."

"Father?"

"You have not disappointed me. Your strength is complimented by your mental agility. You no longer attack with rage. You hunt with thought, with purpose. You read your prey, sense its instincts and intent. You are now the complete warrior, and it is time to claim that which is rightly ours." Lucius paused for a moment, letting his words sink in. Ari sat a little straighter, hanging intently on their meaning. Satisfied, Lucius continued.

"Tonight we will attend the Council of the Elders. There I will ask their allegiance to the House of Nyx." He smiled thinly. "I doubt they will refuse, but should they not see things our way, you must be prepared to do bloody battle."

Ari nodded. The enormity of this meeting would not be lost on him. Lucius had ensured his son understood his destiny well as the firstborn of the Lord of Nyx, heir to this ancient castle and all its titles. His grandmother had once ruled the Council of the Undead until she had betrayed her lineage: turning a human and bearing his child. Claudia of Nyx had suffered the punishment of a traitor. Her grandson's hands were dipped in her blood; the blood of justice, Lucius had assured him. Now, together, father and son would reclaim their lost entitlements and stand, once more, in the highest place of the Gathered Undead.

He smiled at Ari, whose handsome face was set determinedly.

"You should rest for a few hours, Ari, you may need all your strength. The Council of Elders is much like a pit of snakes. You must keep your mind sharp and your talons sharper."

With a quick squeeze of his son's shoulder, Lucius let himself out of the room, knowing he should rest, yet his mind raced in anticipation. For so many years, decades he'd longed for this direct confrontation. These Elders, these ancient vampires with their crusty rules and outdated observances, had rejected him as tainted spawn. In their eyes, he embodied the product of his mother's shame. Humans were fine for feasting and fornication but not for breeding. It mattered not to them his conception occurred moments after his father's bloody initiation. To the Elders, he was less than pure. His mother's exile became his own. Lucius gave a low chuckle. Now they would see the true power of his vampiric heritage. Tonight, the might of Nyx would return and stake its rightful claim. His mother's unfortunate passing heralded the passing of the old ways. A new generation dawned. His son embodied the perfect predator, with enough insight to outwit his enemies and enough strength to overcome them. It may be difficult at first for those dried out vampires to recognize the new order, but Lucius's confidence remained unbridled that by the end of the meeting, the Council of Elders would see things his way.

✳✳✳

# CHAPTER TWENTY-TWO

OIL lanterns dimly lit the cavern, lanterns fueled with human oil. Lucius knew this by the heavy, clinging scent. Shadows flickered across the hard stone walls, marked by time and the small rivulets of water that trickled down their smooth surface. This had been the meeting place of the Elders from time immemorial and Lucius supposed he should feel awed, daunted even, by the scene of ancient power before him.

He didn't. He felt confident and powerful.

The Elders were seated at a huge iron table which rested on a raised platform. They gazed down at him with inscrutable faces, the flickering lamps casting their eyes into deep shadow. He waited quietly until addressed, honoring tradition for the time being until such subservience became useless.

"Lucius, of the House of Nyx. We grant you permission to address the Council of Elders."

Lucius recognized the voice immediately. Lord Valdis, a great uncle of Valdymyr, his mother's puppet, sat on the Council for well over a century. Highly respected by his peers, who deferred to him when matters required a stern hand, he also presented the most dangerous political obstacle to Lucius achieving his objective. By all accounts, Lord Valdis had not taken the news of his nephew's death well. Silas told him the Elder had spewed the darkest invocations against Valdymyr's killers, calling down the fire of Hades and a thousand lifetimes of death upon them. Lord Valdis had a personal score to settle and that made him dangerous. He had no proof of Lucius's involvement in Valdymyr's death, but Lucius held no doubt in his mind that he had his suspicions.

The other five members of the Council were more pliable. They were likely to be more politically motivated and amenable to persuasion than Lord Valdis. Mustering as much humility as his confidence would allow, Lucius bowed his head and stepped forward.

I bring my most respectful greetings to the Council and thank you all for your ear."

"What business brings you here, Lucius of Nyx?" Lord Valdis wasted no time getting to the point. Lucius obliged him with a polite inclination of his head.

"As you know, most honored Members, the circumstances of my birth have been under question for some time now."

A couple of the Elders shifted uncomfortably in their seats at the mention of Claudia's disobedience. Lucius pretended not to notice their discomfort, continuing to speak, his voice calm and even.

"I am here to submit to the Council the right of my birth by Vampiric blood. I have the written testament of my mother, Claudia of Nyx, that I was conceived *after* my father was turned. Thus, my Lords, I lay claim to the same purity of the Vampiric heritage that you, the wisest of the ancients, bear within yourselves."

A long moment of silence fell and an exchange of meaningful glances took place. Lord Valdis's voice was stern when he spoke.

"Your mother submitted this same petition to us after your birth, Lucius of the House of Nyx. We rejected it then, and we reject it now. Your mother's disobedience brings doubt to any word she may have given to us."

"She swore this to me on the name of our ancestors." Lucius's tone was quiet but insistent.

Lord Valdis held up his wrinkled clawed hand, dismissing

Lucius's words.

"It was no doubt a contrivance to spare her child the pain of rejection, Lucius of Nyx."

Lucius allowed himself a wry smile. "My mother hated me, Lord Valdis. She had no reason to soothe me with lies, nor would she have thought to do so."

Another silence again followed by a quick, whispered exchange, then Lord Valdis spoke once more.

"Your mother is dead by your own hand, Lucius of Nyx. Explain to us why we should not cast you into the darkest depths for her murder?"

Lucius had known this was coming and had prepared for this moment. He looked up at the table of Elders imploringly.

"Lords, you all knew my mother well. She was powerful, born of the most ancient lineage. I think most of you would say she was formidable."

A couple of heads nodded in agreement and there were a few quiet chuckles. Encouraged, Lucius continued.

"On the horrible night of my mother's death, I was left with no choice, but to defend myself. I tried to fend off her savage attack, but she was relentless, inflamed by rage."

"What was the reason for her rage, Lucius of Nyx?" A soft voice interrupted him. He turned to the thin, gaunt Elder at the far right of the table.

"Lord Uldryk, you knew my mother from the earliest days. I believe you may have been in receipt of her temper on one or two occasions." Quiet laughter erupted among the Council members.

"Indeed, I did, Lucius of Nyx," the Elder Uldryk agreed with a tight smile. "I thank you for the memories, but now, if you do not mind, what was the reason for your mother's rage?"

Lucius stepped back, making a quick motion with his hand. Ari stepped into the lamplight beside him. His tall, muscular frame cast a huge shadow on the cavern wall behind the Table of the Elders.

It loomed over them, the shadow of the House of Nyx, dark and all-consuming. Lucius pushed Ari forward.

"*This* is the reason for her rage, my Lords. My son, Ariel."

Lord Valdis waved his hand and the platform, supported by heavy chains slung over massive iron pulleys, began to lower. It creaked and whined, grinding to a halt as it touched the cavern floor. The Elders remained seated, studying the young man before them with great interest. Even the three Elders who had already met Ari at the castle strained to peer at Lucius's son more closely.

Ari bowed his head and withstood their inspection calmly. Another hushed exchange broke out amongst the Council. Then a scowling Lord Valdis rose from his chair and spoke.

"Lucius of Nyx, my esteemed colleagues believe that you and your son should be given the benefit of the doubt regarding the purity of your bloodline. They believe you should be reinstated at the head of the House of Nyx, as Lord of that House and all its titles, lands, and wealth. This day, all funds which had been withheld by the Council will be restored to you, as will your title of Lord of Nyx. And your son, Ariel, is recognized as your rightful heir. The succession of your house forthwith is ensured."

"I thank the Council." Lucius bowed deeply.

"Oh, do not include me in your thanks, Lord of Nyx. Although initially outvoted, I have very strong reservations about restoring your title and have only agreed to do so on the understanding that you will adhere to one strict provision."

"'Provision,' Lord Valdis?" Lucius sensed an obstacle.

"Yes. In accepting the reinstatement of your title Lord of Nyx, you accept the provision that at no time and under no circumstance will you seek admission to the Council of the Undead."

Lucius felt his world spin out of control. No admission to the Council of the Undead? How dare they! Only members of the Council of the Undead could challenge for leadership. They were depriving the House of Nyx of their legitimate right to rule. Somehow he bit down on his anger, managing to speak calmly and clearly.

"My Lords, I beg you to reconsider." The word "beg" burnt his tongue; however, he needed to persuade them, even if it meant assuming the appearance of a beggar. "Admission to the Council of the Undead is my birthright. I have as much right to join the Council of the Undead as I have to my own lands and title."

"As I said, Lord of Nyx, it is I who stand in your way in this matter, not the other members of Council. It is I you should address." Lord Valdis stood up. Although no longer young and virile, his reputation alone gave him an imposing air, which he now used to its greatest effect.

Lucius gave a shallow bow. "As you wish, my Lord." His tone was deliberately insolent. The slight did not go unnoticed. Lord Valdis fixed him with a murderous stare.

"You would do well to set a better example for your son, Lord of Nyx."

"With all due respect, my Lord," replied Lucius in a tone entirely devoid of respect, "my son seems to have fared quite well by my example. Perhaps your Lordship would like a demonstration of his prowess?"

"I warn you, Lucius, the spilling of an Elder's blood brings a heavy penalty." Did Lucius detect a waver in the old vampire's voice? He turned and smiled at the table of Elders ingratiatingly.

"You mistake me, Lord Valdis. No blood shall be spilled. It is but, shall we say, a lighthearted demonstration."

His nod was imperceptible to all but Ari. Like lightning, the boy leaped forward, grasping Lord Valdis around his throat, pinning him to the iron table. He held him easily, waiting for his father's command. The remaining Elders, startled from their chairs, backed away from the young vampire fearfully.

Except one.

Ragnar Grettirson, more commonly known as the Huntsman, a robust vampire of undetermined age and ancient Viking heritage, stood his impressive full height, his eyes fierce, his fists clenched, prepared. If any on the Council could directly withstand a direct physical challenge from Ari, he could

Lucius stepped forward, placing a hand on Ari's shoulder, "As you can see my lords, my son has lightning speed and the strength of twenty men."

"Indeed," growled the Huntsman, unwavering.

Lord Uldryk stepped forward nervously. "The Council has had demonstration enough, Lucius of Nyx."

A tense silence filled the chamber. Imploring eyes from the other Council members rested upon the Huntsman,

The giant vampire smiled coldly, baring fangs as sharp as his gaze. "It is demonstration enough for now." His muscles still tightly tensed, the Huntsman stood motionless for a moment, then slowly sat down, his unblinking eyes still set upon Ari. The other Elders followed his lead and stepped forward cautiously to resume their seats.

Lucius breathed in deeply, smiling as he relished his moment of power over the other Elders, but his smile died as he met Ragnar's steely gaze. Even seated, the warrior vampire presented a formidable figure. Lucius's eyes narrowed. The Huntsman proved as much a foe as Lord Valdis, but it was a battle he was not prepared to fight. Not now. Reluctantly, he gave the command.

"Release Lord Valdis, Ari."

Ari relinquished his grip and the Elder vampire straightened himself shakily, avoiding the eyes of father and son. He turned to speak with the other Council members, but Lucius halted him.

"My Lord, did you not say I was to address you? Let this be between you and I, then, as you wished."

Lord Valdis still avoided his eyes.

"I suppose we can reach a mutually acceptable agreement."

"I am all ears, Lord Valdis. Tell me."

"We agree to allow your admission to the Council of the Undead. However, both you and your mother demonstrated a lack of good judgment, which cannot be repeated. Like her, you chose to breed with a human. If you would be accepted, you must prove your loyalty and that of your son."

"My son's loyalty is not in question, Lord Valdis."

"Your son's loyalty belongs to you, Lord Lucius of Nyx." Lord Valdis no longer seemed shaken by his ordeal. His voice rose commandingly, reverberating through the ancient cavern. "We need proof of his loyalty as much as we need proof of yours."

"And how shall we prove our loyalty, pray tell?" Lucius's eyes narrowed, he sensed a trap.

"Send him out into the world. Let him make his fortune amongst the humans without being contaminated by them."

Lucius smiled and looked over at his son proudly. "Ariel will succeed in whatever role is given to him."

"He must prove himself for four seasons," Lord Valdis continued. "We have had a clear demonstration of his superior physical strength. Let us see if Ariel of the House Nyx has the moral strength to equal his physical abilities." The Elder spoke with an authority that dared no challenge.

A wry smile curled the corners of Lucius's mouth. "A vampire with moral strength, Lord Valdis? Surely that's a contradiction in terms?"

Lord Valdis chose to ignore his comment. "Our strength lies in loyalty, Lord Lucius. Without the company of our fellow vampires, our eternal years within the realm of mortality would be a torture of endless days of fools and their follies. Together, we can take what we need from the humans, be it blood or gold, without fear of reprisal. Our strength is greater than theirs and strength in numbers is even greater." He looked at Ariel, and then back at Lucius. "Even you are aware of the importance of loyalty in these matters."

Lucius looked at the Elder, then back at his son. He could hardly refuse without bringing more shame to his family name. The House of Nyx had been tainted by weakness and foolishness. He would not allow it to be tainted by cowardice as well. It was a risk, but he felt Ari prepared for the challenge. He had shown a remarkable level of self-control for many weeks now. Lucius would watch him very carefully, of course. Everything would be lost if Ari's old, bloodthirsty habits returned, but if he passed this probationary period successfully, their rise to power was likely assured. The House of Nyx would be admitted to the Council of the Undead and he, Lord Lucius of the House of Nyx, would directly challenge for the leadership of the dark realms. The time for bloodshed may come, but for now, diplomacy won out as the better option. He smiled at the members of the Council, who had slowly come forward at Lord Valdis's release. They gathered around Ari now, casting their shadows upon him as if they were a dark cloak around his shoulders. Lucius bowed, deeply this time, then straightened.

"I thank the Council for their consideration and—"

"One moment, Lucius," Lord Uldryk interrupted him in his quiet, rustling voice. "There is one other condition of your probation."

Lucius swallowed his words, startled. *What more could they want?*

"Your son will travel into the realm of the humans in order to gain his life experience. You, however, will remain at your castle and manage your household with the diligence required of a Lord of the Clan."

Lucius stared at him, momentarily speechless. He quickly gathered his senses, stuttering out a protest.

"But, my lords, my son is not ready to venture out on his own. I need more time. His inexperience will leave him vulnerable."

"That is the point, Lord Lucius of Nyx," Lord Uldryk

216

responded dryly. "We need to see Ari's moral strength, not your puppetry skills." His words stung Lucius into silence. A cold pit of anger rose in his stomach, mixed with a liberal dose of doubt. This was a disaster. He couldn't let Ari loose on his own, especially now while still adjusting to his new world of thought and feeling. He couldn't take the risk of letting him loose in a world that would test his newfound ability to its limits. Desperately he looked at the Elders, his eyes moving from one stone cold face to another. With a sinking heart, each cold stare convinced him he would find no room for negotiation. He'd taken a risk in subduing a Council Elder by force and he doubted he'd won their favor by doing so. He'd gained their fear, maybe, but not their favor.

Defeated for now, he bowed to the Elders.

"The House of Nyx accepts your terms."

The Council returned the bow and silently withdrew into the shadows, leaving Ari alone on the platform. Lucius motioned him forward. He wondered if the boy understood what just happened. Ari's next words reassured him.

"Don't worry, Father. I will succeed in the human realm. I can read them now."

Lucius smiled at his son.

"I know you will, Ari." His brow creased as a thought occurred to him. How would Ari respond to the lure of the opposite sex? Lucius knew all too well the temptation that lay in a well-rounded breast and the seductive curve of a woman's hips. He'd been seduced by that alluring, fragile beauty, and he'd been betrayed and nearly destroyed by it, too. He'd never addressed this issue with Ari, choosing to focus on honing his son's physical skills while relentlessly guiding the boy's emerging thoughts and feelings towards the singular goal of dominance. However, he realized now that he'd been foolish not to address matters pertaining to the opposite sex. Yes, Ari now had the remarkable ability to read the minds of men, but the minds of women were an entirely different matter. It was hard to read a woman's thoughts at the best of times and doubly so when one's own thoughts were consumed with desire. This had been his own undoing and he couldn't let it be his son's. Lucius put his arm reassuringly around Ari's broad shoulders.

"Ari, there are matters we need to discuss and arrangements that need to be made. Come now, I will have Silas prepare some refreshment and then we will talk about your journey out into the world."

Together, father and son turned their backs to the iron table and, already deep in conversation, walked slowly from the cavern.

MARGRETHE turned at the sound of the latch. It was too early for Silas with her evening meal of deer's blood. She'd lost much of her desire for blood, having seen it flow too often, drinking barely enough to sustain her. Her son needed her; this empty shell that seemed so lifeless yet continued to live, needing neither love nor sustenance. Somewhere deep inside, Margrethe knew that this deathless carcass was no longer her son, yet she clung to his shell with a desperation forged by loss and grief. She needed someone to hold and protect. There was nothing else to comfort her in her endless existence. This room contained her world now and her son's shrunken shell remained her only salvation.

The door swung open. A tall, powerful body filled the frame, blocking out the light from the hallway.

*Lucius!*

Margrethe rose from her chair. Lucius stepped into the room, filling it with his presence.

He seemed relaxed, almost friendly. When he spoke, his voice seemed to hold a note of concern.

"Margrethe, I apologize for the unannounced visit. I thought it time I personally checked on your welfare. And that of Raphael, of course." He glanced at the sad form that lay motionless and empty on the plush lounge. Raphael no longer inhabited that wretched body, but if it kept Margrethe happy, he would go along with the delusion of Raphael's presence. Margrethe followed his gaze. She wondered if the sight of his youngest son would move him. His eyes hovered on Raphael for a moment before returning to her own. His hypnotic gazed mesmerized Margrethe to feel a strange tug of memories; the touch of his lips on her skin, the swell of him inside her. She shook the visions away and returned his gaze warily.

"I appreciate the gesture, Lucius. We are comfortable and well cared for, thank you." Her tone remained civil but distant.

"Good." He paused for a moment, looking at her intently. "I have a proposal, Margrethe."

Her wariness increased.

"What proposal, Lucius?"

"When I leave this room, I am leaving the door open and the key in the lock. You will be free to come and go as you please within the confines of the castle grounds."

Margrethe regarded him suspiciously.

"Why?"

Lucius shrugged. "There is no need to keep you incarcerated, Margrethe. You and your broken son pose no threat to me."

Her broken son! Raffy meant nothing to him. She couldn't trust him. Lucius only granted favors when it benefited himself in some way.

"Forgive me for asking, Lucius, but is there no price for this freedom you offer?"

Lucius gave a harsh laugh. "Today's events have provided payment enough. Your freedom comes without cost or sacrifice, Margrethe."

"Are you not you afraid I will escape?" she asked quietly.

Lucius gave a low, rumbling chuckle.

"You would be foolish to do so, Margrethe. The forest is full of dangers."

She snorted derisively. "Wolves? Deer? An occasional

rabbit? I may well choose to take my chances." She didn't know why she challenged him. She should take his offer gracefully then try to work things to her advantage.

He laughed again.

"Oh, the deer pose no threat, Margrethe, nor do the wolves. And rabbits? Tch! It is the People of the Wolf you must fear."

Margrethe frowned. "The People of the Wolf?"

"Dacians!" Lucius spat the word contemptuously. Worshipers of the Wolf God. If only our youngest son could speak and tell us how he and Edmund found a way past the Dacians. You, dear Margrethe, may not be so fortunate."

"I am not one of you. These wolf people have nothing to fear from me."

"You are one of us! You are the mother of the heir to the House of Nyx. That in itself is enough for them to rip the flesh from your bones."

Margrethe shivered. Lucius saw it and smiled.

"As I said, you are free to come and go as you please, provided it is within the castle grounds, of course. I only have your safety and best interests in mind, Margrethe."

Doubt still gnawed at her. Lucius seemed to sense her hesitation.

"I will leave you to consider my offer, Margrethe. As I said, the door will remain unlocked." With a stiff bow, he turned and left the room, leaving her to wrestle with her thoughts. The door remained open as promised. A cold draft invaded the warmth of her chamber. It whistled down the long hallway. The oil lamps flickered in its wake, their shadowy fingers beckoning her forward. Cautiously, Margrethe peered around the open door and down the empty hall. She glanced back at Raphael lying motionless on the lounge. In spite of her constant prayers and tears, she knew he would remain so. Her son no longer inhabited this shell. He only resided deep within the dark realms of her oldest son's empty soul.

*Ari!*

This sudden gift of freedom meant she could see Ari.

A wave of emotion washed over her; joy, fear, sadness and anger. Her maternal joy at the thought of a reunion with her child suddenly turned cold. It was Ari who had destroyed his own brother, trapping him somehow and devouring him. No, the wolf was not her enemy. Her enemy lay closer, ready to seize any opportunity for victory. It was Lucius, she reminded herself, who held Raffy hostage in a prison with no key. Ari was just another pawn in Lucius's game and she remained Raffy's only hope, yet how could she free him without hurting her boys? Tears of grief and frustration sprang to her eyes. She would find a way to release Raffy. She would play along for now until she could discover Lucius's motive in freeing her, for motive he must have.

With a deep breath, Margrethe stepped into the hallway. The cold air rushed over her bare arms. She wished she'd grabbed a shawl but her courage resided in her hands now and she didn't dare place it aside and go back. The flickering shadows brought the statues to life in their dark alcoves. She could feel them watching her as she tiptoed down the hall. They traced her every step with their sightless marble eyes. She hurried to escape their carved stares.

She found Lucius in the drawing-room. The room was tidy, the curtains flung open to embrace the evening gloom. He turned to greet her, his face polite and inscrutable.

"Ah, Margrethe. I am pleased you chose to join me."

Margrethe looked around the room, expecting to see Ari lounging on one of the chairs. She and Lucius were the only occupants. Ari was nowhere to be seen.

"Are you looking for something, Margrethe?"

Did she detect a sarcastic note? "I am looking for Ari, Lucius. I would like to see my son."

"Our son," Lucius corrected her. "I am sorry, Margrethe, I fear I must disappoint you once again. Ari is not here."

"Not here?" Her heart dropped like a stone. What had he done to Ari? She stared at Lucius accusingly. He caught her look and held up his hands as though to protect himself from the daggers in her eyes.

"No, no, Margrethe. I assure you, Ari is fine. Perfectly fine! In fact, he is on his way to North America right now."

"America?" Margrethe stared at him, not quite comprehending his words.

"Yes, America. The brave new world. The land of the free. America."

"But, but, why?" Her head reeled. The questions spilled out of her. "When did he leave? Who is with him? Surely he is not traveling without a companion!"

"Hush for a moment, Margrethe. I will answer your questions, but please, be seated." He waved her to a chaise lounge. She sat obediently, still stunned by his announcement.

"Now, let me explain it to you in simple terms." He spoke as to a child. It grated on Margrethe's nerves, but she kept her silence.

"Ari is traveling to America to seek opportunities for our financial advancement. The family coffers are a little low after the war?" A flat out lie, Lucius had more money than he ever dreamed of now that the family's confiscated riches were soon to be returned in full by the Council, but the lie proved suffice for his current needs, Margrethe need not know of his full return to undead grace.

Again, she ventured to ask, "Does he have a companion, Lucius? Surely you have not let him travel alone?"

"Of course not. Silas is with him."

Ah, so her jailer now guarded her son. There in part rested the reason for her freedom. Well, it was better than no escort at all, she supposed. Silas may be dour and his loyalty most certainly laid with his master, but her son stayed in capable hands. The realization dawned on her that with Silas and Ari gone, she'd be left alone with Lucius. She visibly squirmed. The thought did not comfort her in the least.

Lucius seemed to sense her discomfort. He reached for a crystal decanter and two matching glasses, raising the decanter towards her.

"Would you like some refreshment, Margrethe? You must be tired of deer's blood by now."

She nodded wordlessly.

"Good. This is my finest, highborn vintage blood. It is much smoother than peasant's blood with a far more, shall we say, pleasant taste." He poured the crimson liquid into the glasses. It splashed thickly against the sides. In spite of herself, Margrethe felt the thirst rising within her. Deer blood repulsed her. Weakened by her incarceration and the strain of events leading up to it, she needed sustenance. Gratefully, she took the cup he offered her, drinking thirstily. The blood stained her lips and her teeth, coursing through her being, revitalizing her. Her eyes sharpened, her skin tingled. For the first time in a long while she felt alive. She glanced down at the half-empty glass, then looked up at Lucius. He smiled.

"As I said, my finest beverage." He raised his own glass to his lips and drank deeply, draining the contents. Margrethe did the same. He poured another glass, offering her a refill. She accepted automatically. He sat down beside her, his powerful body only inches from hers. She could feel him, almost taste him. She struggled against the intoxication, sitting with an outward calm that belied her sudden inner turmoil.

Lucius seemed aware of his effect on her. He wrapped an arm behind her head and sat back, breathing in deeply then exhaling. His breath formed a cold mist in the warmth of the drawing-room.

"So, Margrethe, we have an eternity to fill. What shall we talk about?"

She didn't respond, choosing to stare into the crimson depths of her glass. He moved quickly, cupping her chin in his strong hand and turning her face towards him. His eyes were black, burning coals. They burned into her, searing her resolve. He didn't give her a moment to protest or resist. He pressed his mouth hard against hers. She could feel the sharp sting of his fangs on her lip and pulled away, managing to struggle free from his embrace momentarily before realizing that the years of loneliness and loss had left her with no will to resist. Her body went limp. Casting all her lingering fears aside, Margrethe allowed herself to fall into her enemy's strong arms once again.

***

# CHAPTER TWENTY-THREE

ARI stood in the busy city street, drinking in the hustle and bustle around him. He'd insisted that Silas remain at the hotel. His father's servant had protested, but Ari convinced him of the importance for him to prove himself to the Council and his father as quickly as possible. Reluctantly Silas had agreed. Freedom was a new concept for Ari, and he embraced it with enthusiasm. The journey from the Carpathians had been arduous. At his father's insistence, they'd avoided the Dacians, choosing to take the safer, longer route through the forest. Silas had been dour company and the long silences only made the journey seem even longer still.

Now, standing in the thriving, crowded street, Ari realized that the journey had been worth the effort. New York City inspired him beyond his wildest dreams. Unlike Europe, it seemed relatively untouched by the ravages and concerns of the Great War. Skirts were shorter, and smiles were wider. People buzzed around with a sense of purpose, like bees in a hive, creating an energetic life force he found intoxicating. A pretty girl caught his eye, dressed in the latest fashion. Her hair was styled simply, framing a delicate face with large brown eyes and painted red bow lips. He felt himself swell with desire, and hastily turned his gaze away, mindful of his father's warnings. Lucius had been most forceful about it. Under no circumstances was Ari to give way to fleshly desire. He was to return to his father in a year, pure and untested by feminine charm. In return for his obedience, Lucius had promised him a suitable wife of noble vampire blood. Ari had agreed, supposing that it would not be too difficult to suppress his desires by strength of will. Had he not endured many months of testing at his father's hand? Could the allure of a woman test his endurance more than the rigorous training and endless instruction that had molded and shaped him?

Time would tell.

Ari's eyes slipped back to the girl. He caught a glimpse of her disappearing into the crowd, sauntering seductively, her hat perched jauntily on her head. He sighed, thankful that Silas had not been there to observe his weakness. It seemed that resisting the allure of a woman was going to prove much harder than he'd thought.

Drawing himself back from sensory intoxication, Ari focused on the task at hand. His father had given him the name and address of a fellow clan member who'd taken residence in New York City over sixty years ago. Ari had followed a map, hastily drawn by the hotel doorman, to an Italian restaurant on a busy, tree-lined street. The honks of automobiles chorused in the background winding through the horse and carts that still made their way through the busy city streets. The war had brought a fresh wave of advancement, but the old world still intruded on the new. Attitudes were slowly changing, but some people still clung to tradition as a child to a treasured toy.

Romani's Italian Restaurant shone as an outstanding example of tradition, a family concern, run by Orfeo Romani. The Romani Clan was not as old as the Clan of Nyx, but they were still powerful and respected as being one of the oldest Italian Clans. Their influence stretched from Sicily to Brooklyn. His father had been close to Orfeo as a child, and after Claudia's bloody death, the

Romani Clan had been first to accept Lucius's plea of self-defense and his right to be admitted to the Council of the Undead. Lucius thought it provident to forge an even stronger alliance with the Orfeo Clan. Thus, Ari found himself standing in front of Romani's famed Italian restaurant. He peered through the windows, looking for any sign of movement. A lone figure sat at a table shuffling through a pile of papers. Ari rapped on the window. The man looked up, startled. His hand went to his coat, then hesitated. Ari waved the map as if it were a letter of introduction. The man walked cautiously towards the door. Dark and thickset, he looked like he hadn't shaved in a couple of days. He unlatched the door, and a blast of garlic and warm air hit Ari's face.

"Who are you?" The tone resounded unmistakably brusque, the accent strange to Ari's ears.

"I am Ariel of the House of Nyx. Lord Lucius Ruthven's son."

The man's brow furrowed for a moment before realization dawned in his eyes.

"Ah, you're Lucius's boy? Well, whaddya doing standing out there in the cold? Come in, come in!"

Ari accepted his invitation gratefully. The wonderful aroma enveloped him as he stepped into the restaurant. Contrary to popular legend, garlic held no terror for vampires. Orfeo embraced him with big, bearlike arms before placing two kisses of greeting on his cheeks. Ari endured the crushing embrace, breathing in relief when finally released. The man had the strength to rival his own!

"Welcome, son of Lucius. I've heard many tales from home, some of them quite disturbing. After your grandmother's death, I've wondered many times how your father has fared."

"He is well, Lord Romani," Ari assured him.

Orfeo waved a hand. "No need to use titles here, Ari of Nyx. In Brooklyn, I'm just Mr. Orfeo Romani, owner of the best Italian restaurant in New York City." He beamed proudly, and if the delicious aromas drifting through from the kitchen were any indication, Ari could well believe this restaurant had no rival. Orfeo Romani led him through the restaurant and the kitchen with its bubbling pots full of enticing sauces, past the young apprentice rolling out pasta dough, and out to a small, cramped office. It barely contained the two chairs and the desk that furnished it.

"Please excuse the mess." His host hastily cleared a pile of papers from the chairs. "I've just lost my accountant and the books are a mess."

He looked up at Ari. "Don't suppose you're good with numbers, Ariel of Nyx?"

"Ruthven. I have taken my father's human name as a surname. And my friends call me Ari." He smiled at Orfeo, who smiled back.

"Ari it is then. In turn, please call me Feo. I insist. That's the name *my* friends know me by."

They settled into the newly cleared chairs and their newfound camaraderie. Orfeo didn't mention the offer of work again until he'd caught up with the details of Claudia's demise and Lucius appearance before the Elders. Ari recounted events, skipping quickly over the details of Claudia's bloody death while assuring his new friend that Lucius had only acted in self-defense Orfeo shook his head sadly.

"The House of Nyx is one of the most ancient of all the Clans. It's not right that the heir and his son should have to prove their worth to lesser Clans."

Ari hunted in his coat pocket, pulling out a carefully folded piece of paper. He handed it to Orfeo, who opened it and read it carefully before looking at Ari.

"So you're here to make your fortune, Ari?"

Ari grinned. "So it seems, Feo."

The big man stood, his head nearly touching the ceiling of the tiny office.

"If that's the case, your father's sent you to me at just the right time. Come with me, I wanna show you something."

Ari followed him obediently, stopping at a cellar door at the back of the restaurant. Orfeo yanked on the door. It opened easily, and both men climbed down the steps, ducking under the beams that barely missed the top of their heads. At the bottom of the stairs, the room opened up to a cavernous expanse lined with rows of bottles stacked to the ceiling. Mercifully the rows were much higher than the cramped entrance.

Orfeo stood proudly, surveying his collection.

"This is the future, Ari. They've just passed the Prohibition Act. We can still serve alcoholic beverages, but they have to be below the prescribed limit. Once they ratify the 18th amendment, the sale of alcohol will be banned altogether. These bottles of fine wine are already valuable, but their value will triple once they bring in Prohibition."

Ari looked at the gleaming rows of bottles and wondered how the sour juice of grapes could hold such currency. He supposed that wine was to humans as blood was to vampires.

"How will you sell it if it is illegal?"

Feo laughed. "There are ways, Ariel Ruthven. We've been building clubs all over Brooklyn. They're hidden away: some in warehouses, some behind shops, all connected by secret tunnels. They'll be heavily secured by our men, who will check everyone at the door. People will find out about the clubs by word of mouth, under the trust of secrecy."

Ari's eyes widened as he looked around. "You must have a lot of trust in your men, Feo."

"The Familia Romani are bound by loyalty or death." Orfeo's voice sounded hard. "There is no need to doubt the loyalty of my family or my friends. They respect me, and they fear me."

Ari turned, studying the man standing next to him. Orfeo Romani was tall and built like a bear. His age was indefinable, as was the case with most vampires. His face was square with a powerful jaw. His eyes were the dark, cold eyes of the Undead. There was no doubt that Orfeo Romani would be a formidable foe. Ari was glad he was on the right side of an alliance with his new friend.

Feo caught Ari's stare.

"If you join us, Ari, you will have riches beyond your dreams in far less time than you could imagine."

"I know nothing about wine or restaurants," Ari protested.

Feo shrugged. "Start with the books. If you can sort that mess out, you can sure help me run a few jazz clubs."

"Jazz?"

Feo laughed and flung a big bear arm around Ari's shoulders. "We're going to have to give you a quick education in American culture, Ari Ruthven. Welcome to New York City and welcome to the Romani family."

LUCIUS sat beside the bed, watching quietly as Margrethe slept. His eyes followed the delicate curve of her neck, bloody and swollen from their vigorous lovemaking. He'd not been gentle with her, his pride demanding her surrender as much as his flesh desired it. She'd seemed to enjoy the harsh demands he'd placed upon her body. She'd groaned in ecstasy as his fangs had sunk into her, writhing against him in a heady mixture of pain and desire.

She stirred under his gaze, the silk sheets tangling around her ankle. The movement dragged the top sheet from her breast, exposing a delicate pink nipple bruised and bleeding from the small puncture wounds that surrounded it. He'd ravaged her mercilessly, tearing and thrusting until his lust and rage were spent. She'd taken the punishment willingly. Perhaps she believed she deserved it.

Perhaps she did deserve it.

No doubt, she'd be horrified upon waking and remembering their intimacy. It didn't matter. She remained his prisoner. He would keep her dosed with fine blood and subdued with fear.

Margrethe stirred again. Her eyes fluttered open.

"Good morning, Margrethe."

She looked over at him, sleepily at first. Gradually, her eyes widened as her surroundings dawned on her. She sat up quickly, pulling the sheet up to cover herself.

"Dear God, surely we didn't?"

"Oh, I assure you, we did." Lucius teased her like a cat with a mouse. "You were quite passionate, actually, Margrethe. Abstinence seems to have sharpened your appetite."

"Do not be ridiculous!" Even as she said the words, he could see the flashes of their lovemaking coming back to her. Denial filled her eyes. "You must have put something in my drink."

"Of course not," he assured her. "It was the purest of untainted, noble blood, Margrethe. In fact, it was my mother's blood."

Margrethe stared at him in horror, then began to gag. He relished the moment.

"Are you feeling unwell, Margrethe? Perhaps the blood of Nyx does not agree with you, eh?"

She covered her mouth with her hand, staring at him with accusatory eyes.

"You seemed to enjoy it well enough last night, just as you enjoyed my lovemaking." Lucius stood up, stretching lazily. "I will be traveling to Budapest on business. I will be gone for three weeks. You are free to do as you please within the castle grounds, but again, I must warn you that any attempt to venture further will expose you to great danger."

"The greatest dangers are usually to be found close at hand." Her voice froze as cold as her stare.

Lucius smiled.

"I am not your enemy, Margrethe. You are the mother of my child, my heir. I am sworn to protect you."

Raffy's face swam before her eyes.

"You killed our child!" Anger sprang into his eyes as her

words cut into him. He leaped beside her in a moment, gripping her face hard between his fingers. Her eyes met his defiantly.

"Margrethe, I did not kill our son," he hissed. "I saved him. His body was weak. He would never have survived in the realm of the Undead. Now he is safe. He lives within his brother. He breathes with his brother's strong lungs and walks with his brother's strong legs." He released her, pushing her back onto the bed.

"Do you really believe Raphael lives in that shriveled shell in your bedchamber? Do you not understand, Margrethe? Raphael lives within Ariel. Your son is not dead. He is alive, and he lives within his brother. Together, they are complete. Two sides of the same coin!"

Margrethe shrank back against the ornately carved bed head. It dug into her bare flesh, pressing on the bruises she only now began to feel. She continued to stare at him wordlessly. The hatred never left her eyes. He wasn't sure if she'd even heard his words, much less understood them.

He sighed.

"Margrethe, you can take your rightful place beside me as Ari's mother or you can remain my prisoner, with only an empty shell to hold for comfort. If you desire to hold Raphael close, then you must hold Ari close. The two are now one."

She remained silent. He shrugged.

"Very well, I will leave you to think about what I have said." With that, he gave a stiff bow and withdrew. He could feel her eyes burning into his back as he left the room. The wounds on her flesh would heal, but he'd inflicted other wounds that ran deep into the dark recesses of her soul. He would never be able to trust her. One day, he would have to face the inevitable task of disposing of her, but for now, he still craved her presence, no matter how much she hated him.

MARGRETHE watched Lucius leave. Every fiber of her miserable being loathed him. She couldn't believe she'd allowed him to seduce her. She was sore and bleeding, but the worst part was knowing that she'd drunk Claudia's blood. The thought sickened her, as though she'd drunk in the vampire's evil heart and violent last moments. She felt poisoned, violated once again at Lucius's hands.

His absence would give her time to gather her thoughts and formulate a plan. She thought briefly about escape. It would serve no purpose really. Where would she go? She no longer had any family or fortune. She remembered Lucius's last words. He'd said that Raphael lived now in Ari, that they were one. Complete. She wondered if, in some strange way, he spoke the truth. Yes, the shriveled body of Raffy lay on a lounge in her bedchamber, but his life essence was glaringly absent. Where, then, was Raffy? Did he reside in the shrunken body in her chambers, or within the body and mind of her eldest son? She knew the answer, deep in her heart. She couldn't abandon her youngest son's body, no matter how useless it had become, but she no longer could cling to his empty shell in the vain hope that he would return. She would reach him through Ari. Her oldest son would return to the castle in a year. A year was but a drop in the ocean of eternity. She would wait. Perhaps she could bring Raffy forth by encouraging his spirit in her eldest son. Perhaps Lucius, much as she despised him, was right. Perhaps she could have both her boys by embracing one.

For some odd reason, the thought gave her hope.

LUCIUS hated Budapest. He had hoped to travel to America with Ari, but the Council's demands had put that idea to rest. He'd thought to stay for a while, but Budapest was battle-weary and unwelcoming. Even worse, the mistrust that gnawed at him every time he thought of Margrethe. Perhaps he was wrong to leave her alone at the castle. It had been a challenge, a test of sorts. At first he'd been confident that she would be there when he returned, but today he'd begun to doubt his own judgment. She may be foolhardy enough to escape. He didn't want to risk leaving her for three days, much less three weeks.

Impatiently, he pushed the papers forward. The elderly bookkeeper peered at them, then looked up at Lucius quizzically.

"This is quite a substantial transfer, Lord Ruthven."

Lucius checked his temper, answering the old man calmly but firmly.

"I am well aware of the details of the transaction. My only need is for you it to transfer it to my son. I did not come here to solicit financial advice."

The old man nodded and signed the paper. Satisfied, Lucius rose from his chair.

"Thank you. Please transfer the remainder at the same time next month."

Again, the bookkeeper nodded. "As you wish. Have a good day, Lord Ruthven."

Wordlessly, Lucius tipped his hat and emerged from the darkened office, blinking at the sun's harsh glare. He could tolerate daylight, but he couldn't say he found it comfortable.

He half expected to see Silas waiting with the car then remembered that his manservant was otherwise engaged. He hoped he was keeping a tight rein on Ari. The old bookkeeper's observation had been accurate – this was an extraordinary amount of money. Ari had been confident and insistent in his letter. If his instincts proved true, this investment would add the wealth he so desperately coveted, as well as an alliance with the Romani Clan that would serve him well in the Council of the Undead. Lucius had to admit his surprise at Ari's entrepreneurial spirit, although he could not help but wonder how much could be attributed to Raphael's inner presence. His younger brother had always been quick to seize an opportunity and see its potential. For a brief instant, a wave of guilt engulfed Lucius. He'd been fond of Raffy, as the little imp liked to be called. It had hurt him when his youngest son had chosen to flee the family castle. It felt as though Raphael had rejected all that Lucius offered him. He'd left his father no choice, really. At least now, he still had a life of sorts, even if only through his brother's body and mind. Raphael had sacrificed himself to save his mother. Perhaps he'd saved himself as well.

ARI was drunk. He sat back in the plush booth, surrounded by pretty girls with perfect hair and carefully applied makeup. One, in particular, had caught his eye, a cute little blonde with the bluest eyes he had ever seen. She curled up under his arm, her small pert breasts pressing against him, her head on his chest like a fragile bird. She reminded him of his mother. The thought doused his desire immediately. He pushed the girl away and tried to sit up straight. His head swam, and a wave of nausea rose up in his stomach. Silas leaned towards him.

"I think it is time we took our leave, Master Ari."

Ari nodded silently. He allowed Silas to hook his hand under his arm. The old man had amazing strength, lifting Ari's dead weight quite easily. Feo hurried over to help him, sharing Ari's weight with the older vampire.

"Well, I think young Ari knows a bit more about New York City now, Mister Silas."

"Aye. Possibly a little too much, Mr. Romani." Even through his alcoholic haze, Ari could tell by his tone that Silas was not impressed. He shouldn't have brought the old man. He hiccupped. It had been a night filled with music, women, and far too many bottles of wine. Silas had tried to stop him a few times, but Ari had waved him away, enjoying the camaraderie of his newfound friends and admirers.

This was his new life now. He'd messaged his father, who in return, had sent the first installment of their financial future. The money had arrived earlier in the day, and now he celebrated his new partnership in his new business, jointly owned with Feo Romani. Ari staggered a little and looked up at his helpers, smiling happily. Life was good and could only get better. He staggered again, bumping his head as they helped him into a nearby cab. He barely felt the blow and sank back into the leather seat. Silas climbed in beside him. The sway of the cab made Ari a little ill. He closed his eyes against the nausea and let the blessed relief of unconsciousness drift in and take him away. By the time they reached the hotel, he had fallen asleep, dreaming of fine cars, pretty girls with bow mouths, and mountainous piles of cash.

***

# CHAPTER TWENTY-FOUR

A YEAR seems like a lifetime to humans. It stretches ahead, its days pregnant with promise, dotted with holidays and the changing of the seasons. A year is a mirage of hopes and dreams, a seemingly endless opportunity to right the wrongs of the past and create a new future, yet it passes in an instant, in small moments where fortunes are won and lost, hearts are captured and broken, and right becomes wrong. The future, no matter how carefully planned and nurtured, can be destroyed in just one of these fleeting moments.

For a vampire, however, a year is but a day, a mere drop in the ocean of time. Days stretch endlessly. There is no rush for a vampire to achieve fulfillment before death. In the face of such a lack of desperate motivation, a vampire lives in the moment and for the moment, desiring only that which brings immediate comfort and gratification. A vampire's plans rarely stretch beyond the need to satisfy these desires and to avert the boredom that constantly threatens to overtake those whose days have no end.

For Lucius, this year had passed more slowly than any he could remember. It was a year of waiting, impatiently, for his destiny to unfold. It was a year of preparation and anticipation, marred only by the reports of his son's bloody adventures, both in the bedroom and out of it. Lucius had already chosen an appropriate wife for his son; a fine boned, feisty girl of ancient lineage and immaculate vampiric heritage. He only could hope that news of his son's messy antics had not reached her ears, nor those of her noble father. Ari needed a superb match and this powerful alliance would be most beneficial for the House of Nyx. Lucius just hoped that Silas could keep the boy in line long enough to see him wedded, bedded, and presented to the Council unblemished and intact.

ARI sat in his stylish and masculine Manhattan apartment, accented with a minimalist style that suited his needs. Ari led a busy life. His days were taken up with running his club and organizing consignments of booze and food. His nights were spent at the club, entertaining distinguished guests who relied on his discretion and, more importantly, courted his favor. Outwardly, Ari had it all; wealth, comfort, and respect. He enjoyed the company of good friends and the attention of beautiful women, yet he dared let none of them close, preferring to keep them all at arm's length. Feo remained his closest ally, both in business and personally. The two formed a strong bond and a formidable team.

Feo's loyalty was without question, and he expected the same in return. The Italian vampire worked the streets of New York City smoothly, hustling deals and making a quick profit. He ruled his kingdom with an iron fist and a gun in his belt. Ari studied his friend closely, observing his strengths and weaknesses and learning from both. He picked up the intricacies of business quickly, and his club soon began to show a healthy, steady profit. The amendment passed, and Prohibition ushered in an era of prosperity for illegal booze joints. Ari and Feo rode the crest of that lucrative wave and Ari's Lounge Club became the place to be seen, secretly, of course. The younger generation put the Great War well behind them, dancing and drinking the memories away. Prohibition had turned the experience into a deliciously illicit adventure, drawing the bright young things like moths to a flame. They were happy to spend their wealthy parent's money, and Ari was more than happy to take it from them. His overheads were high. It was expensive to get a cop to look the other way, or to pay extra cash to a friend on the docks to slip a shipment through. Nonetheless, even with the expenses, Ari was in a very comfortable position financially.

Inwardly, however, no comfort could be found. Ari looked around the room with a sad smile, his gaze coming to rest on the original Klee that hung above the mantel. Ari loved the painting. He understood that face, with its stylized, fractured features and empty eyes. The Klee reminded Ari of himself. It was a mask, holding together the pieces of a puzzle that didn't quite fit.

Every day, Ari struggled to know himself. He knew he was strong. He knew he was smart. He knew he could read people like a book. He just couldn't read himself. He walked through each day with a calm outer shell that belied the battlefield within. Lust battled with a tangible sense of the sacred, anger wrestled with patience. His mind and heart constantly warred as the sharp insight of Raphael fought against the raw instincts of Ariel. His sleep was restless and punctuated by ghastly visions that left him exhausted and irritable.

He glanced over at the bedroom at the girl sprawled across the bed. Her head hung over the edge, the last look of surprise captured forever in her sightless eyes. Her skin was white, like alabaster. He'd drunk deeply, draining every last drop from her exquisite body. Unable to resist the lure of the flesh, Ari had learned to focus his desire on his bloodlust. The warmth of a woman's body pleased him, but the warmth of her blood on his tongue pleased him more. Women became his prey. He would toy with them, charming them and winning their hearts, only to shock them with small moments of cruel insensitivity. He would learn their innermost thoughts and fears, and use them to advantage, luring them closer until the scent of their blood drove him to attack. Silas was always on hand to clean up the remains of Ari's passion. The old vampire would gather up the bloody sheets with his usual taciturn grunts and disapproving looks and Ari would ignore his disapproval with studied indifference. People disappeared all the time in Ari's world and a missing showgirl or prostitute could be easily overlooked, especially when one had the right people on the payroll.

He wasn't careless, of course, but both he and Feo had an army of people to take care of any little problems. However, one slightly bigger problem that no one else could take care of loomed over him, casting a dark cloud in his sunny sky. A year had passed, and it was time to return to the Carpathians and present himself to the Council of Elders. He'd done well enough financially to ensure a healthy return on his father's investment. Morally, he'd been less successful, although the objects of his lust never lived more than a few moments beyond his orgasm. His thirst for blood ensured they were dead before his seed could spark new life within them, so while he'd broken his promise to remain pure, he hadn't tainted his family bloodline any further by bringing forth a half human bastard. No doubt Lucius wouldn't be happy about his carnal lapses, but Ari knew the abundance of wealth he'd bring with him on his return would be more than enough to ensure his father's good favor.

He wasn't looking forward to the visit. Business continued to be brisk and Feo wanted to expand their territory, a bold move considering their market. They weren't the only entrepreneurs to take advantage of Prohibition, and fierce competition for bootleg dollars grew by the hour. Ari had absolute confidence in Feo's ability to run things while he went away, but he longed to pursue even greater success. The affairs of the ancients held little interest for him. He would help his father secure the family's position on the Council of the Undead and then he would go back to the life he'd built for himself in America.

Truly, the Land of Opportunity.

Only one thing he looked forward to on his visit to the

ancestral castle: his father had promised him a wife. Humans were little better than prey unless they served some advantage. He enjoyed the company of some, yet tired quickly of the company of most. The ability to read the minds of men was often a gift, but sometimes more of a curse. The weaknesses of men knew no end. They could be ruthless, but their egos often stood in the way of good judgment. They were easily seduced by the swell of a woman's breast or the empty promise of riches. Ari had yet to meet a human that couldn't be bought. From poor men to politicians, every man had his price and every man had his weakness.

Ari's weakness was loneliness. It wasn't the warmth of a lover's touch he sought, but companionship. He needed someone who understood, who could still the turmoil in his warring mind. He needed a confidant. He was surrounded by vampires, yet none of them could be trusted. Even Lucius, with his lectures about family honor and inheritance, was mindful first and foremost of his own well-being. His father had used him to secure his position on the Council. Ari knew it was Lucius's grand ambition to rule the realm of the Undead and Ari was happy to help. He had no desire to remain in the Carpathians, enslaved to centuries of tradition and hierarchy. He had his own kingdom to rule and by the time he returned to America, Ari hoped to have his queen by his side. Buoyed by the thought, he turned his attention to the tedious task of packing.

"Silas, where are my black dress pants?"

Silas bustled in with the missing trousers. Ari watched him thoughtfully. He couldn't truly trust Silas, either. Not entirely. Silas took good care of him, but the old vampire's loyalty still remained first and foremost to his father. If, at any point, Lucius decided that he proved a liability, Ari had no doubt that Silas would assist in his immediate disposal without a moment of regret.

Even his mother, the woman who nurtured him in the womb, could not be trusted. He knew she loved him, but now he knew she feared him too. He'd seen the accusation and horror in her eyes as Raffy had crumpled before her and he would never forget it. He knew she would still blame him for the loss of her youngest son. He knew her fear would be mixed with hatred and vengeance. That made her dangerous.

And untrustworthy.

Ari knew that Raffy could not be truly lost, remaining alive and well within the fibers of Ari's being. He sensed Raffy's presence deep within when he woke from his bloody feasts, prodding his conscience as he stared at the lifeless eyes of his victims. It was Raffy who held Ari's tongue and reined in his temper when a foolish human tested the boundaries of their acquaintance. It was Raffy who thought to toss a coin to the beggar on the corner of 74th and 16th or tip the laundress with her plain face and old eyes. Ari wouldn't have noticed these people if it hadn't been for Raffy's compassion. At times, Ari felt comfortable sharing another consciousness within him. In fact, Raffy's presence often proved helpful. At other times, however, Raffy's conscience pervaded Ari's thoughts and produced such guilt that he would double over from the physical pain, resulting in a torturous existence of constant inner turmoil, but he supposed it was the price he must pay for accepting his brother's reluctant sacrifice. Therein lay the greatest guilt. At his best moments, Ari embraced his brother's presence within with a sense of inner power. At his worst, his body became his brother's prison, a cage of muscle, sinew, and bone trapping Raffy deep within its dark depths.

Ari sighed and swallowed hard against the sadness that welled up within him. He hoped his father had chosen a suitable bride. He needed the distraction.

LUCIUS roared with laughter, slapping his guest heartily on the back. Annoyed by the display of false camaraderie, Margrethe turned to study the girl Lucius had chosen for their son. Isabelle of the House of Erebus was beautiful, with fine bone structure and perfect skin. Her pedigree was impeccable. She was intelligent. She was witty. She was also incredibly self-absorbed and coldly ambitious. Margrethe had no doubt that Lucius would find these last traits most attractive. Focus and determination, he would call it. It didn't matter what she thought in any case. Her son's future had already been decided. Margrethe smiled at the girl and passed her a dish of thinly sliced pieces of raw meat.

"Do try the venison, Isabelle; fresh game from our forest. I promise you, it will melt in your mouth."

Isabelle helped herself to a slice of deer, tearing it delicately with her sharp fangs. She paused for a moment, savoring the moist, rich flavor.

"You said this is your own game, Lady Margrethe? It is remarkably fresh."

Margrethe smiled thinly. "Yes dear, we kill our own here." The meaning of her words was not lost on their guests or on Lucius. He glared at her, his knife raised mid-air. She smiled again.

"I do hope everyone has left room for dessert."

Lucius put down the knife slowly, his eyes blazing with anger.

"Lord Erebus and I will withdraw to discuss the upcoming nuptials. Perhaps you and Isabelle could spend some time getting to know one another."

Isabelle smiled at Lucius, then at Margrethe. "I would enjoy that Lord Ruthven. Perhaps Lady Margrethe will be kind enough to tell me more about Ari. I still know so little about your son."

Margrethe returned her smile wearily. Her son? Which son? The son she'd lost, buried deep within his stronger sibling, or the son who devoured his weaker brother and who now laid claim to everything Raffy had ever felt or thought? Did she even have a son? Was Ari half a son or a son made whole? Margrethe couldn't think anymore. The matter tore at her heart and frayed her nerves. Lucius would no doubt chastise her for her inappropriate comment later. He'd no doubt accuse her of saying it to sabotage the union, but, in truth, she would be relieved to see Ariel settled with a wife. Ari would find Isabelle attractive, but if anything of Raffy still existed in Ariel, Margrethe knew the girl's cold, selfish nature would not endear her to her youngest son.

Margrethe knew that, sooner or later, one brother would have to triumph over the other. She deemed it impossible to wage a never ending battle within oneself without some kind of clear-cut resolution. One must have a victor or face self-destruction. Eventually, one or the other would prevail; the dark or the light, the younger or the elder. One thing was certain. Right now, Ari needed a wife. The possibility of Ari's bloody urges overtaking him provided an ever present worry and a wife would give his desires focus. Isabelle seemed to be a determined girl. Margrethe hoped her strength would enable her to contain her husband to be in his darkest moments.

With his brother's influence coursing through his body and mind, Margrethe hoped that Ari had found a sense of balance and peace but in all honesty, she knew her son as little as Isabelle knew him. Ari might return to her a complete stranger, molded by his father's hand and the ways of the world. On the other hand, she might catch Raffy's warm gaze in Ari's eyes. She dreamed of touching her youngest son's spirit and holding it close, if only for a moment. If she could be reassured that Raffy still existed within Ari, she would accept the union of her boys within one body and submit herself to domestic imprisonment in the House of Nyx. She just needed a glimpse of her youngest boy. With a sigh, Margrethe beckoned Isabelle to the chaise lounge.

"Come and sit beside me, dear. We will talk about Ari soon. First, tell me more about yourself."

LUCIUS stretched contentedly. Apart from Margrethe's

inappropriate comment, it had been a pleasant evening and much to his delight; he'd found Isabelle of the House of Erebus to be infinitely suitable. Not only was the girl beautiful and smart, she was ruthless and ambitious, two qualities he found most pleasing. She'd seemed eager to join Ari in America. Lucius knew she would fit in there. Her easy confidence and vibrant nature would endear her to Ari's smart, New York City friends.

He hoped it would also endear her to Ari.

In any case, her noble family lines were impeccable. An alliance with both Erebus and Romani placed the House of Nyx in an even stronger position to take control of the Council of the Undead. Lord Erebus had seemed impressed by Ari's achievements. Of course, Margrethe's deliberately provocative comment had created an awkward moment, but Lucius remained determined that the match would be made. He would smooth things with his guest over a few glasses of fresh, sweet blood; a toast to the union of their children and the Houses of Erebus and Nyx.

Yes, everything appeared to be going perfectly. Well, almost. The small matter of Ari's personal aberrations still had to be addressed. Silas had contacted Lucius from New York City, concerned that his charge's bloody instincts were rising within him again, despite Raffy's constant inner influence. For the most part, Ari seemed to be in absolute control of his thoughts and actions, blending easily into the human realm, moving between his human and vampire friends without any disruption to his routine or attitude. However, when it came to intimacy or dealing with adversaries, Ari's bloodlust knew no limits. Lucius instructed Silas to continue to monitor the situation and continue cleaning up the bloody remains of Ari's romantic dalliances. Little could be done about the tortured and bloodied bodies of Ari's business rivals, but that gave Lucius scant concern. Violent death was an accepted result of the gangster lifestyle and Ari's stable of crooked cops kept him well covered. Lucius envisioned his son's true nature would remain successfully hidden for now. He turned his attention to Lord Erebus, now pouring more of the intoxicating blood into their glasses.

"Here's to the betrothal of our children and the alliance of our clans!" Lucius raised his glass, clinking it against his guest's. They drained the rich red liquid and sat in comfortable silence for a moment as the blood coursed through them. Finally, Lord Erebus spoke.

"When is Ariel due to return, Lucius?"

"He returns tomorrow evening, Lord Erebus. We meet with the Council in three days."

"Ah, yes," Lord Erebus nodded. "The Council." His voice trailed off, and again there reigned silence, only this time not as comfortable. An unasked question hung between them.

Eventually, Lord Erebus spoke. "I trust the Council will be satisfied with your son's progress and your management of your position?"

Lucius smiled reassuringly. "There is nothing that would prevent the Elders from admitting the House of Nyx to the Council of the Undead."

"Ariel has fulfilled his part of the agreement satisfactorily?" A loaded question, indeed.

"My son has met every requirement laid down by the Elders," Lucius lied. So far, Ari's sensual deviations were known only to himself and loyal Silas, and it would do their cause no good if that knowledge spread any further. The necessity of an early marriage pressed upon Lucius's thoughts. He decided to broach the subject, hoping that his guest would not find his eagerness suspicious.

"Lord Erebus, I was hoping that I would be able to present Ari to the Council with an honorable wife by his side."

Isabelle's father stared at him in consternation. "Lucius, you said you meet with the Council in three days. That is hardly enough time to prepare a wedding!"

"I realize it is a most unusual request, Lord Erebus, and, of course, I, like you, would wish to have the grandest wedding for our children." He paused. "However, I believe Ari's status as husband would benefit him greatly before the Elders."

"Would their betrothal not be enough to please the Elders?" Lord Erebus sounded irritated. Lucius shifted in his seat, choosing his next words carefully.

"I am sure it would please them to no end, Lord Erebus, but I am convinced a marriage would please them even more. Ours are the two most ancient Clans in the Realm of the Undead. The Council cannot help but look upon our alliance with favor. A betrothal is the mere promise of alliance, but marriage, ah, now *that* is the eternal fulfillment of that allegiance."

Lord Erebus nodded slowly. Lucius knew his words gained the desired effect.

"Very well, Lucius. The ceremony will take place and be witnessed by our immediate families. After their presentation to the Council of Elders, the new Lord and Lady of Nyx will celebrate their nuptials in a manner befitting their standing. No expense will be spared, and the expense will fall to the House of Nyx." He held out his hand. Lucius grasped it firmly.

"Agreed, Lord Erebus. Our children will marry in two days' time and after their presentation to the Council of Elders, I will throw the most elaborate celebration in the memory of the dark realms."

***

# CHAPTER TWENTY-FIVE

ARI sat at the head of the lavishly laid out bridal table. His wife sat beside him, resplendent in an elaborately embroidered gown. A wreath of roses, white and blood-red, encircled her auburn hair. White for purity, red for blood.

A few hours ago, he'd stood in front of the Council of Elders with his father and his freshly wed bride and presented himself as worthy and unsullied by human desire. His noble wife's purity was under no doubt. His own, however, seemed highly questionable as the Council of Elders scrutinized him with narrowed eyes. He had assured them that the world and its vast temptations had left him unsullied. Ari acquitted himself well under their examination. The fact that his emotions had played no part in his bedding of wenches should have been enough, Ari believed, to present himself as pure and untainted to the Elders and his bride's family. The Elders were impressed with his respectful demeanor and his quiet confidence and seemed pleased, too, with the wife who stood beside him. Lord Erebus beamed down happily at his beloved daughter and his son-in-law as the Council declared their support of the noble union of The Houses of Nyx and Erebus.

Lord Valdis regarded Ari suspiciously, but the old vampire kept his thoughts to himself, unwilling to challenge Ari in the face of his marriage with the daughter of such an ancient and respected Clan. The only one who might have dared a challenge proved conspicuously absent. Ari was admittedly relieved when he observed Ragnar Grettirson's empty chair.

His father, on the other hand, noted the ancient warrior's absence immediately with a frown. The Huntsman's refusal to attend the wedding and his and Ari's presentation before the Council unmistakably rejected the union—a direct insult to the House of Nyx. Even as Lord Erebus stood and warmly commended Lucius on his management of his household, Ragnar's absence ensured his father's mood remained dark, vanquished only by the admission of the House of Nyx to the Council of the Undead. A broad smile quickly replaced the frown as Lucius realized that his nearly complete victory drew to fruition, in spite of the censure of Ragnar Grettirson. With the blessing of the Elders, the House of Nyx would continue to rise and thrive until they ruled the realms.

Another loud toast brought him back to the present. Absently, he raised his glass. As promised, Lucius had spared no cost with the wedding celebrations. Ari noted his father's expansively good mood concerning the entire affair by the proof of Lucius willingly opening the purse strings. The grand hall was draped in rich, red silk and illuminated by hundreds of candles that hung from the ceiling in massive, wrought-iron candelabras. White roses cascaded down the walls and over the silk covered tables, which were laden with platters of delicately sliced slivers of raw venison, rich blood puddings, and delicate, sweet blood jellies. Carafes of the purest blood sat alongside bottles of the finest wine, both imported from the farthest parts of the world. Wine and blood flowed freely, guests imbibing liberally in both. The heady scent of roses and blood filled the air. Ari's head reeled a little. He'd drunk far more wine than anticipated, and the festivities suddenly felt overwhelming. He felt a hand press against his arm. His wife looked at him, concern reflected in her strange golden eyes. She was the daughter of fire and her warmth touched him now, even through the alcoholic haze.

"Are you unwell, my lord?"

Ari smiled at her blearily. "No need for such formality, dear wife."

Isabelle inclined her head graciously. "Perhaps you would like to retire early, my dear husband."

Ari looked around the grand hall. His carousing guests were thankfully oblivious to his presence, and he supposed his absence would not draw their attention. He stood unsteadily, offering Isabelle his arm, not so much for chivalry, but from a need to lean on something. She took it without a word, resting her pale hand solicitously on his finely tailored suit. A wave of warmth flowed through him. He staggered a little and leaned on her heavily. With a nod to Lucius and her father, Isabelle led him from the room. She was surprisingly strong. He clung to her like a moth to the flame, his eyes mesmerized by the glint of the lamps on her fiery hair. Desire stirred within him, not for her blood but for her body, which lured him seductively from beneath the embroidered folds of her dress. He wanted to know her inside and out, this fiery beauty who now shared his bed and his life.

As they neared the bridal chamber, he stopped and pulled her towards him. Without a word, he lowered his head and kissed her. She tasted sweet and warm. His tongue explored her gently at first. After a moment's hesitancy, she returned his embrace and his kiss. He cupped her face in his hands and pulled her closer. Her breasts crushed against his chest. He swelled with desire, not caring if she could feel him. He pressed against her urgently. Ari expected her to pull away, but she pushed herself shamelessly against him. He felt like he was going to explode. Gathering her roughly in his arms, Ari strode the remaining few steps to the bridal chamber and threw her on the bed. She laid there, auburn hair splayed on white sheets, a small, knowing smile on her lips. He set upon her in a mindless instant, ripping at the carefully stitched gown that kept him from his prize. She opened herself, and he dove into her warmth. An ancient fire lit between them, coursing through his cold body and fueling his passion, lost in the heady haze of alcohol and desire. She wound herself around him, entwining him in her long limbs and drawing him deep inside her. As he thrust into her, he felt her sharp fangs pierce his flesh. The exquisite pain enlivened him further. He tried holding back, trapped at her mercy. He cried out as his seed spilled inside her. Isabelle's fingernails raked his back as she reached the peak of her passion. They came together, darkness and fire. Finally spent, they lay beside each other in exhausted ecstasy. Ari gave a small shiver as her tongue delicately probed at the mark she'd left on his skin. In the midst of his slowly subsiding passion, Ari realized that he'd bedded many women, but known only one lover.

IT was done. For better or worse, their son had been joined in unholy matrimony. Margrethe had been excited to see Ari when he returned from America. He'd grown even stronger and more handsome than she remembered. His muscular body strained against the silk suits he seemed to favor. New York City style he'd told her. He'd seemed happy to see her, but Margrethe could sense something different. He had become wary, slightly reserved. She searched her oldest son for a glimpse of Raffy only to be met with Ari's dark eyes that gave nothing away. She asked him questions. What was New York City like? What business was he in? Ari answered her questions patiently. New York City defied imagination. She would love Broadway and the shops with the latest fashions. He was less forthcoming about his business dealings, however. His lounge club seemed to take up most of his time. As he regaled her with witty anecdotes about his more famous customers, Margrethe thought she could hear Raffy in his voice. Ari's descriptions of society ladies with their airs and graces and

251

shameless cavorting seemed infused with Raffy's impish humor. For a blissful moment, Margrethe felt her youngest son's presence, then it faded away. Ari seemed to sense her confusion. He stopped speaking, and his mood changed abruptly. From that point on, Margrethe had sensed an invisible wall between them. Her subsequent meetings with her oldest son felt terribly constrained. In the end, she sensed him watching her even as she searched for signs of his younger brother. Ari's eyes were always guarded, his manner deferential, but distant.

She hadn't been present at the Council of Elders, but Lucius had left her in no doubt later as to the success of their appearance. Lucius had been in a particularly good mood after his victory before the Elders, even ensuring that Margrethe took her place at the bridal table as the mother of the groom. He didn't have to, of course. As they'd never taken their vows, she remained no better than a whore in the eyes of the Undead. In reality, she was nothing more than Lucius's prisoner. She didn't have the appearance of a prisoner, but Margrethe knew that her freedom was an illusion. She'd played happy families with Lucius and Ari in the hope that she somehow would be able to retrieve Raffy from the dark depths of his brother's soul. It was her last hope, and it seemed to be a vain hope. Raffy remained trapped within his brother, infused forever in Ari's soul. Margrethe's influence over Ari was waning. There was another woman to soothe his brow and drive him forward to greater success. Isabelle of the House of Erebus had both her sons now.

Tears welled up in her eyes. If Lucius had wished her to suffer, he should be well pleased. She suffered intolerably, inconsolably. Days stretched before her, long days without end. She would shut herself away and find solace with the shell of her son. Raffy's essence was nowhere to be found in his brother and even if she found him, she had no way of bringing him back. He'd sacrificed himself to save her and in doing so, condemned her to her torment.

A sharp rap on her door jolted her from her thoughts.

"Come in."

Lucius stepped into the room. She shrunk back instinctively. He saw it and looked theatrically hurt.

"I did not mean to disturb you, Margrethe. I will leave if you prefer?"

She shook her head.

"No, Lucius, it is fine. Please sit down."

He accepted her invitation, stretching his long legs in front of him. He smelled of wine and cigars. As the father of the groom, he'd reveled in his role as master of ceremonies. He'd been gracious to their guests, humbly accepting their congratulations. He could afford to be gracious, Margrethe thought bitterly. He'd achieved his dream. The House of Nyx had been restored to its rightful place, and at last, Lord Lucius Ruthven would become a member of the Council of the Undead.

Margrethe had little interest in his achievement. It made no difference to her existence. Lucius had destroyed her life and everything she'd held dear. He'd broken her trust and her heart, then destroyed her brother and her sons, leaving her empty and hopeless. He could do nothing more to her. There was nothing left to take.

"Well, finally our son is happily wed." Lucius stared at her pointedly. "At least one Lord of the House of Nyx has found wedded bliss."

"Perhaps it is as well he found bliss before he could destroy it." Margrethe couldn't keep the bitterness from her voice.

Lucius fell silent. She couldn't tell if he was angry or indifferent. She didn't care either way. She could suffer Lucius's displeasure more easily than she could suffer his affection. Displeasure kept him at a distance.

Eventually, the silence became uncomfortable. Margrethe tried to ease back into the conversation.

"Isabelle seems to be a good match for Ari."

Lucius nodded.

"She is born of the noblest vampire clan, Margrethe. Isabelle Erebus is quality, and she carries her power as gracefully as she carries her beauty. She is the perfect match for the House of Nyx."

Margrethe couldn't suppress a wry smile.

"Surely you mean she is the perfect match for our son."

Naturally, Lucius would see the marriage as a political maneuver. Lucius's sense of romance seemed to be confined to opportunities for advancement.

"Of course, that is what I meant." Lucius dismissed her observation with a nonchalant wave of his hand. "It is one and the same, after all, Margrethe. With marriage comes alliance."

"Yes, of course." Margrethe folded her hands in her lap. The conversation died again, and this time she made no attempt to revive it.

Lucius sat for a few moments, then rose stiffly.

"I hope you will take the time to get to know your son's wife, Margrethe." It came out more a demand than a request.

"Of course I will." Her tone was dull, disinterested. "I only want Ari's happiness." *And Raffy's*, she thought. Somewhere inside Ari, her youngest son would be feeling all Ari felt. If Ari were happy, Raffy would be happy. Maybe. The two brothers had always been so different. Margrethe only could imagine Ari's inner turmoil now that the two were one.

Lucius's voice interrupted her thoughts. "I also wish for his happiness. Do not forget that, Margrethe."

She doubted if he cared at all about his son's happiness. Ari was a means to an end, like everyone in Lucius's undead life. Slowly, an idea began to germinate. If she could coax Raffy out of the dark realms of Ari's inner being, he might overthrow Lucius and free them all from the curse of Nyx. She would need Ari's wife as an unwitting ally. She would need to stay close to Ari and watch for any sign of Raffy's presence. She wouldn't give up. She had only a grain of hope left, but it was enough.

"I will not forget, Lucius. I am sure you have Ari's best interests at heart." She tried not to sound sarcastic.

With a curt nod, Lucius bid her good night. Margrethe breathed a sigh of relief as the door shut tight behind him. The key turned in the lock, a sharp reminder of her true position. She wondered if Lucius would be as vigilant once Ari had returned to America. Perhaps she could persuade him to ease her bonds. If she could escape, she could follow her sons to America. In her current situation, the possibility of escape seemed remote. Margrethe pushed any thoughts of freedom out of her head. She couldn't allow herself to speculate so far into the future. A day had many hours and fortunes could change in a minute. She would wait and watch for Raffy to emerge from Ari's dark soul.

ISABELLE thoroughly enjoyed her new position as the Lady of Nyx. As Ari's mother was not married to his father, the title of Lady of the House passed to Ari's new wife. While Isabelle was secretly pleased, she had no wish to offend Ari's mother, who had lately been spending a significant amount of time with her. They often would stroll in the castle grounds, enjoying the rich scent of pine from the surrounding forest as they walked and talked. Occasionally Margrethe would relate a funny tale from Ari's childhood, but, for the most part, she remained strangely silent on the subject of her son's past. Isabelle had heard there existed another son who had been struck dumb by disease. It was said he'd wasted away to a mere shell. She'd never seen this other son and doubted his existence.

She'd thought to ask Ari about it but found it difficult to broach such a secretive subject with her new husband. Ari's temper seemed somewhat unpredictable and she had no wish to anger him. Her husband appeared to have two personalities. He was usually charming and attentive, but his mood could change in an instant, taking him from mellow reverie to cold indifference or blazing anger. Isabelle had not yet been a target of that anger, but she'd seen unfortunate servants on the receiving end of Ari's fiery temper. Isabelle had been taken by surprise at his first outburst but, gradually, she'd learned to read the signs, soothing his inner rage before it could take hold. Ariel of Nyx was an enigma. He often seemed uncomfortable in the ancient surroundings of the castle. His smart shirts and pants stood out against the more traditional garb of his parents. He'd bought dresses over for her from America. They were shorter than she was used to and she felt awkward wearing them at first, but, gradually, she grew to like the well-cut clothes with their city sheen. She asked Ari many questions about New York City. What was it like? How big was it? How busy? What were the houses like? Were there castles?

He always answered her questions patiently, chuckling at her childlike curiosity. He drew vivid mental pictures for her. She listened as though she were already there. She could see the lounge club, smell the heady scent of fine wine and smoke. She could hear the beat of the music and see the couples dancing with the lack of inhibition that alcohol produced. The mental pictures made her impatient to taste New York City. She'd hoped that Ari only would remain at the family castle for a short time after the wedding, but for some reason he seemed to delay their departure. She wondered if she was the cause for his seeming reluctance to return to his life in America. Perhaps his lifestyle would be changed for the worse by the burden of marriage.

Isabelle shook away the thought. She would be an asset to her husband, no matter where they lived. She was of noble blood, and she carried loyalty and power in her veins, the daughter of fire. The fire of Hades now aligned with the House of the Night. She would light the way for Ari of Nyx. She would be his beacon in the darkness. The powers of the Underworld lay in their hands.

A strange vision struck her. She saw Ari cloaked in the blood-red robes of the Council of the Undead wearing a wreath of thorns on his head; two ravens, one on either side of him, each with a wilted rose in its beak. One red rose, one white rose. The vision dispersed as quickly as it had appeared. Isabelle put down the embroidery she'd been working on and gazed out the window. The forest reveled in vibrancy with the renewal of spring. Birth and rebirth, the endless cycle of life continued their passage through time. Time was her friend. Isabelle placed a hand on her smooth belly. She'd hoped to be with child soon after marriage. It was her father's wish that she seal the alliance between the two clans with an heir and Isabelle had no desire to disappoint him. However, it wasn't just her father's wishes that drew her thoughts to motherhood. Isabelle wanted to bear Ari's child. She wanted a son to bear witness to their union, to carry the bloodlines of the ancients through to the next generation.

In a moment of unguarded weakness, she'd confided as much to Margrethe. Ari's mother had seemed surprised at first, as though the thought of a grandchild had not occurred to her. She'd quickly regained her composure and assured Isabelle that a grandchild would be a lovely addition to the family. She seemed warm and sincere, but for some reason Isabelle sensed that the idea did not particularly appeal to her mother-in-law and she never mentioned it again. From that moment on, an invisible wall had been placed between them.

Sighing, Isabelle picked up the discarded embroidery and halfheartedly began to stitch again. Ari had gone hunting with Lucius and Margrethe had retired to her chambers. An oppressive silence hung over the castle like a dark cloak. The needle pierced the tip of her finger. She stopped and sucked on the blood, savoring the sweet tang. Life was in the blood, and her bloodline was strong. A child would strengthen it even more. Theirs would be a child with the bloodlines of Chaos and Night, a child that could rule not only the underworld but the human world. There were no boundaries in eternity, only endless possibilities. With those possibilities in mind, Isabelle submitted herself to the hands of the Gods of Hades and made a silent vow to trust in their providence.

\*\*\*

# EPILOGUE

*"Life is but a dream for the dead." - Gerard Way*

RAFFY watched the wolf dart through the trees. He hated these times when Ari's bloody instincts rose within him, but he'd learned not to resist his brother's bloodlust unless necessary. The battle of wills always left him drained, and hunting usually proved not worth a battle. As Ari raised his shotgun, Raffy withdrew deep into himself, shutting out the howls of pain as the bullet found its mark.

This was his existence now. His prison walls consisted not of stone, but of flesh and bone. He felt every movement Ari made, feeling the stretch of his muscles and the heaviness of his step. He could feel the force of his brother's bloodlust and the coldness of his heart, immersed in Ari's being, hostage to his brother's thoughts and instincts. It took constant vigilance to stay true to his own essence. There were many times he felt like giving up. It would be easier to allow himself to become absorbed, to become nothing, and let Ari take over, but then something would inspire him to keep fighting. Many times, he would see Margrethe searching Ari's eyes. He knew she searched for him, trying to catch even a glimpse of him. He tried to reach out. Sometimes he succeeded but only briefly. He thought she might have sensed his presence, but he couldn't be sure.

At times, he could barely sense his own presence. Ari's business in New York City led him into some shady dealings with even shadier characters. There was often violence, with Ari relishing the torture of his rivals and their bloody demise. Even more difficult to deal with, however, were Ari's amorous adventures. The bloody excess always left Raffy shaken. His horror would rise in Ari as guilt, causing his brother many sleepless days and restless nights. Ari would try to push down the unaccustomed conscience that followed his feeding frenzies and Raffy would resist, unable to relinquish his righteous horror at his brother's bloodlust. He knew it was only he, Raphael, who stood between Ari and the dark oblivion of his true nature. It was a heavy load to bear, especially when imprisoned in that dark oblivion with no promise of release. That is, until the day there came the light of fire, an auburn beauty with golden eyes and pale skin.

Ari's wife.

*His* wife.

Suddenly, Raffy had a reason to fight. His strength was renewed, and he soared with passion each time Ari bedded the beautiful Isabelle of the House of Erebus. He quelled his brother's bloodlust, filling Ari's thoughts with the scent of her skin and the light in her burnished hair. He craved her, and his craving became Ari's. He touched her skin with Ari's fingers. He kissed her blood-red lips with Ari's mouth. He filled her with his brother's manhood and felt the sweet release as she drained them both of all their strength and thoughts. He lived for these moments of bliss and gradually, he began to fight for them. He could feel himself getting stronger, slowly gaining more control over Ari's thoughts. His brother's outbursts of temper were slowly lessening in frequency and ferocity. Even so, it remained a hellish existence Raffy wasn't sure how to escape, but if there existed any chance at all to do so, he knew he would need all his strength and more.

Ari shouldered the wolf, grunting under the dying animal's weight. Feeling his brother's impatience, Raffy withdrew further into the dark depths of Ari's soul, blocking out the glare of the morning sun and his brother's miserable thoughts. One day, his thoughts would be his own again, and he would be master of his own destiny. On that day, he would take back that which he had lost. He would find a way to set himself free from Ari's dark depths, but until then, he would sleep his brother's sleep and bed his brother's wife. Comforted by the thought of Isabelle, Raffy shut down his senses and allowed his brother to have his bloody way with the dying wolf. He would awaken later when his beloved gave herself to her husband, but until then, he would sleep like the dead and let the will of the undead prevail. As Ari's fangs ripped through the wolf's flesh, Raffy allowed himself to drift into blackness, accompanied by the cries of the ravens circling overhead.

**THE END**

# AFTERWORD

WE would like to personally thank you for buying and reading this book. Producing this novel has been, and continues to be, fulfilling for us, and we hope that it is enjoyable for you to read.

Please consider taking a little extra time to help others find this book by leaving feedback where you purchased it. Your opinion about this book truly matters, both to our authors who have contributed to the anthology and to other readers.

If you have any questions, comments, suggestions, or just want to say hi, please visit our publisher's web page on www.salgado-reyes.com and follow our publisher's twitter account: @Indie__Authors.

~Indie Authors Press~

SOME of the characters from *Blood of Nyx* also appear in the short story "Blood Bond" in *Corpus Deluxe, Undead Tales of Terror* also from Indie Authors Press.